James J. Owen

Spiritual Fragments

James J. Owen

Spiritual Fragments

ISBN/EAN: 9783337332662

Printed in Europe, USA, Canada, Australia, Japan

Cover: Foto ©Andreas Hilbeck / pixelio.de

More available books at **www.hansebooks.com**

SPIRITUAL

FRAGMENTS

———

By J. J. OWEN,

Late editor, for 24 years, of the "San Jose (Cal.) Mercury,"
Editor of "Golden Gate," and author of
"Our Sunday Talks."

SAN FRANCISCO.
THE ROSENTHAL-SAALBURG CO.
1890.

TO THE HELPFUL COMPANION,

EARNEST WORKER,

AND

FAITHFUL AND UNERRING ADVISER

IN ALL THINGS,

MY GOOD AND PRECIOUS WIFE,

(TO WHOM THE SUGGESTION AND INSPIRATION

OF MANY OF THESE "FRAGMENTS" IS DUE);

IS THIS BOOK LOVINGLY DEDICATED

BY THE AUTHOR.

INTRODUCTION.

This is a busy world, and life is too short, and too busily occupied for one to go a roundabout way to truth, when the end can be more readily reached by a short cut across lots. Most people prefer advice in homœopathic doses, and religion in a condensed form—the latter, especially, they would have divested of long prayers, and everything that squints at cant. These "Fragments' are the mere flashes of thought, and as such, we imagine, will arrest the attention of many minds when the obscurity of a bewildering argument, or tiresome essay, would only inspire indifference. It is with this thought we send this book of "Fragments" adrift, claiming for the many and varied topics treated the rare virtue of brevity, if nothing more, and craving for it the kind indulgence of a discerning, but not always sympathetic public.

THE AUTHOR.

CONTENTS.

CONTENTS.

DRIFT OF CIVILIZATION.

The drift of civilization is in the direction of the enlargement of the field of human reason. The time was when to think outside of a certain prescribed formula was heresy, punishable with all manner of pious cruelty. That time has past. There is nothing now too venerable with age, or too sacred with tradition, that man does not claim the right to investigate and subject to the scales and crucible of human reason. If you confront him with a "Thus saith the Lord," he is determined to know when the Lord said it, who said He said it, and how, when, where and to whom it was said. If you bring forward written authority to prove that the sun stood still to enable a certain ancient general to prolong the slaughter of his enemies, or that another prominent personage survived the digestion of a big fish for three days, human reason will naturally question your authority. The fables to which the religious world has so long given credence, are brought under the scrutiny of science and enlightened judgment, and if found unreasonable are cast aside, as moral and intellectual rubbish.

And why should man not reason upon the improbabilities of an ancient book just the same as he would upon any other subject? There can be no better guide than reason, quickened by intuition—notwithstanding we once heard a good Presbyterian clergyman thank God that he had "a religion that was not based on human reason!" What would be thought of the sailor who should cast his compass and quadrant into the deep, and trust to the winds and waves to bear his vessel safely into port? When man sets aside his reason he simply throws his compass overboard. The time is at hand when he will have no religion that does not square with his reason. Why is it that our church pews are mainly empty of brainy men and women, unless it be because thoughtful people are not content longer to listen to doctrines repugnant, not only to reason, but to every sense of human justice. Habitual church-goers are mainly good and respectable people, who haven't the time or inclination to do much religious thinking for themselves, but are passively content to take their religious opinions second-handed.

MEMORY.

Memory! How like an avenging demon it will follow one through life, and out and on into the infinite realm of spirit —the memory of unholy deeds! True, the conscience may be seared by many and oft repeated wrongs, until the memory thereof may make but little, if any, impression upon the mind. . But there comes a time, as God is just, when the spirit will reach its lowest depth of indifference, and feel the first gentle promptings to a higher life. Then memory will do its work, if never before. What ages of agony may not the darkened soul experience in its long, sad journey towards the light! And so, also, the pleasures of memory to a life well spent—what can be more delightful! The pleasing incidents of childhood—a mother's tender love and care ; a father's thoughtful guidance to a manly career—the joys and pleasures, the fond associations, the happy dreams of love—how they will be borne to us on memory's silver wings, sweetening the years of time, and adding rich argosies of gems to the treasures of eternity ! There is no accusing angel so relentless as that of one's own soul—no all-seeing eye so penetrating as that where-by man shall see himself. And this is the true way of life from darkness to light—from the night of ignorance, to the glorious day of man's spiritual unfoldment—when he shall be a law unto himself forevermore.

HOMESICK.

What a dull, leaden thing is a human heart away from its home nest and longing to return. The man or woman who was never homesick has missed just one note of agony in the gamut of human suffering, that would vastly enrich their experience to realize. We well remember, when a boy of twelve years, we left the shelter of the paternal roof to solve the problem of life—to learn the printer's trade. Eleven miles away! What an infinite distance, and what æons of time were involved in that first week of absence! Strange faces and scenes all around, and such an aching lump in the breast! And when Saturday night came, with what eager joy we walked those eleven miles to be once more coddled in the dear old home nest. What a joyous welcome from the six noisy brothers and the one wee sister, as the traveler (?) returned to them, and the sainted mother gathered her wanderer of a great long week to her loving heart. Ah, that was in the "lang syne." Where now is that happy household? All except the writer and the then baby girl in some of the many mansions of the Infinite Father in the Beyond! And we toughened and grizzled with the footprints of time, sit here dreaming of the good time coming in the evening—the Saturday evening—when our task shall be finished, and we can go home !

MISSIONARIES.

Twenty missionaries sailed from the city of San Francisco recently for Siam, China, and other places in the Orient, to teach the people of those lands something about Jesus. What a waste of good men and women! Missionaries, from a country that licenses rum-selling ; from a people far less honest, or moral, in a general sense, than those to whom these missionaries are sent ! How the chains of a perverted education must cling to the limbs of these poor missionaries. They give up their lives for the imagined welfare of the poor heathen, who care nothing at all for their teachings, unless it be that they may thereby acquire a knowledge of another tongue. The Hindu doesn't want our religion, for the very good reason that he thinks he has a much better kind of religion of his own. He *might* profit by some of our science—our superior knowledge of many things ; but that isn't religion, and that isn't what these men and women go out to teach.

MOTHER.

Beautiful mother ! How patiently and gently she bears up under the heavy burden of her almost desolate life. Desolate, did we say ? Not so. Loving angels are her daily companions ; they walk by her side, through the fields and over the hills of her lonely mountain home—wherever duty calls her—and they brood her with their sweet presence through the silent watches of the night, ever enthusing her heart with an abiding trust in the All-Good. At her tasks, early and late though not strong for such arduous toil, yet never complaining' —always the gentle word and the kind thought, and always the comfort of others in preference to that of herself. Grand, unselfish soul ! There is a brighter day dawning for you. Think not the clouds that have so long lowered over your widowed life have no silver lining. Already the light is breaking, and the glow and warmth of happier hours are near at hand. There are years of happiness before you in this life, and a crown of peace, the guerdon of a beautiful womanhood, in the life Beyond.

SECRET OF STRENGTH.

A lady friend, nearly sixty years of age, who had tramped all day through the busy streets, preparatory to departing on a

long journey by sea, dropped in to spend the evening with us recently. She bore not the slightest appearance of fatigue, and was bright, convivial and full of life. We inquired the secret of her freshness and strength. She replied that she had learned the art of holding herself together, as it were, and not exhausting her vitality in her physical labors. She could find rest while walking along the crowded streets, by not allowing other persons or things to draw upon her strength. If she found herself becoming wearied in the least, she immediately called a halt of her forces and rallied to the support of herself. Thus by a prompt and wise exercise of her will powers she was able to ward off physical fatigue, and at the same time perform a vast amount of work. Here is a fine illustration of the power of mind over matter, and one which we recommend others to imitate.

STRANGE.

It is indeed strange that so many believers in spiritual truths should be averse to permitting the fact to be made known—as though some surrender of reputation depended upon a concealment of the truth. The time has past when to be known as a Spiritualist was attended with any disgrace, if indeed there was ever any such time. The attitude of Christians who reject the positive facts of Spiritualism is simply puerile. They have pretended to believe in the existence and communion of spirits in a sort of general or deific way, it is true, but without any postive proof thereof. Now, for them to ridicule Spiritualists for confirming them in their belief, with proof, "in confirmation strong as proof of holy writ," is not only unjust, but it emphasizes their own illogical attitude of believing without proof! But there are too many good men and women in the world, men of broad intellectuality and acknowledged worth, who are open and avowed Spiritualists, for anyone longer to hesitate to be known as such.

SICKNESS.

Sickness is nothing more nor less than the body at war
with the spirit. A good lady, who had been an invalid for
years, and is now a great sufferer from a combination of ailments, said to us a few days ago that she did not believe in
Spiritualism—thought it all fraud and humbug, that she did
not want any of her spirit friends coming near her. "'That,"
we replied, "is just what's the matter with you, and fully ac-
"counts for your ill health. Your attitude of mind towards
"your spirit friends, who would gladly bring you health and
"strength, prevents their coming into your aura ; hence, they
"are powerless to aid you." How much misery could be
averted in this life if people only understood these spirit laws
better, and brought their own spirits into harmony with the
world of spirit forces on the other side of life. How pained
must be the spirits of our loved ones, who have left us for a
brief season, to be rudely repulsed when they would come to
us, with loving purpose, from their shining homes.

THE DIVIDING LINE.

The dividing line between "God's patience and his
wrath," as the old hymn has it, is something too fine for human
reason to determine. For instance, the church teaches an
eternal heaven of infinite happiness for the saints, and an
eternal hell of infinite woe for sinners. There is no intermedi-
ate or graduated state of happiness or misery. The two
places, or conditions, are separated by an impassible gulf as
wide and deep as eternity. But we find no analogy in mortal
life to warrant any such division in the life to come. Here
the bad are not wholly bad, nor the good, except in phenom.
inal instances, wholly good. There are the very good and the
good who are almost bad, the very bad and the bad who are
almost good. They live side by side here, and closely impinge

upon each other's lines of life. If the good in the bad is to receive no consideration, what is the use of the bad trying to be good? Why punish a soul for the bad there may be in it, and give it no credit for the good, especially when it is trying hard to overcome its evil tendencies, which may be the result of heredity, or of unfavorable environment? These are questions that only the orthodox clergy can answer most unsatisfactorily! The more they try, the more they find themselves, like the poor fly in the spider's web, inextricably involved in the meshes of illogical logic !

MAN MADE THEORIES.

Compare the man-made theories of the future, supposed to be founded on the teachings of a special revelation from the Creator, with the truths brought back to us by those who have solved the mystery of death. They tell us a simple story that confutes the religious teachings of the ages; hence the church will have none of it. They, our risen friends, assure us that just as we leave this life we enter the next, developed or undeveloped, saint or sinner; that our status there, at first, is just what we made ourselves here; that growth, by good conduct, is possible there as here; that we suffer there for our misdeeds here—not eternally, but until we have paid the full penalty of violated law. They invaribly tell us that they have found no heaven nor hell, no God nor Devil—in short, that life there is a continuation of life here, but under better conditions for improvement, and that every soul that tries can find happiness sometime and somewhere, and that without any vicarious atonement.

PERVERTED MEDIUMSHIP.

Perverted mediumship may be defined as that kind of mediumship where spirit intelligences of a low order lend themselves to dishonest purposes. It may be the medium's own spirit, working independently, or, perhaps, in concert with spirits outside of the body, that produces the false message, or dishonest result. It was a frequent occurrence with a dishonest slate-writer, formerly of this city, (who was addicted, with other vices, to that of gambling, and spent large sums at the gaming table,) for messages to appear upon the slates, signed by the name of the medium's guide, or some spirit friend of the sitter, directing or entreating the latter to lend money to the medium, under plea of house rent to pay, or great distress of poverty. In this way he obtained large sums which were recklessly squandered to gratify his vitiated taste for gambling. This medium's guide, through another medium, protested to a lady of the writer's acquaintance, from whom over five hundred dollars had been extorted in this way, that it was not he that indited the begging messages, but the medium's own spirit !

––––––

These are important facts that every investigator of psychic powers should understand. They teach us that we never should surrender our own judgments in matters of spirit communications—nor should we accept as genuine, without question, all messages that purport to come from our spirit friends. The moral status of the medium should always be considered in such cases, ever remembering that the message from your friend is liable to be perverted, or distorted, by the impure channel through which it comes. While mediumship is not a question of morality, nevertheless, morality in the medium is an important factor in obtaining honest communications. Hence it is that we should demand an upright, honorable life, and a high standard of integrity on the part of our mediums, if we would avoid the unsatisfactory results of which so many complain.

––––––

But the fault of a deceiving message may not always lie with the medium. We should consider well, in approaching the sacred altar of spirit communion, whether our own hearts are clean and honest, and in a fitting frame to receive the truth. The man who spends his days in an endeavor to circumvent his neighbors and get the best of a trade—the one of impure life and dishonest tendencies,—what right has he to expect absolute honesty of communication through any medium? His spirit friends may be on the same moral plane as himself, and who would delight in leading him astray. If we would have the best from the other side of life, we should seek for the best in our own lives, ever aspiring for the truth, ever living and acting the truth, and ever drawing nearer and nearer to the Infinite Good.

TWIN MONSTERS.

Prejudice and jealousy are two of the meanest attributes of the undeveloped human mind. The former appears at its worst advantage when it condemns without just cause, and refuses to listen to that which might tend to remove an unjust conclusion from the mind. The Church has so roundly and so long condemned all other ways of going to heaven, except the narrow one through its own dooryard, and especially does it look upon Spiritualism with such disfavor, that some persons within the shadow of its influence, whose habits of independent thought are not strikingly pronounced, have come to shape their opinions therewith, without really knowing why or wherefore. With narrow minds prejudice becomes a raging demon that will not reason nor listen to reason, and so nothing can be done with it but to remove the cause, or let it tire itself out with its own cussedness. We know a grand soul and a good husband, in fact more than one, who would dearly like to enjoy his belief in our beautiful philosophy, but can not because his wife will not assent to it. And so, for the sake of peace, he is obliged to forego what might be a source of the purest and sweetest joy to them both.   Isn't it pitiful?

The other of these twin monsters of the undeveloped spirit is jealousy, the instigator of more domestic ill than all other causes combined.   Not even rum, the fierce demon of destruction that has dragged down to ruin and death so many of the fairest and brightest minds of the world, can compare with it. Men and women, who live largely on the physical plane of life, enter into the marriage relation wholly ignorant of themselves as spiritual, immortal beings.   A sense of absolute ownership in each other, utterly regardless of the needs and duties of the unselfish higher nature of the soul, dominates every thought, until neither can trust the other out of their sight, and they make themselves wretchedly miserable if either merely exercises the common amenities of friendship toward persons of the opposite sex.   They continue in this error of the mortal mind until they become disgusted with themselves, and repulsive to each other, and they fly asunder, through the divorce courts, to make themselves again miserable in some new alliance.   There is no jealousy in true marriage.   The love that is enduring is too pure and beautiful to admit of suspicion or jealousy.

MORE GOOD THAN APPEARS UPON THE SURFACE.

There is much more good in the hearts of men than always appears upon the surface.   They may seem cold and thoughtless of the welfare of others, and even indifferent to the ordinary appeals of charity ; but let some great calamity befall a community—some wide and fearful devastation by fire, flood, famine, or pestilence, and straightway they become heroes. Their hearts and purses are open to the cry of distress.   The fact is, our business methods are calculated to close the avenues of sympathy to the needs and distress of others.   The strife and struggle necessary to hold one's own in the competitive grab for even the humblest means of existence, all operate to dim the divine glow of humanity in the soul, and make us mean and unnatural.

AM I MY BROTHER'S KEEPER?

That, Cain, is just what you are. When he is weak and you are strong, you owe him of your strength. When he would wander in by and forbidden paths, it is your duty to show him the better way. If you see a snare in his path that might cause him to stumble, it is a crime in you not to remove it. For what purpose, Cain, were you given superior wisdom or strength, but to assist those less endowed along the journey of life? But do you do it? See the multitude of young men sowing the seeds of disease and death in the thousands of liquor saloons in the land. What are you doing to save them? Are you not responsible for those deadfalls in licensing them to sell poison to those young men? Behold the wretchedness, misery and crime all around, the results of man's weakness and cupidity. Are you sure that your skirts are free from all responsibility for this condition of things? These are serious questions, Cain, and they appeal to you for an answer. You cannot escape your duty and responsibility in these matters any more than you did that fearful homicide you tried to conceal with the evasive question, with which we commence this fragment.

LOVE ALONE THAT SAVES.

One may belong to all the churches in the land; he may keep all the Sundays and holy days in the calendar; he may even abstain from the use of meat on Fridays, and if he be not charitable and have love in his heart for his fellow men, it will avail him nothing in the life to come. And so, after all, it is love that saves, and not the ordinances of the Church.

Then why not dispense with all ecclesiastical machinery and appliances in the work of salvation, and depend upon love alone, which any one can have without the aid of priest or church. One doesn't need to "believe and be baptized" in order to be good ; he need subscribe to no creed or confession of faith in order to love his fellow men, bind up broken hearts, or minister to the wants of the needy. And that is all the religion that Jesus taught.

SIX DOLLARS A WEEK !

That is the uniform wages paid to thousands of shop girls —clerks, cashiers, saleswomen—employed in this city of San Francisco! (Many girls are obliged to work for much less.) And out of this munificent (?) income, these women are expected to board and clothe themselves, and often to support an invalid mother or sister, or perhaps take care of a family of their own? "Expected," did we say? No; they are not "expected" to do anything of the kind. Their employers know that it cannot be done. At the lowest estimate, board of the very plainest kind, and room rent, would absorb the entire amount, leaving nothing for clothing, (and they must dress tidily,) or car fare (as they cannot always live near their work,) and nothing to make good lost time from sickness. This last is an important item, when it is borne in mind that many of these women are required to work from fourteen to sixteen hours a day, and often most of the time standing on their feet. What right has society, that tolerates a system of competition in trade that makes such wrongs possible, to condemn these girls when they go astray? It will not do to blame their employers, for if they paid higher wages they would be undersold and driven to the wall by their neighbors across the way. The fault is with the system that places every man's hand at the throat of his neighbor ; and, as always, the wrong falls heaviest upon the weakest, woman, in this case, is necessarily the greater sufferer.   In the light of these facts, should we not hail the day when Bellamy's dream of the future, or something like it, shall become a reality?   The life we are living is the struggle of hungry dogs for a bone, when there is an abundance for all, if we only go to work right to obtain it.

COARSENESS.

It cannot be other than a coarse nature that would needlessly wound another in his cherished religious opinions.   Thus, to ridicule what another has been taught to believe as sacred—the Bible, the Church or the Christian religion—indicates a great lack of refinement, as well as of that thoughtful consideration of another's feelings which always ought to belong to the true gentleman.   Such manifestations of coarseness, whether from the public platform, through the public paper, or in private conversation, always arouse a feeling of disgust in the reader or listener.   If such offences against good taste, and ordinary common sense, are offered for the mere purpose of insulting or humiliating another, we can only pity the perpetrator as a shameless blackguard, but if done with a view to compel or induce one to change his opinions, we would suggest that it is the very worst possible way to accomplish the desired result. No man was ever converted by ridicule or abuse.

KINSHIP OF HUMANITY.

The kinship of humanity!   By what indissoluble ties are we not linked to each other and to the entire race—rich and poor, prince and peasant, black and white!   The same in physical structure, and the same, in degree, in all the passions, impulses and emotions of the soul—hope, love, memory, anger, joy, hate, envy, jealousy, benevolence, kindness—all in one and one in all, more or less developed in each, but enough in each individual to make each one an epitome of all humanity. If we know ourselves thoroughly we shall thereby understand mankind generally—what is best for their advancement, and how best to touch the secret springs that uplift the lowly. We should never drift away from this thought of universal kinship ; we cannot if we would ; for Nature steps in with its constant reminders of sickness and sorrow, pain and misfortune, and finally with that all potent and universal leveler, Death, to teach us the oneness of humanity. Think not, ye proud and haughty ones of earth, that wealth or station are yours of right ; for there comes a time when you must descend from all worldly fortune or eminence, and take your place with the lowliest of earth—in the grave. The King will furnish no daintier morsel for the worm than the beggar. Know, then, that true and lasting preferment can be attained only in proportion as we love our fellows, and kindly help the weak and erring over the rough places of life.

INTELLECTUAL SLEDGEHAMMERS.

And now comes "John Ward, Preacher," on the heels of "Robert Elsmere," to stagger the faith of thousands in the cruel and unnatural dogmas of ecclesiasticism. And so the leaven is working, and the churches will ere long swing into line, and join hands with all who have the love of humanity at heart. These intellectual sledgehammer blows must tell, for man is a reasoning being, and cannot always consent to accept the foolish fables that have been palmed off upon him by designing men as the truth, and which he has been taught that it is sinful to question. If God is love, as we are taught from the pulpit, how is it possible that he can create souls for eternal punishment, knowing that when he created them that that would be their inevitable doom? "The John Wards," and

" Robert Elsmeres" of the churches, who have stumbled upon these questions, are bothering the preachers considerably about these days.

QUALITY OF GOODNESS.

What can there be in the quality of goodness possessed by the Christian, that is in any manner different from that possessed by the Atheist, the Spiritualist or the Jew? Even take the church standards of goodness requisite to salvation, no churchman will pretend to say that they are in any respect different from the goodness practised outside of the church ; neither will he presume to say that there is any saving virtue in belief, or ordinances, separate from goodness. So, we are brought down to the simple proposition that if a man is saved for his good qualities within the church, he must also be saved for the same qualities out of the church. The conclusion is unavoidable. And then, what is salvation? Is it, or can it be, anything more or less than the happiness which is the natural outcome of a well ordered life? If the infidel lives to bless the world with loving thoughts and kind acts, surely the Christian could do no more. Hence, in the Court of Eternal Justice both would be entitled to the same reward.

It is far better to be educated to a life of usefulness, no matter how humble, if honorable and worthy, and earn your way through the world, than to carry a diploma from some college in your pocket, and live on your friends. Culture is a good thing to have if the brain is of the right quality to profit by it. Many a man who would have made a good mechanic or tradesman, or manual laborer of some sort, has been spoiled by too much culture, or perhaps we should say false education, and educated out of all usefulness to himself or the world. You can't make a razor out of a piece of hoop iron, but you may spoil a good hoop trying.

INFANT DAMNATION.

There is not a Presbyterian clergyman in existence, who would dare to stand before an intelligent audience of the present day and preach the doctrine of infant damnation. And yet that is a part of the creed of election, or pre-destination as published to the world in their Westminster Catechism. The clergy do not believe it, they dare not preach it, and yet they subscribe to it. Is this fairly honest? Jonathan Edwards, one of the fathers of the Presbyterian Church, taught the doctrine of election with an unction and vehemence that sent a shudder of horror through the heart of humanity; and the great lights of Puritanism held that no man could be saved until he was willing to be damned for the glory of God! The church is getting over such monstrous conceptions of the Infinite, Father.

LIFE AND DEATH.

How beautiful is life! To the child so full of innocent glee; to the young man so bright with promise; to the middle-aged, so rich in fruition, if rightly lived; to the aged so encompassed with the smile of Infinite Love and so joyous with fond anticipation of the life beyond! How brief at most, and yet how full of rich experience! This is a good world to live in; but for the burdens of time—the infirmities of age—we should never want any other; at least we should be content to wait a long time for the next. In proportion as we make the best use of this life will we be prepared to get the truest enjoyment out of the next. And then no one need be troubled about the next life. If he lives to do good, and make others happy here—if he fill the air around him with the aroma of kind thoughts and loving deeds—he will find everything to his liking "over there."

How beautiful is death! The tired nerves have become insensible to pain; the sorrow of parting is over; consciousness is enfolded in sleep; angel lullabys fill the dreaming soul with a soft melody of bliss! And now so gently—so very gently—the spirit is withdrawing itself from its environment of matter,—from the old worn out body—inward from the extremities, and outward through the spiritual brain. What a wonderful change is this! *They* are there, the loved ones appointed to be present at the second birth and receive the newly born spirit. How carefully they watch its reorganization just above the still body! How eagerly they note its first indication of conscious-ness! If enfeebled with a long illness, the spirit, sympathizing with its earth condition, may require rest for many days, as we measure time, ere it come to a consciousness of the great change. In all this how beautiful! The bud expanding into the full blown rose is not more so. What a delightful study it must be to those upon the other side, though mixed with tears of sympathy for mourning friends here. To many of us that glorious change is near hand.

A CALIFORNIA WINTER.

Now comes the beautiful dreamy days of our California Winter, (Nov. 16th.) The cold winds that so long have swept down from the North, are lulled to gentle zephyrs, and the budding hopes of a new year are everywhere apparent. The bare, brown hills, that seemed so desolate and desert-like dur-ing the later Summer and Autumn months, are already clad with a rich mantle of green, and will soon blossom into purple and yellow with myriads of wild flowers. No fierce blasts of East-ern Winters here; no dreadful winding sheets of ice and snow. Our rivers run joyfully to the sea. The air is soft with mellow haze, and fragrant with the freshness of Spring. The birds are nesting in the trees, and tender flowers bloom all around and through the Winter months, as during the Summer. What a land of beauty and of grandeur is this, our loved California.

THINGS THAT WEALTH CANNOT PURCHASE.

There are many things that wealth can purchase to minister to the pleasures and needs of the mortal; but the things
that concern us most it can not buy, and therein the poor man
is the peer of the prince.   It can not command any sweeter
sleep nor any better digestion than that enjoyed by the home-
less tramp.   It can not purchase health, nor hope, nor happiness.   It can not avert death.   That which many a rich man
would give millions to possess—a sound pair of lungs, or kidneys, or a well ordered heart or liver—many a reader of these
Fragments is richer than a very Vanderbilt in.   And so, after
all, how empty and unsatisfactory a thing is wealth, especially
when the shadow of sickness falls across one's path, or the
rider upon the Pale Horse appears in sight.   We are none of
us as poor as we might be, even though the sod were our only
pillow, and our roof the starry canopy of night.   He, the gentle
teacher of Nazareth, "had not where to lay his head," and yet
He possessed all wealth.

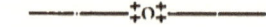

THE CHRONIC GROWLER.

The chronic growler—we find him almost everywhere,
wherever men and women congregate.   He is never satisfied
with his surroundings; something is always wrong with him,
and he is not backward in showing it, and thereby striving to
make others as uncomfortable as himself.   If at the table, his
food is never properly cooked or served ; if in the public con-
veyance, the managers and servants are sure to come in for a
measure of his execrations ; if at the communion table, he
would remember with disgust the quality of bread and wine.
Such a man should never marry, or if he does his wife should
be made of that sterner stuff capable of taking the growl out of
him on his first attempt to practice it.

VALUE OF PHENOMENA.

It is nonsense for lecturers on the philosophy of Spiritualism to under-estimate the importance of spirit phenomena in the work of bringing the world to a knowledge of the truth. Man must first be convinced of the truth of Spiritualism before he will listen to the philosophy thereof. You may talk forever about the continued existence of the spirit of man beyond the grave, but unless you can and do prove it, the intelligent skeptic will only laugh at you for your presumption. Take test mediumship out of the Cause, and all lecturers on the philosophy of Spiritualism would have to close up their halls, and turn their attention to some other pursuit as a means of livelihood. The spiritualistic press, now all too poorly supported, would have to surrender to the inevitable and quit. Give us more mediums of this class, and better ones, if possible. They are the foundation stones, and the pillars, that uphold the temple of Spiritualism.

———‡o‡———

GRAVITATION.

What slaves to gravitation we all are while imprisoned in these mortal bodies! A bird with wings weighted with lead would not be more so. True, we have harnessed steam and electricity into our service, and journeys of months have, within the last few years, been reduced to days, still we must ever bear the heavy load of a cumbersome body, while on this plane of life. But won't it be grand when the spirit can master space entirely, and on the electric car of thought can flash away to the most distant star, and in an instant of time? We do not apprehend that it is possible for all spirits to take such mighty flights, if indeed any can. Those of the planet earth may not be able to go beyond our own solar system, which contains fields of space quite broad enough to satisfy any ordinary taste for traveling. We know that disembodied spirits can move over the face of the earth with the rapidity of thought, and that some are permitted to go on long journeys to other planets of our system. The power to accomplish such marvels of loco-motion must be a source of amazing delight to the spirit.

————‡o‡————

ENLIGHTENED THOUGHT.

The drift of enlightened thought is in the direction of ab-solute infidelity to all man-made creeds—to everything that hampers the freest investigation of all things relating to man's present and future welfare. The old ecclesiastical bugbear, "Believe or be damned," no longer frightens anybody. The people have come to see that it is only a scarecrow with an imitation gun. Thus, from one position to another, have they advanced, until the intelligent world has come to see that the whole plan of salvation, with all of its dogmas of God and the devil, the creation and fall of man, the vicarious atone-ment, heaven and hell, etc., are only the foolish fancies and fictions of undeveloped minds, which must be swept aside for something higher and better ; and that the only things in the traditions of the church worth preserving, and of which the church even has never been overstocked, is LOVE, the all-potent factor in man's redemption and exaltation.

————‡o‡————

When we remember the centuries of fierce theological teaching to which the race has been subjected, we can but wonder that there are so many good people in the world as there are—so many generous hearted and sympathetic people. The thoughts of an all-loving purpose in creation, and that all seeming evil is but undeveloped good that will disap-pear with man's spiritual unfoldment, is but just dawning upon the world. It is breaking in streams of roseate light all around the sky, and the dark shadows of Omnipotent wrath are rapidly melting away.

A LOST FORTUNE.

That was an odd and somewhat suggestive way of stating the case, as we read the other day in a smart newspaper—"Henry R. Simpson lost two million dollars last evening in "less than a minute—from heart disease." It was a great misfortune to Henry Simpson, that he should have had that amount of money to *lose*, for what else does any rich man, who does nothing for the world, do with his money when he dies but lose it? The only way not to lose it is to make a good use of it before he dies. If he leaves it for imprudent and unthrifty heirs to squander, he not only loses it, but he does them an incalculable mischief as well. If man were to live on this plane forever, and especially if the infirmities of age should render it impossible for him to acquire more, there might be a good reason for his holding on to all he could get; but old age should remind him that he is about through with this mortal existence, and that the time is at hand when he will no longer have any use for money, or property of any kind. There is nothing so tests the quality of a rich man's nature, as the appeal of approaching dissolution, to "render unto Cæsar the things which are Cæsar's, and unto God the things which are God's." Governor and Mrs. Stanford, guaged by this test, are not found wanting; neither is Eunice S. Sleeper, nor other royal souls we could name.

"No man can be wise without love, and no woman can truly love and not be wise," so says Ernst von Himmel, in his new and charming book, "The Discovered Country." Wisdom and love must go through life hand in hand, or there is no reality or happiness in either. All of the inharmony growing out of perverted love results from the absence of wisdom. In the life beyond they understand these things better than they do here.

DESTRUCTION OF INNOCENT LIFE.

What preverted taste—what cruel ideas of pleasure, men have who destroy harmless birds, for the mere love of killing. Of all this cruel pastime, that of trap shooting seems the most heartless and diabolical. The most harmless of birds, usually the dove or wild pigeon, is placed in a small box, from which by means of a trap door and string, it is sent forth into its native air, only to fall bleeding and dying at the hand of some savage lout, who stands ready, with gun in hand, to kill. And this is sport! If there was such a place in the universe as a bottomless pit and a personal Devil, and the latter should lay in wait by the mouth of the former, with his regulation pitch-fork and pitch the unwary trap shooter therein, at the first opportunity, could any one be blamed for objecting,—that is, if there was a way provided for pulling him out when he had properly profited by his experience?

————‡o‡————

EDWIN ARNOLD.

No sweeter singer ever climbed the holy mount of song —none ever swept the lyre to a grander purpose, than Edwin Arnold, author of "Light of Asia." His poetry is full of soul, as well as of that nameless grace of art that rounds out every part, and stamps the seal of genius on each classic line. Schooled in the glowing imagery of the Orient, familiar with its deepest lore and oldest language, and yet an adept in all the sweet forms of English speech, he can play upon the deepest emotions of the soul with a master's hand. His "Good Night! Not Good Bye," written in memory of his wife, who passed on to her home among the angels a few months ago, for tender pathos and exquisite sweetness of expression, has no equal in our language. No one can read such poetry without feeling himself drawn nearer to the heart of the Infinite Good.

THE VIRTUE OF SELFISHNESS.

Selfishness is usually condemned unqualifiedly as a deplorable vice, and yet we cannot see how, in the present incongruous condition of society, it can well be wholly dispensed with. There is a kind of ravenous selfishess that " wants the earth," which of course is a curse to the world, and cannot be too loudly condemned.   But the selfishness that prompts one to take good care of himself, and look out for the welfare of his family becomes a virtue under the existing social order. If one " sells all that he has and gives it to the poor," as Jesus suggested was a proper thing for a certain rich man to do in his time, there is a probability that in this day and generation, one would find himself, when too old to work for his daily bread, an inmate of the poor-house. We could never see any virtue in poverty, at the same time who can but admire the sterling unselfishness of the one who would share his last dollar with a suffering brother mortal.

———‡o‡———

A GRAND HUMANITARIAN.

That noble woman and grand humanitarian, Mrs. Leland Stanford, who, with her husband, has given vast sums for humanity's sake, is reported as saying that she hoped it might be her lot "to die poor."   Ah, that is the sweetest poverty the world ever knew, that surrenders all worldly wealth for the good of others.   How such deeds blossom into glory, and clothe the immortal spirit in raiment of light.   The wealth that belongs simply to the things of time bears no comparison to the riches of the spirit.   One is dross, the other pure gold— one the shadowy thing of a day, the other the substantial riches of eternity, that shall increase and grow brighter with the ages. Go on, royal souls ; there is preparing for you a home in the life beyond, in comparison with which all earthly palaces are the veriest hovels.   Only a few years hence, at most, and you will enter upon your possessions. Life will then have for you a meaning and a grandeur of which this life is but the faintest suggestion. How like unto Him who gave his all, even his life, for the good of others.

————‡o‡————

DEATH NATURAL AND PAINLESS.

The thought of death is a great terror to many people— the thought that they must grow old and die, and their bodies be consigned to the grave. But why should it be? In sleep the body simulates death in all except the physical awakening. The spirit passes out and into other scenes and enjoyments, and no doubt, often, to the companionship of spirits on the other side of life. We do not dread sleep; why should we dread death, which is quite as natural and painless. Even were there no hope of a hereafter, there surely could be no de- sire to live, if life were unendurable from pain or other causes; But that which most reconciles one to endure the ills of time and the pains of sickness to the end, is the knowledge that the spirit needs all these experiences to best prepare it for the real- ities of the life to come. While no true Spiritualist has any doubts or misgivings as to the future, he is nevertheless willing to remain here his allotted time, and endure patiently until the end.

————‡o‡————

OLD TRADITIONS.

It appears to us that our religious teachers spend altogeth- er too much time in studying the ancient writings which have been compiled into a book (millions say The Book), and alto- gether too little in studying themselves, and teaching the laws of life and health as they find them engraven on the tablets of their own constitutions. It would seem to be self-evident that whatever may be a revelation to one person, in a past age, can- not, in the nature of things, be a revelation to another person in another age. We would not deprecate the grand precepts of life and duty embodied in the Christian Scriptures, although— — we would much prefer to have said precepts and teachings disentangled from the mass of rubbish in which we find them involved ; still, there is so much we need to learn, of which the Bible tells us nothing, that it does seem as though some of the time spent in Bible-class and Sunday-school, as well as in church service generally, might better be devoted to lessons in hygiene and the science of right living. What better is a man off from listening to a sermon from a Second Adventist, on the destruction of the wicked, or a Calvinist on predestination, or infant damnation? What more does he know after being taught the doctrine of three Gods in one, or the necessity of killing one of the three, which was the entire three, to satisfy the sense of justice of the other two, which was himself, as the only means of saving man from the consequences of his imaginary fall? In the light of the new truths now breaking upon the world, these old traditions are fast fading away.

THE SHADOW OF ECCLESIASTICISM.

How dark the shadow of the grave that the Church has thrown across the pathway of human life ! Centuries of horror ! A world plunged into a vortex of everlasting woe, with no escape except by a method repugnant to every honorable soul ! No man can shirk the responsibility of his own sinful acts, in a vicarious way, without lowering himself, thoughtlessly it may be, in the estimation of every bright and manly intelligence in the universe. And then so very few, comparatively, are permitted to escape by " casting their sins upon Jesus." The great multitude, including mighty nations, cast into hell because they reject a narrow, priest-made plan of salvation ! Great minds, like those of Edwin Arnold, Huxley, Humboldt, Spencer, Wallace, Darwin, and hosts of others, all consigned to eternal torment, because they have a grander conception of the Creator, and a truer appreciation of man's proper place in the universe, than to believe in the monstrous dogmas taught from Christian pulpits today!

And yet, how the Church has garnered the spiritual thoughts of millions of the human race. It contained all of spiritual truths they knew, cruel, despotic and vindictive as it often was, and on its altars, red at times with the blood of martyrs, has been laid the purest and holiest faith, the sweetest love, the most undying devotion of the human heart. How grandly have devout men and tender women gone to the stake, and amid the cruel flames that rioted through every avenue of mortal agony, sang hosannahs to the Lamb, the gentle Nazarene, in whom they placed their trust. No doubt that same Jesus was able, in many instances, through laws that Spiritualism has revealed to the world, to sustain them in that mortal hour, and give them happy and painless exit from this world of sorrow. It is not the religion of Christianity that we condemn, by any means, but only the fungus growths of ignorance, barbarism and superstition that have fastened to its vitals.

THE TRUE HERO.

He who gives himself up to the indulgence of aught that injures the body or degrades the spirit surrenders to the enemy without making his best fight. He virtually throws open the gates of the citadel and invites the enemy to enter in. Life is a constant struggle, and he only is the true hero who makes the most valiant defense of himself against all the encroachments of evil. Victory over self is within the reach of every one. That some fail is simply because they do not do their best. And so they must needs try again, on another plane of existence, or perhaps on this. We may not know where; but this we know, the victory must be gained somewhere.

SLEEP.

Sweet sleep! That comes like a balmy wave of forgetfulness over the spirit, and all the troubles and cares of the day —its heartaches and sorrows—

> " Fold their tents like the Arabs,
> And as silently steal away !"

O, beautiful Sleep! Faint counterpart of death! Blessed friend and comforter! Who does not love to rest in thy sheltering arms! When the shadows of night curtain the drowsy earth, and the stars come forth to hold their silent watch in the sky; when the wanton bee, lawless ravisher of the flowers, returns from his last flight at eve, and the mother bird gathers her brood under her faithful wing,—then the tired toiler in the field or by the forge, lays his burden down, and bows his head to thy gentle caress. And thus, on and on, day by day, till the last sleep shall come to the weary eye-lids, the sleep that knows no waking on an earthly morrow! So may it come to the tired heart, stealing over the senses as gently as falls the summer dew, and all mortal pain shall be dumbed forevermore.

———‡o‡———

MORAL DEATH.

If all the people were buried who are dead the cemeteries would not be large enough to contain them,—that is, morally dead, which is simply indifference to the growth and needs of the spirit. When a man closes his heart to the appeals of his sorrowing and suffering fellow beings, and lives simply in himself and for himself, he is dead, and the sooner he is placed under the ground the better it will be for the living. There are other kinds of death than those followed by immediate decay of the physical body. Petrefaction, crystallization, and stagnation of the spirit—what is this but death, and death in its most repulsive form. Blessed be the man that can rise superior to this kind of death.

COLD COMFORT.

The editor of *Freethought* is asked to publish a death notice of the little two year old son of a friend, with the added request that the editor would "add what consolation there may be to offer." Here is the proffered consolation (?) : "We can say that there is no consolation except the "knowledge that merciful Time may lessen the acuteness "of grief; that sorrow consumes itself at last; that whatever of "trouble might have been in store for the littleone, had he "lived, is spared him now." If we had nothing more to offer a stricken heart, we would ask to be excused and say nothing. Why will our freethought friends persist in repudiating evidence of the future life that is as palpable as sight, as positive as touch, and as clearly established as the proof of mortal existence—that is, to millions of the race. There is not a whit more improbability of a continued existence of the spirit of man beyond the confines of the grave, even were there no evidence of the fact, than there is that he exists here. There is no more mystery about the one life than the other. If there was no future life (and we *know* there is), then Nature is an infinite cheat, as far as man is concerned. She completes everything else she undertakes ; why should she make an exception of him? She brings him up to a point where his longing soul has just begun to aspire for knowledge, and then she snuffs him out of the universe ! No, no, neighbor ; you are on the wrong tack.

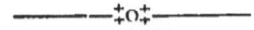

It is your small man that makes the greatest fuss about little things. He will fume and fret, and abuse his wife, about the loss of a gimlet, and work himself into a rage over trifles that would not ruffle the repose of one of larger capacity. No one, perhaps, can help being small, but surely he ought to be able to avoid showing it.

MODERN SPIRITUALISM.

How grand the prospect. Out from the caves of darkness and superstition—from crypts venerable with age and hoary with tradition—steps forth a beautiful maiden, radient with the light of a new day. Her name is Modern Spiritualism. In her hand she bears a banner on which are inscribed the words: "Love, the fulfillment of the law, the redemption of the race." She is greeted with derision by the conservatism of science, and the intolerance and bigotry of the Church. The respectable cowardice of the world gathers her garments aside to let her pass. But steadily onward, following the sunlight of Eternal Truth, she moves forward with the air and mien of an angel from the upper planes of life. And following her lead, behold the mighty hosts, coming up from all nations, and all walks o life! The shackles are falling from their limbs—the scales from their eyes. Truly, the day of jubilee, the dawning of the new era, is at hand!

——— -‡o‡——

The heart that is not touched with pity at another's failings and weaknesses, as well as at his misfortunes, has only learned one-half of its lesson of humanity. What credit is it to you that you are not a beggar, a drunkard, or a thief? Had you been fashioned of poorer stuff, and environed with wretched associations from infancy, then what? Be thankful for yourself, and press on in the better way.

* *
*

He who saves all his smiles and kind words for his neighbors, and bestows nothing but frowns and abuse upon his wife and children, has not yet learned the alphabet of life. He needs the chastening hand of some great sorrow to make his heart tender and teach him his duty to his family. Nothing so undermines the natural meanness of such a man, as the sight of the white, dead face of the wife, who, in his better moments, has nestled lovingly in his arms.

BRAINS.

"Blood will tell," is an old but somewhat inelegant adage, borrowed from the race-track. So will brains. If one expects to get the upper hand of the world, he must not imagine he can do so without an effort, nor that he can succeed without putting into vigorous exercise his keenest faculties. The number of people "born with a gold spoon in the mouth," is very few. And even the pampered sons of wealth naturally find it a hard task to hold on to their possessions without brains. They generally possess so many expensive vices that ere they are aware, they find themselves broken down in health, and their wealth scattered to the winds. It is an actual blessing to most people that they are born poor, that is, if they are naturally good for anything. They thereby acquire habits of thrift and economy most essential to health as well as to success in life. Where the material is bad it makes but little difference how they are born —rich or poor. They will be apt to make a bad job of it in any case.

————⁘○⁘————

Kindness is the only true educator for an erring soul. You must develop his better nature—call forth the good there is in him—and the bad will naturally cease to manifest. You cannot do this by harsh words or cruel treatment. You can educate him in the better way only by the exercise of a tender sympathy growing out of a proper understanding of your relations to each other.

* *
*

We pity the stricken one, who, standing by the open grave of his heart's idol, believes that "death ends all." O, the night of dark despair! the impenetrable gloom of hopeless woe! What! Is such to be the horrible fruition of human love—of the tender yearning for another's welfare that reaches out to the very stars? No, no! the All-Father and Creator is no such monster.

NATURE'S LESSONS.

All nature is pointed with useful lessons for man's spiritual and intellectual unfoldment, if he will but open his understanding to the meanings of her many voices. She pleads with him from the stars to look upward for light to guide him through the tangled ways of life, and lead him to his eternal home. She woos him from her mountain peaks of everlasting snows to pattern his character after their spotless whiteness. She invites him in the fragrance of the rose, in the murmur of the brook, and in the song of the birds, to make his own life rich with the aroma of good deeds, and melodious with the beautiful symphonies of loving fellowship with all that is good in earth and heaven.

Leave the dead past alone in its sepulchre. Why chain the living with the dead—why tread forever its dismal vaults, feasting the soul on its cruel and bitter memories. If a friend has wronged you, forget it ; if suffering has been your lot— —if misfortune and disappointment have shadowed your life —let it all go. Bury your ills, and resurrect your joys. Gather the lillies and roses wherever you find them, and tread the nettles and thorns beneath your feet. Life is too short to burden the spirit with unpleasant things.

THERE IS NO DEATH.

The lessons of our translated loved ones is that there is no death—that what seems so is only transition—the birth to a new life, as real, aye, far more real than this; for here we bear the changing conditions of time—youth, with its bright hopes and golden dreams; manhood, with its fierce contests in the battle of life, its struggles with the busy world ; old age, if we have lived rightly, with its sheaves of ripened grain, its pleasant memories, and its calm outlook upon the future. But there, in that new life, these mortal changes and conditions do not exist. He who has profited by his earthly experiences, goes onward in the path of eternal progression, amid scenes and surroundings that are real and tangible to spirit sense. Here all is change. There is no permanency in matter. The hills wear away and melt into the sea; the rocks themselves crumble to ashes at the touch of time; the "firm set earth" is growing old, and in some distant æon, will doubtless become a dead world to be buried, perhaps, in the bosom of the sun. Spirit is the eternal, unchanging substance, while matter is the evanescent shadow of things, upon every atom of which is written "change."

It is a beautiful thing to grow in years gracefully and wisely—to carry down into the sunset of life the gentle graces and sweetness of a spirit enriched with good thoughts and noble impulses. Age is not measured by years nor whitened locks, to one who lives rightly. The soul never grows old. It may lose its elasticity of expression through its worn out instrument; the footsteps may become faltering and the voice feeble with time, but the soul is there just the same, with all its garnered earth experiences, all its lustre untarnished. It has only withdrawn a little within the veil, whence sooner or later it will step out into the open day of a new life.

When Death comes to a good man or woman, in the fullness of time, it comes as a welcome friend. One after another their hearts' treasures have been gathered to the home of the spirit, and at last they stand alone, like ripened grain ready for the sickle. The struggle of active life is over; the battle has been fought; the world's stern work has passed into younger hands, and they stand alone with the evening's calm around them, and with ear bent for the sound of the boatman's oar that shall bear them over the silent waters.

In proportion as the mind is empty of knowledge does it engage in the frivolities and little things of life. Show us a gossiping scandal-monger, and we will show you a person with many rooms to let in the upper story. Imagine George Eliot, Alice Cary and R. W. Emerson crooning together and back-biting a neighbor across the street!

GENEROUS DEEDS.

Like the fragrance of the flower exhales the aroma of kind thoughts and generous deeds. The soul shines out through the face, and radiates the very presence of a good man or woman. In their daily walks among their fellows they shed blessings on every hand. They have gentle words of sympathy for the suffering, kind deeds for the needy, and are ever, like their great Teacher, the beautiful Christ, offering the waters of life to him that is ready to perish. This is the kind of humanity that must supplement the multitudes of selfish and soulless men and women, now existing upon the earth before the figurative New Jerusalem, the city of God and his angels, foreshadowed in the Apocalypse, can come down out of heaven and become the everlasting abode of the saints—of the "spirits of just men made perfect." Let the good not grow weary. The millennium is slowly but surely coming. Centuries are but moments in the reckoning of eternity.

INVOCATION.

Infinite spirit of Nature, thou that pervadeth the universe of matter, quickening into life and being all forms of beauty —radiating in the sunlight, blossoming in the flowers, filling the air with melody in the song of birds and the murmur of brooks; —thou that art everywhere and all things—in the pains of motherhood, in helpless infancy, in the joy and gladness of youth, in the struggles and trials of manhood, in the bowed form and feeble step of old age, in the sinking pulse of death;— thou that holdest the universe in thy keeping, and in the mighty sweep of suns and constellations, filleth immensity with glory—may we not feel that we are a part of thee, and realize that thy infinite purpose in us is that we may become like unto thee in all symmetry and beauty of spirit, in all nobility of character, in all grandeur of goodness. May thy ministering spirits from the shining shores of immortal life, touch all hearts with a tender sympathy for those that suffer, and kindle anew in each soul a firmer purpose to subdue all the lesser good in the undeveloped nature, and to rise to the higher planes of being, where all is honor, and purity, and true manliness of soul. And thus we will ever pray.

The mole burrowing in the dark earth, the thistle down floating on the summer breeze, the rootlet of the plant groping for moisture and nutrition,—all are moved by a divine energy, the same that called the world into existence, and bespangled the infinite spaces of ether with star gems.

WHAT WERE YOU MADE FOR ?

Young man, would you make your life, financially or otherwise, a success? Find out as early as possible in your career, what vocation, or art, or line of life, you are best suited for, and then pursue the object persistently and zealously to the end. Turn neither to the right nor the left, but press on to the goal of your ambition, and you will surely win. It is the undecided, irresolute man, one who is "everything by turns, and nothing long," that fritters away his young manhood, and his maturer years, and ere he is aware of it old age creeps up on him, and finds him with nothing done. But he must remember that in pursuing his object, whatever it may be, he should consider the needs of his spiritual nature. "Man cannot live by bread alone." He needs other aliment to round out his character and make him the complete man he should be.   This spiritual culture should interblend with his business pursuits, and go hand in hand therewith.   It should be remembered that some of the grandest successes in life were of men who could never find time to acquire wealth.

EVER AND FOREVER.

The old orthodox idea of eternal punishment—of never throughout all the countless ages of eternity, giving the once mortal sinner a chance for repentance or reform ; but ever and forever holding him to the rack of unforgiving agony for wrongs done—is not, surely, the true spiritualistic idea of making the world better.   And yet some there be who would ransack the earth to find some blemish in one's character and conduct— no matter how long repented of, or condoned by subsequent good conduct—to condemn him, in the eyes of an uncharitable world, and bring him to mortal disgrace and ruin.   In the eternities we would rather be such a wrong doer than his unmerciful judge.

There are two standards of judgment among men concerning their fellow men—one to regard every man a rogue until proved honest ; the other, to look upon all as honest until they demonstrate in their lives and conduct that they are unworthy of confidence.   This seems to be the better way, and we would apply the same rule of judgment to mediums for spirit communion.

* *
*

A bad digestion and a diseased liver have turned many a very fair article of Christian into a confirmed cross-patch and wretched human porcupine.   It takes a fine quality of spiritual grace and goodness to enable one thus afflicted to turn the better side of his nature to the sunlight ; thus, when your enemies abuse you charge it to their deranged internal economy and pass on.

SUSTAINING GRACE OF SPIRITUALISM.

"But for the sustaining grace of Spiritualism," remarked a stricken brother to us the other day—one who had recently been called to part with the mortal companionship of a dearly loved wife—"I should at once follow her to the grave." But now he knows of a verity that it is her wish that he shall stay till his work is finished; he knows that his angel is ever near him, giving him the assurance and sweet satisfaction of her loving sympathy, and that she will be there to greet him when he shall lay aside the mortal. And so he will walk bravely to the end. His anchor is cast, sure and steadfast, within the veil, and his eternity of hope and unending love is begun.

He who seeks for the highest and best in his own life is sure to find it. He will certainly develop those spiritual faculties in his nature that will draw him nearer to the divine life. But to do this, he must rise above all unkind thoughts, all domination of evil, into an atmosphere of unselfishness and harmony. He must "enter the path" and "live the life." Then will peace, like a river, flow into his soul, and happiness and rest—the rest of persistent endeavor for the welfare of others—be his forevermore.

The crowded streets! What a medley of humanity! Eager faces, glad faces, puzzled faces; faces sodden with dissipation and distorted with crime; thoughtful, frivolous, wicked faces; young and joyous faces, wrinkled and careworn faces, loving and gentle faces—how they meet and mingle and flash by me, an unceasing, ever-changing kaleidoscope of humanity —never the same and yet always the same! Where will all these faces be ere long? All gazing upward with sightless eyes. A generation passes away and a new one takes its place, and the world moves onward without a break.

OPPOSITION.

After all, what effect has opposition upon Spiritualism—what the ignorant abuse by pulpit and press—but to advertise it to the world, and make for it new friends? Hasn't such been the case with all new systems of religion and philosophy, in all times, the world over? The church once sought to punish heresy with the faggot and the rack; but did the crop of heretics become any less? Did the pagan persecution of the early Christians have any other effect than to fire the hearts of the votaries of that religion with additional zeal? So is it with Spiritualism. "Let the heathen rage against us;" it brings us strength. Woe unto our cause when it is no longer considered worthy of abuse.

Slain again and again in the house of its friends, defiled by its ministers, waylaid, and beaten down, and robbed in high places, nevertheless our beautiful Spiritualism still lives. It comes forth bleeding but never crushed from every disaster, to grapple again and again with error, and win men to a belief in the glorious truths of immortality and the higher life. It pervades many homes where love dwells, and where it has erected its holy altars, before which the inmates gather in sweet and reverent devotion. The storm of fierce opposition but gives it new strength, treason in its councils, and betrayal of its sacred trusts, but add to the potency of its energizing forces to subdue the hearts and understandings of men, and bring the two worlds together in one mighty purpose to uplift and ennoble humanity.

When will man learn that all bitterness, rancor, unkindness—that all manner of ungenerous thought and feeling—are but clogs and bars to the spirit's advancement and growth. And then these moods of minds grow upon what they feed, until all the springs of charity and gentleness, that ought to gush forth in every human nature, are dried up, and the fallow ground of the heart becomes parched and arid as a desert waste. What a dark and wretched karma some people are creating to carry with them to the other life. The lesson of love and good will should be learned here, and not wait till we get "over there."

THE ONE BRIGHT STAR.

Spiritualism is the one bright star that shines down into the stricken heart, radiating the entire being with the light of peace and hope. It spans the river of death with a rainbow arch of glory, along which tread the shining feet of angels. It broadens our outlook upon the physical plane of life and enables us to realize that it "is not all of life to live, nor all of death to die." Before this new light, now streaming into the hearts and homes of humanity, the hideous phantoms of a false theology, founded in the barbarism of the race, must flee away. "The bottomless pit," like the great mælstrom of the Northern Coast, has been found to be a myth—the "impassible gulf" a hideous fantasy of a distorted brain. Spiritualism gives us a Being of infinite love at the head of the universe, and not a monster of implacable hate, who will "laugh at our calamity and mock when our fear cometh."

The nightmare of the soul, has it not been, through all the ages—the theology of Christianity? It has taught the separation of kindred souls for all eternity, and furrowed out of space an infinite vortex of everlasting woe for the ignorant and undeveloped. It demands what is an impossibility to many intelligent minds, under pain of eternal banishment from happiness, and then asks us to render to such a Being the love and worship of our souls! Not such the God whom Spiritualists would adore.

MY SOUL AND I.

Fragments from a Sunday Outing.

I have wandered forth, this beautiful Sunday morning (July 21st, 1889), from the quiet country home of my friends, Mrs. S. M. Nunn and her gifted artist daughter, Miss Ella (where the writer and niece are spending a few restful days)— have strolled forth, my soul and I, to hold communion with nature, among some of her wildest and most beautiful forms. Here are dense forests, deep and dark ravines, mighty masses of rocks, towering redwoods, and rippling streams. Here, also, are sloping hillsides, and wide stretches of fertile vales, all combining to make as rare and lovely a picture as any that can be found elsewhere, even in this land of nature's wonderful variety and beauty, (California.) What a home for an artist or a poet, and what a charming place for a brief outing from the noisy city !

Among the hills, the grand old hills, for two glad days. The air is pure and soft, and fragrant with the odors of the fir and the laurel, and the breath of wild ferns and climbing vines, while the purling brook at my feet makes laughing melody among the rocks. A great silence broods the earth, save the sharp hum of the bee on its errand of sweetness, and the chirp to the brown linnet on yonder branch. Have no fear, little mother, your tiny brood is safe. I am here to sit with you at the feet of our common mother, to gather strength and courage for other struggles. So, go on with your housework, my timid little friend. Your being's end and aim is complete in rearing your young brood. But you have a little time, now and then, to spare for a song of joy to gladden other lives ; and so we take heart of you. Nature has fulfilled her purpose in you, and you are happy, except when some great shadow falls across your life, as now ; and I am that shadow. I'll move farther up the brook, and leave you at your task.

The cattle grazing on yonder hillside—they are not troubling themselves about the ownership of the lands upon which they feed ; nor whether they are mortgaged or not ; nor whether one of their number is richer or better than another. They do not chafe their souls in prayer for better pastures by and by ; nor do they worry over their sins ; nor are they concerned about their respectability. They do not sell rum to other cattle, nor do they organize great trusts to rob their fellows of a fair share of food. They are not troubled about the ownership of houses, or lands, or bank accounts, to leave to their heirs ; nor do they ever die of Bright's disease from imprudent habits. Not one of them uses tobacco in any form, nor slanders his neighbors, nor lays awake nights planning how he can get the best of a bargain. They have no use for lawyers, or doctors, or preachers. Happy brutes !

Will she not come to you, pretty dove, at your plaintive call? Surely, it was not always thus ? I remember with what joy your heart was filled in the golden days when your wedded life began. The world was very bright and fair before you then. You thought you would never weary of each other's attentions. You floated in a fairy shallop on a sea of golden dreams. But care and toil and anxiety came, and left their furrows in your heart ; and then, neglecting the growth of your spirit, you became worldly-minded and sordid ; your heart grew cold and indifferent towards your mate. She drooped for a while, and then a beautiful light shone in her eyes one day, and she unfurled her wings and flew away to the sweet Summerland. And now, sad and lonely (for you loved her better than you knew), you sit and mourn all the day long for a joy that is dead. Quit that nonsense. Be a happy dove again in striving to make amends for the past by helping to assuage the griefs of other mourning doves, and by sharing in their burdens, ever remembering that she waits for you in that better land. Now, get thee out of the shadow and into the sunshine, and cease that sad refrain.

———

Ah, little bright eyes ! Who are you, scudding along the dead branch, in your brown dress, and peering askance at this intruder? Haven't you something gayer for your Sunday attire, or don't you care? Are you not aware that all over this great earth evangelical Christianity is teaching, from tens of thousands of pulpits, that a peculiar sanctity attaches to this day, because the Maker of the heavens and the earth, after six days' labor at world-building, rested on the seventh? What right have you, little lizard, to be breaking the Sabbath in this way? Now, don't look at me in that quizzing kind of way, as though you would say, What do you know about it? (Honestly, we know nothing, but then we preachers think we do.) You needn't tell me that God never rested, that the work of creation is going steadily forward from eternity to eternity, and that all days are alike holy? Doesn't the Book say otherwise? Get thee hence from off that log, and leave me to my meditations. I will not listen to thee.

———

"God wants a little fun once in a while, dosen't he ?" queried a nice little boy of his mother the first time he ever saw a dude. So it would seem, for some of his creations are surely suggestive of the ludicrous. See with what gorgeous apparel, what colors rivaling the ocean's blue or the rainbow's marvelous dyes, he bedecks some of his creatures. Take that rare little tid-bit of a humming-bird, flitting among the flowers of the wild rose bush just upon the bank above me. What a little flashing gem of light and beauty it presents to the eye ! Ah, what is this but one of God's bits of pleasantry, uttered to amuse me? So of many quaint and beautiful shapes of bird and flower. In fact, all nature is bubbling over with mirth for our delight, when we would have it so.

The mountains? **How** they appeal to us to come up higher! How proudly they lift their mighty crests to the heavens, as though they were the monarchs of the earth and sea! Behold them from afar!   Seamed and gullied though their rugged sides may be with the attrition of ages of storm and melting snow, there upon their placid brows sits enthroned the majesty of eternal repose.   Volcanoes may rage within their bosoms, and earthquakes struggle and gasp at their feet, still they stand forever as mighty finger-posts pointing the way upward to the All-Good.   O mountains, grand and glorious, I love you! Let me rest in your arms for aye, and dream, and dream.

———

"'There is a pleasure in the pathless woods," sang Byron, and so there is; but, until one can find time to make new and better paths, it were wiser that one keep in the old ones.   To be torn and wounded by briars, to lose one's way among the thick furze, and all to accomplish nothing, is not well.   Some would-be reformers work on this principle.   They step out from the old paths, and slash around in the brush of new ideas, without any other purpose, seemingly, than to get themselves into a great sweat, and think thereby they are opening up a better way of life and thought for those who are to follow them.   Until one can say, I have found the better way, he should advise no one to follow him.   It is true that we must first tear down before we can build anew, still we should remember that we may need a shelter in the meantime.   An old house and a leaky roof are better than none at all in a storm.

———

What a rollicking good time we have had, my soul and I, out here in these vast depths of shadow, in these grand old woods! How we have romped among the birds and brooks, and drank our fill of the divine nectar that dreams are made of.   And now the night steals on apace, whose early morning sun will light us on our way back to the great city and to the sober realities of a busy life.   Good night!

WHERE RESPONSIBILITY LIES.

Every act of our lives—every thought of good or evil—leaves its impress upon the spirit, moulding, and shaping it for the life of the spirit within other and finer environments, in that world "beyond the river." Thus it is that we make ourselves what we really are. We shall be grand and radiant in that new life —the fit companions of grand souls,—or we shall grovel in the slums of the hells we have created for ourselves, just as we will. But, it may be asked, Is the spirit wholly responsible for its mortal expression? We would answer, Most certainly not, Neither is the child responsible for its carelessness in falling into the fire,-but it must suffer the pain of the burn all the same. We are not responsible for inherited tendencies to evil, nor for the bias of early erroneous education, but we suffer from their impress upon our natures just the same as though we were.

POVERTY OF RICHES.

" I never felt so rich in all my life as now, and never had so little of this world's wealth," said a grand, good woman in our presence the other day. It was the true riches of the spirit that she possessed—riches that " neither moth nor rust can destroy, nor thieves break in and steal." She is a woman in perfect physical health, made so because of her harmonious life, and one who holds daily and almost hourly communion with the spirit world. The spirit of a beautiful girl, who passed to the other life in early infancy, now just developed into spiritual womanhood, came into her life a few years ago, and now is her constant companion and friend, and the gentle guardian of her home. This spirit entrances her, and speaks through her lips, and is to her all that a loving daughter could be in spirit. Into the heart of this woman has been instilled the beautiful lessons of love, charity and true happiness. She has learned that there are riches of the soul, priceless jewels of wealth, with which naught of earth can compare. And these are the treasures that are filling her life with joy.

He who is ever thinking evil of others must have that in his own nature to call forth like thoughts in the minds of his fellows. The mind is apt to dwell upon that of which it possesses most. There is an old adage that "it takes a thief to catch a thief." We would that there were no thieves to catch, and none to catch them!

MORE! MORE!

"More! More! That was the sad refrain of poor Oliver in Dickens' touching story. It is the cry of the great world of humanity in its struggle for the things of earth. More land, more houses, more income! Never contented or satisfied ; always, as long as life lasts, seeking for more! It is a preverted spirituality that prompts this unreasonable longing for temporal possessions. If men would put forth the same energy in the acquisition of the treasures of the spirit that they do to pile up worldly wealth, how grandly they would mount to the upper heights of being—become gods, as it were, both in this world and the next. Thus they would build for eternity, whereas now they mostly build for time.

HOW TO MAKE SPIRITUALISM RESPECTABLE.

If we would make Spiritualism respectable we must first learn to respect it ourselves. The world is full of erring and sinful ones. Some there are in our ranks, of the " holier-than-thou " kind, who delight in hunting out the erring and following them through life like sleuth hounds of perdition. Puffed up in their own conceit and oblivious of the beam in their own eyes, they are ever on the hunt for the motes in their neighbor's eyes. And the fuss they make, and the dust they stir up would naturally lead the outside world to believe that Spiritualist are a very unsavory class of people; when the fact is they are no worse than their defamers. What are a few dishonest or immoral mediums and preachers, to the millions of believers in Spiritualism? Haven't all religions had their Judases? Why should we expect Spiritualism to be an exception to the rule? When we find a black sheep in the fold, is it highly important that we should parade it up and down the world, and keep at it, and after it, until by very force of habit and association we become black sheep ourselves? Let us quit our groveling in the slums of pernicious thoughts; let us learn to be amiable, at least, if we cannot always be just.

EARTHBOUND.

One of the startling lessons we learn from spirit communication is the suggestive one that countless multitudes of spirits on the other side of life are what is called " earthbound." That is, they are chained by an immutable law of their being to the conditions of life that environed them here. The duration of this condition depends upon the state of spiritual unfoldment of the individual, and of the spirit's aptness to learn the law of progression, and tear itself away from its pernicious habits. A man, for instance, who has been a rumseller, under protest, as it were—following the business for a livelihood, while at the same time he despised it—will rise much more rapidly than one who followed it for the mere love of the vile traffic. The latter, together with the spirits of misers, or those who accumulated wealth on earth by dishonest practices, or by oppressing the poor, find themselves earthbound when they enter spirit life. They live and grovel in spiritual darkness near their old haunts, often for ages, or until they are ready for advancement; and then some gentle, guiding hand will come to them to assist them into the light.

FREE THOUGHT.

"Free thought!" Is such a condition of thought possible? Freedom to think is itself a condition of the brain, or of environment. Because we think differently from, or in opposition to, other people is no indication that we are *free* to think. The free-thinker, so-called, is one who denies the possibility of the existence of any form of life independent of a physical body, or that is not tangible to the physical senses. In other words, his thoughts are the veriest slaves of matter. He can not think beyond matter. He is chained to the atoms of matter that compose his material form, and there he must remain until enfranchised by the uplifting of his own spirit, or the disintegration of death. To designate thought thus enslaved as *free* thought is a misnomer. Freedom belongs to the spirit, and is something altogether superior to matter. To deny or make light of the "things of the spirit" is no more indicative of freedom to think than was the jeering of the slaves of superstition that bound Bruno to the stake, or shouted, "Crucify him!" to the ignorant rabble that nailed Jesus to the cross.

CLINGING TO LIFE.

It is hard to let go and give up, for one who has been wholly wrapped up in the things of time and sense. This world is his all. His elegant home, his lands, his accumulations of wealth—how can he give them over to other hands who never toiled to win them? Then life has been so sweet to him; he has had such a good time; and now he finds himself slowly drifting away. Old age, that once seemed so far away, is at last upon him. His energies are waning, and he realizes that he has nothing more to live for. But still he clings to life and to his possessions with a tenacity born of despair. If he could only turn his eyes from the past, away from the perishing baubles of time, and look forward to the life upon which he is about to enter ; if he could only realize that the spirit can soar best that is least encumbered, and that only his good qualities will be of any use to him over there, we think he would not be long in cutting himself loose from all hat chains him to earth.

HUMILITY.

One of the essential conditions to spiritual growth is humility. "Unless ye become as little children," etc. And why not? What is man that he should be puffed up with vanity or pride? Did he come into the world inheriting a fortune accumulated by his ancestors? A few years hence he will go out of it owning positively nothing—not even his coffin. Was he born to honor or fame? A little while hence and not even the worms will respect his titles, even though he were a king. Is he the child of genius, swaying multitudes by the eloquence of his tongue or pen? Soon his right hand will lose its cunning, his voice be heard no more, and his ears will be deaf to the once welcome plaudits. And so, in all these things, wherein has man any . "pre-eminence over the beast"? Should not this fact make him humble and modest in all his relations with the world? Here we are all learners in the prim. ary school of life, and we know so very little of anything that we can hardly afford to consider ourselves great in any sense.

Only as woman is exalted, honored and enlightened can we expect that the world can become better. As the mothers of the race, women are necessarily its saviors. The man who would speak slightingly of woman, or who would drag her down into the mire of his own lusts or evil thoughts, is a shame and disgrace to the mother who bore him. He should blush for his iniquities, and seek by the refining fire of discipline to purge himself thereof. Only the pure in heart are fitted for the companionship of good women.

MISFORTUNE.

Think you, tired heart, that there is no place in the world for you—no honest work, no way to earn even a humble livelihood? You have tried, and tried, but nowhere do you find the door of opportunity open to you. You know you are deeply in earnest; you know, also, that you have ability and could fill many a niche in life far more capably than some who are less worthy, and far less qualified. And yet you have to wait and wait, till your soul tires trying, and the clouds of misfortune seem to gather dark and thick over your spirit. Ah! do you know what misfortune is?—You, fair of form and features, with sound limbs and two good eyes and ears?—You, clad in comfort, and with a roof to shelter you?—You, with the flush of health on your cheeks and the elasticity of a grand womanhood in your footsteps? In yonder hut lies a poor mother, with features pinched and pale, dying of consumption. The father of her helpless children—one a little crippled boy —is a victim of the accursed demon strong drink, and his humble earnings go to enrich the rum-seller. Come with me, let us together enter within. No carpet on the floor, and only a few articles of dilapidated furniture—nothing but squalor and rags; and that poor, forsaken mother's life slowly fading away. O, it is a long, sad story—a story of woe and wretchedness in comparison with which yours is a dream of Paradise. Give her your rich sympathy and love, and you will forget yourself, —forget that you are poor, and that your lot is a hard one. It is thus, dear friends, that we mount as on eagle's wings, to the upper sky.

A WELL-ROUNDED LIFE.

A well-rounded, harmonious life—a life devoted to kind thoughts and good deeds, no matter in how humble a way—should be the highest aim of human existence. Such a life fills the measure of earthly experience necessary to prepare the spirit for a continuance of life on another plane of existence, upon which all must enter sooner or later. Here is something to strive for. How to make the most of this life, is a question that concerns all. But one must bear in mind that no life is complete that is not a foretaste of the higher life to come. Reader, take an account of stock with your own soul, and determine, if you can, if called hence to-day, just what, and how much, you could take with you. It would certainly require but little figuring to show you what you must leave behind.

"How can I best and most completely adjust myself to the universe?" should be the question that every intelligent mortal should ask of the divinity within his own soul. He needs to know what he is here for—what is meant in his creation. His mortal life, he must realize, is but a point of time in which to prepare for an eternity of existence; and he must know that to secure the largest measure of happiness here or hereafter, he can not well afford to let the present opportunity for doing good to others pass by unimproved.

The old idea of death, with its horrible uncertainty of happiness in a future state of existence, and its remote prospect of a physical resurrection, is no longer generally believed in by the Christian world. The fearful picture of a burning lake of actual fire as the abode of lost souls, is no longer presented from any intelligent pulpit in the land. To Spiritualism is largely due this transformation of public sentiment on this question, at the same time it holds man to a strict accountability for all his acts. There are worse hells than lakes of fire.

AN AWFUL MYSTERY.

Sleep—sweet, refreshing sleep! How like a gentle balm it distills through the tired nerves, and fills the senses with a soft, dreamy feeling of rest. The toils and cares of the day are over, and Night broods the earth with his sable wing. All nature invites the weary body to repose. It is then comes the awful mystery of sleep. The spirit, ever bouyant with eternal energy, sails away on the ocean of dreams, to some fair haven, it may be, in Soul land, there to meet and mingle with kindred spirits, whose bodies, like its own, are at rest, some, perhaps, forever. How very like the sleep that knows no waking—the last sleep. Each day we die, and each morn we come forth to a new life—just as we shall come forth from the sleep of death, to live forever on another plane of being.

THE FIRST AWAKING.

Imagine yourself, dear reader, just waking to a conscious existence in spirit life. It may be that the funeral is over and the old body consigned to its mother earth; or, perhaps, you have come to consciousness in time to attend your own funeral, if you so desire, as you might. You find yourself clothed upon with a new body, not unlike the one you have cast off, but more perfect! This is the spirit body spoken of by St. Paul, and it is made up of rarified matter, tangible and real to spirit sense. O, wondrous change! You are alive and well. What must be your thoughts on awakening to that new life? How they must flash back over your earth life—over your business affairs, which, perhaps, you have left all unsettled—over the loved ones who are overwhelmed with grief at your departure—over every act of wrong you have ever committed;—and then, as you begin to take in the situation more clearly, and realize that now and henceforth you must take your place where you belong, irrespective of earthly wealth or fame, how glad you will be if you can feel in your inmost soul that all is well with you. If you do your best here it will be all right with you there.

TWIN GRACES.

A clear head and a sound heart is the best capital possible to go through life with. But the two must go together to produce the best results. A clear head alone will make one cold and calculating. It will succeed in accumulating wealth, utterly thoughtless of those who fail; in fact, it will thrive on the failures of other, and sleep soundly at the same time. But couple the two together, then, with proper spiritual unfoldment, Nature and Grace will present to the world a type of manhood akin to angelhood. It is this happy combination of elements in his own life that each individual should aspire for. And he need not imagine that he cannot become such if he only will. It may be harder work for some than for others ; but the harder the struggle the greater the glory of victory.

KINDNESS.

Kind treatment will win in subduing an obdurate nature, where harsh measures fail. Instance the case of the prison convict at Folsom, in California, who was believed to be entirely incorrigible. For three years he had been shut up in solitary confinement, and for some months prior to a change of warden, his hands and feet had been shackled with heavy weights. The new warden found him thus, and resolved to try an opposite course of treatment with him. He first removed the shackles from his hands, and, two week's later, the heavy irons from his feet, all of which was accompanied with good advice. The man was a stone mason, and a skillful workmen. He was soon put to work, working faithfully, and gave the very best of satisfaction. He continued thus for over a year, when he was accidently killed by the fall of a derrick. From what was supposed to be the worst convict in the prison he became one of the very best, and all because of a little kindness wisely exercised in his behalf. This man would have gone to his death loaded with irons, under the treatment to which he was at first subjected.

PLAINT OF THE UNWISE.

It is very hard to break through the crust of a selfish man, —one that has given his life to the acquisition of wealth,—and by any earnestness of pleading, or honesty of logic, induce him to disintangle his spirit from the encumbrance of his possessions, the better to prepare him for a state of existence wherein worldly gain constitutes no element of happiness. He will hold on to his wealth, even though it be far in excess of any possible earthly needs, to the bitter end, and finally pass on to the other life, there to suffer, perhaps for ages, pangs of regret over opportunities for usefulness lost forever. Such spirits, returning to earth, come with the one sad plaint, "Oh, would that I had done what I could for humanity's sake!"

HOME.

The home is the bulwark of society. Given, a nation of homes, and the result is a nation of patriots. The promiscuous, feverish, unsettled life of great cities, is destructive of all the finer sentiments that cluster around the true home. The French language has no word equivalent to that of "home," for the reason, probably, that there are no homes in Paris, and Paris is France. In our great cities there are numerous places where people sleep and eat, but few homes. The lodging, tenement, or boarding house—these are not homes. It is only in the country, or removed from the whirl and din of the city, that we find the true home—a pretty cottage, embowered in flowers and vines, musical with the laughter of happy children, and radiant with bright, sunny faces. There is no rumbling of wheels over the stoney street; no careworn, stolid faces to meet you at every turn; no fierce, unholy eyes to gaze into yours,— but only the sweet peace and contentment that comes of harmonious living. Why will people throng into the great cities when the country offers such rare charms.

WHY WAIT FOR HAPPINESS?

Why wait for happiness in some future and far off heaven? Why not have it now and here? Heaven is not a thing of time or place, but a condition of spirit into which all must come before they can find true happiness. There is just as much heaven in this world as the spirit is capable of enjoying, or as can be found in the next. Wealth can not purchase heaven,—nor kingly power create it. It is more often found in the poor man's cottage, than in the palace of the rich. A gentle nature, a loving heart, a contented mind—these are heaven, and all there is of heaven in God's vast universe. No one need wait for death to enable him to enter upon the enjoyment of this eternal heritage of peace and rest.

We are living in an age of the rankest kind of materialism, and nowhere is its spirit manifested more completely than among Spiritualists. True, they claim to believe in a future state of existence, and yet they live as though this life was the all in all of being. They gather in the perishable treasures of earth, often entirely neglectful of the everlasting riches of the spirit, which alone will be of any worth to them a little while hence. They pass on, one after another, and do little or nothing for humanity, and then they return to us with the set plaint, "O, that I made better use of my opportunities! O, that I had my life to live over again!"

Persecution for opinion's sake, like abuse of the individual, is the strongest possible promoter of the cause that it is sought to crush. There is a just principle in human nature that rebels at abuse or persecution of a fellow mortal. Let a man or woman be roundly berated, and in all true natures this principle at once asserts itself, and rallies to the defence of the wrongfully accused. Persecution first gave Christianity to the world, and when it became strong, tyrannical and corrupt, its martyr-fires made Protestantism first possible, and then a mighty success. No Spiritualist need fear for his Cause because of the abuse of the ignorant.

SORROWFUL SATISFACTION.

The aches and pains, griefs and disappointments of some people constitute their standard themes of thought and conversation. They seem to derive a sort of sorrowful satisfaction in being able to oversize the pretentions of their neighbors in the matter of grievances and misfortunes. To them a first-class article of rheumatism, and a No. 1 brand of cholera morbus, are sources of delight which will answer for many years of neighborly chat; and they tell their ailments and infirmities over "each in its accustomed place, from morn till night, from youth till hoary age." And thus their weaknesses and imperfections are made to grow upon what they feed, until their mortal bodies become animated bundles of disease, and finally and prematurely "food for worms."

How the harassing cares of this life—the worry, the strife, the worldly ambitions—encompass the spirit as with an armor of steel, and make it almost impregnable to the humanities and charities—the tender thought of the welfare of others—so essential to the unfoldment of the spirit, and to fit it for the higher enjoyment of that realm of existence upon which we must all soon enter.

SCIENTIFIC METHODS.

How glibly we talk about scientific methods of psychical research, as though it was one thing to be scientific and another to be careful and truthful. What is science but a few collated facts in certain departments of nature? Wherein does the astronomer, or the geologist, or the naturalist, possess any peculiar qualifications for the investigation of psychic phenomena? He can apply none of his methods here. Here is a new realm of natural facts that can only be explored in ways peculiarly its own. The one who enters this realm with mind divested of the prejudices that a scientific knowledge in other departments of nature is apt to engender, is the better qualified, in our judgment, to discover the facts that abound therein. It is no discredit to Spiritualism that its facts are rejected by Dr. Carpenter and the Seybert Commission. The judgment of Professors Crooks, Wallace and Zollner, is quite as conclusive to the contrary; while there are thousands of plain, practical people, who are not scientists in the general acceptance of the term, whose judgment in these matters is quite as good as if they were.

HEALTH AND HARMONY.

If you would have health of body you must first have harmony of spirit and peace of mind. When all of the bearings are properly oiled, the machinery of the mill runs smoothly and without friction; but once admit an element of inharmony, and the friction of discord is felt through all its parts. As a particle of dust will stop the movement of a watch, so, with a finely organized, sensitive nature, will the indulgence of a single, unkind or unworthy thought often produce great disturbance in the physical system. We do not say that *all* sickness is the result of inharmonious conditions of mind, but that much of it is beyond question. Some people think they are harmonious when they are greatly otherwise. True harmony is that condition of the spirit which is at one with the All-Good—that thinks no ill, that rises superior to all the petty annoyances of life, and reposes sweetly and serenely on the bosom of Infinite Love. Below this there is more or less discord to work havoc with the delicate machinery of the body—just how and to what extent we may not fully know.

A HOPELESS PLACE.

To the materialist what a dreary, hopeless place is the grave! With no knowledge or thought of life beyond, he consigns the remains of some idol of his soul to the cold earth. To him the life that faded away in his arms marked the end of being for that loved one, absolutely and forever. There is nothing left for him now but memory, and the consciousness of a dead joy. He shuts his ears to the voice that would gladly speak to him out of the silence, and give him the assurance that his idol still lived. He will not have it so, for has he not reasoned himself into the conviction that there can be no such thing as spirit separate from the mortal body? And so he turns homeward from the place of the dead, with the light gone out of his life forevermore. All the logic and reason of all the schools of materialistic thought cannot possess a feather's weight in the scale against the demonstrated fact of one little spirit rap, nor all the agnosticism of the universe against a single grain of positive knowledge.

When we look out even upon the very little of the universe that the mind can grasp or comprehend, and consider, if we can, that we are but mites, held by the mysterious law of gravitation to the surface of one of the most inferior of the countless millions of worlds that roll through the mighty vastness of the skies, how insignificant seem all human pomp and greatness. In humility of soul we may well exclaim, "What is man that Thou art mindful of him!

BUILDING BETTER THAN SHE KNEW.

We know a lovely soul, aglow with the highest and holiest thoughts of human life and duty—a mother of a noble son, whose nature is unfolding beautifully under her loving care,—who thinks only good continually, and carries her thoughts into all her acts, which are ever for the uplifting of the lowly and the advancement of truth; and yet this grand soul is distrustful of her own merits, and of her power and influence for use in the world. It is well to be modest and unpretentious; it indicates a well-disciplined spirit. But, if this good woman could see herself as the bright ones of the other life see her, she would lift up her soul and rejoice that she is able to be the instrument for good that she is. Take courage, sister; you are building better than you know.

How easy it is to be obliging and civil, and gentle—to speak pleasantly, and considerately of the presence and opinions of others—in short to be a lady or a gentleman, in all the walks of life. Human nature, undisciplined of the spirit, is not far removed from the beast. Its tastes, appetites and habits are all of the animal, and full of the suggestiveness of the flesh. It is only through the domination of the spiritual nature of man that he rises in the scale of being above his brother animals. And the first step to a better order of life lies in the direction of those little amenities that make one thoughtful of the feelings and happiness of others.

* *
*

Many a noble soul finds expression through an unattractive body, just as the sweetest kernels are often encased in rough exteriors. It is the gentle expression, the kind and loving thought, the sympathetic heart, that indicate the noble spirit—the true man or woman. It is impossible for a noble nature to be unkind. Truly, " of such is the kingdom of heaven."

TRUE BEAUTY.

A pretty form and face, when not accompanied by vanity, are attractions that every woman may be pardoned for aspiring to. Symmetry and beauty of person, like all other forms of beauty, have a spiritual side which is uplifting and ennobling. Who can deny the inspiring effect of grand natural scenery—of majestic mountains, of restless oceans and summer sunsets. It is only when we learn to comprehend the spiritual significance of beautiful forms that we derive the highest and purest delight therein. True beauty must belong to the spirit to be rightly appreciated. A beautiful spirit makes the plainest features of the human face beautiful. In searching for the beauty which survives the ravages of time, one must delve beneath the surface of things. There is a beauty of form and face that grows more beautiful with time, but it can be seen only with the eye of the spirit.

SPIRITUAL DISCERNMENT.

When one's own spiritual nature becomes sufficiently unfolded to enable one to discern the "things of the spirit," he then has no further use for those manifestations of spirit power that appeal only to the physical senses. There are thousands of Spiritualists, who believe in all the physical phenomena known as spiritual manifestations, and yet who are never seen in seances for such manifestations. Why is it? Simply because they have outgrown the conditions making such manifestations necessary for their communion with their spirit friends. They have learned the way of communing in spirit on the higher plane of their natures; in other words, they have learned to meet their spirit friends on their own grounds and in their own elements. While physical phenomena is necessary to arrest the attention of the skeptic, it should be regarded but as the primary school of Spiritualism, from which the truly progressive soul will naturally seek to graduate as soon as possible.

A MONSTER OF INIQUITY.

What a monster of iniquity has man, in his ignorance, made of the All Father! He is held up to the world as a being of omnipotent power and infinite cruelty, who can be placated only by the most obsequious worship, and a belief in a stupendous absurdity. To question the existence of such a being is to cut oneself off from all hope here or hereafter. It is to force the Father to consign the children of his creation to ever lasting woe, with never a chance to reform, but forever and ever to suffer torments untold. How can any just man make himself believe it possible for him to love such a being! How unlike the Infinite Spirit of the All Good that the unfolded spirit of this more enlightened age has come to recognize! The old faiths of the world are being slowly undermined by the newer and better philosophies of life, and ere long they will disappear altogether.

ONE WORLD AT A TIME.

" One world at a time," is a wise maxim, in a general sense, at the same time it is by no means unwise to so make use of the "one world" as to best fit one for the next, or other world. The first point to be settled is that involved in the main question, Is there any other world, or any future state of existence? All Spiritualists claim to have settled the question, and all Christians think they have—the first by actual knowledge, and the latter by faith. Then, knowing that this life, at best, is of but short duration, and that in the nature of things it must be simply preparatory for one of vastly longer duration, is it not evident that the highest and best use of this world is to prepare one for the more enduring realities of the life to come? Can any sensible mind arrive at any other conclusion? Why then, in our declining years, should we cling so tenaciously to the things of earth, not one of which can we take with us into the Beyond?

ALMOST THERE.

"Almost there!" said the grand old veteran, as, with tottering form and feeble step, he returned my friendly greeting as we passed. Yes, indeed, methought, you are "almost there." A very little while and the pale boatman will bear you away to "the land of rest," where all your "possessions lie." How grand it must be to feel that one's work on earth is finished, when it has been well done, and that the time is near at hand when one can lay the old body down, and step forth into the new life! Thrice happy day! No more the bent form and feeble step! No more the wrinkled features, nor the dull senses! But from the old tenement of clay steps forth a spirit form, radiant and fresh with the lustre of perpetual youth. Happy, ye aged one, who can say, "All hail the day of my deliverance."

————‡o‡————

THE DEVIL'S PHILOSOPHY.

"Eat, drink and be merry, for to-morrow ye die." That is the Devil's philosophy—if there be a Devil. It is the philosophy of the devil of man's undeveloped nature—the devil of appetite, of lust, of sordid purpose. It is the practice, if not the philosophy, of the great, selfish, masses of humanity, who are rushing and drifting along as though this life were all. But should we not "eat, drink and be merry" in this life? Certainly, in a rational sense, but not because "to-morrow we die," but because to-morrow we live, and shall live forever. We should make our lives joyous with the sunshine of health, harmony, and true happiness here, that we may all the better be prepared for that "to-morrow" which will come to all, and to many, very soon. "What profiteth it a man if he gain the "whole world and lose his own soul?" That is, not for eternity, for in the wisdom and justice of the Creator that cannot be; but it will be quite long enough, we doubt not, to burn away the dross in the furnace fires of remorse.

COME WITH ME.

Come with me, ye sons of wealth and daughters of fashion—ye who live in the complacent belief that you are doing your duty to yourself and to your fellow beings—let us walk forth together through the by-ways of this great city. O, the shame of bartered womanhood, the agony of dissipated and degraded manhood! O, the nights of revelry and debauch, the deeds of crime, the homes of wretchedness and woe! Behold the fiery torrents of ruin and death flowing unceasingly from over three thousand fountains of hell! See ye the army of young men, the vast multitudes of "foolish virgins," building for dishonor, for disease, for the grave! What can you do to prevent—to save? Ask your own conscience, What are you doing? Place your firm, young feet upon the eternal rock of truth, and by example, by precept, by all the energy of your being live and labor for the All-Good.

No man has a right to live upon the vices or weaknesses of his fellow-beings, and none can so live without sinking his own spirit into the depths of unutterable misery. He may not realize it in his years of earthly prosperity—in the enjoyment of gold coined from the heart's blood of his fellows,—but there will come a time when he will call upon the rocks to hide him from the eyes of an offended God—the remorse of his own conscience. "Am I my brother's keeper?" do you ask? You are, sir. If you are stronger, or wiser, or better than he, you owe him of your strength, wisdom and goodness, to protect him in his weakness.

*
* *

How small the range of vision that sees not beyond the boundary of this little planet, with its one moon, and imagines that the Creator of millions of worlds greater than ours, and of vastly more importance in the plan and economy of the universe, should have to embody Himself in immortality and cause

Himself to be executed upon the cross, in order to avert a moral catastrophe to the human race !   Can it be that after trying His practiced hand on systems of worlds innumerable, He should come, in the awful perfection of His skill, to make such a terrible mistake with this little earth ?

*
* *

Large souls are never envious or jealous—never seek to build themselves up by pulling others down.   They delight in the success and good luck of their neighbors—are glad when others are made glad, even though their own pathway may be beset with thorns.   And when fortune smiles upon their lives, they are always ready to share it with their less fortunate friends and neighbors.   The world needs large souls to bear its mighty burdens of truth to humanity—to carry forward its grand reformatory and uplifting work.   Thereby are the children of the One Father led onward from age to age, and from lower to higher planes of spiritual unfoldment.

*
* *

How eagerly the storm-tossed mariner watches for the land—for the haven where his loved ones dwell.   They, too, are waiting and watching for the gleam of his welcome sails— little "faces by the pane," a fond mother, perhaps a loving wife—all eager to greet the wanderer and fold him in the heart of home.   How typical of the journey of life; and how precious the thought to the " homeward bound"—those of us who are nearing the silent shore.   Soon the shadowy hills will break upon our vision—soon we shall drop anchor in calm waters, in the beautiful harbor of rest.

* *
*

Of all the evils that ever beset the human race there is none so great as that of the indulgence in strong drink.   It is the giant's heel that crushes out manhood—the poison breath that blights and blisters the lives of all with whom it comes in contact.   It turns angels into demons, happy homes into hovels of wretchedness, and fills the world with misery and crime.

And yet there be good people who seek to justify the traffic in rum as a sort of necessary evil! Would they permit a mad dog to run through their streets to bite their children! Is hydrophobia a blessing?

SWORD OF THE SPIRIT.

"The sword of the spirit!" How few understand the meaning of the phrase; certainly none who have never felt its mighty power. Words, as the garments of thought, may be expressive in an intellectual sense, as appealing to the intellect; but it is only when charged with spirit power that they strike home to the hearts and consciences of men. To make this power effective, the writer or speaker must feel its animating and beautiful chemistry, its electric thrill and glow, surging through his own being like a mighty tidal wave of divine strength and power. Then the words he utters are made "the sword of the spirit," to overcome all opposition, and pierce their way to the quick of the understanding—to the living soul. Armed with this formidable power one man becomes a host in the battles of life.

STUPENDOUS MISTAKE.

It is a stupendous mistake for anyone to imagine that he can add to the measure of his own happiness by destroying the happiness of others; in other words, that he can derive any lasting benefit to himself by circumventing his neighbor. The competitive usages of trades are inimical to the highest welfare of society. Competition is based upon the law of might, and not upon the higher spiritual law of right. It presupposes a superiority, skill or judgment, in the one whereby that one's advantage becomes another's disadvantage. When the principle of co-operation shall prevail, as it will some day, then the highest interest of one will become the best interest of all, and no one will think to advance himself except by the advancement of all. There is a deep spiritual significance in the saying, "He who would lose his life shall save it;" that is, to give is to receive, in the highest sense. We cannot do for others without doing for ourselves.

ENLIGHTENED CO-OPERATION NECESSARY.

Is ours the highest and best form of government possible for man? Most of us seem to think so about once a year—on the Fourth of July; but a fair consideration of the iniquities and wrongs practiced under our laws, or against their enforcement, would hardly warrant any such conclusion. A government that permits the existence of great trusts to speculate on the staples of life, or that sanctions the traffic in, and use of death-dealing stimulants, cannot be other than a standing iniquity. In fact, our system of competitive industry, in which the weakest are forced to steal or starve, when once they are driven from the field, is anything but to the advantage of the multitude. A condition of society, abounding in prisons, poor-houses and insane asylums, cannot surely be a wise or healthful state of affairs. It is only by enlightened co-operation that society can find rest from the turmoil, agitation and wrong now everywhere apparent.

What a crude if not cruel idea of Supreme Wisdom or justice, it is to suppose that, in the economy of creation, evil should be accorded any especial advantage over good. If undeveloped or evil spirits are permitted to return to earth to ensnare the feet of the unwary to their eternal destruction, and good spirits are not allowed to make use of the same law of return to counteract the influence of the evil ones, then wherein, pray, consists the justice and goodness of God? Can some of our smart ecclesiastics—believers in the Devil theory of creation—answer?

ONWARD.

Onward, ever onward, from childhood to old age, with swiftly gliding footsteps, moves the mighty procession of human life. To some it is the butterfly of a spring morning, with wings purple and golden, flitting from flower to flower, followed by the dull chrysalis of old age, as the sum of wasted years. To others, it is the struggle with, and mastery of self—the outreaching of the soul for the Infinite—the enlargement and ripening of the spiritual powers, growing brighter and more beautiful with the years—brushing away the cobwebs of mortality, the rust and corrosion of time, and at last entering upon the life beyond full grown and ripe for its infinite unfoldments and possibilities. It is only by the constant exercise of our powers, in any direction of being, that we can hope to grow. If we would wear the laurels, we must win and merit them by our own efforts.

HIGHEST CONDITION OF LIFE.

If everybody sought the truest welfare of his neighbor is it not apparent that there would be no poverty, sin or suffering in the world? Hence, that must be the highest condition of life, the most conducive to the welfare of humanity, that exercises the broadest charity and liberality among men. Should the rich man "sell all that he hath, and give it to the poor," as Christ recommended the one who came to him in trouble, to do? By no means. That was doubtless a capital case, and one that required heroic treatment. Wealth, in the hands of the good man, becomes a power for good in the wise and noble use of its accumulations. For such an one to "give all that he hath to the poor," would be to place beyond his reach the means for doing great good. Besides, the poor should be assisted into ways of self-support, rather than made the recipients of charity, which should always be the last resort, where all means of self-sustenance fail.

THE SWEETEST PLEASURE.

The sweetest pleasure the spirit can know is that which it shares with others. What joy so dear to the mother's heart as that she experiences in ministering to the needs of the helpless babe that nestles upon her bosom? Thus in giving she receives, even more bountifully than she gives. And herein we catch a glimpse of the philosophy of happiness—in the devotion of ourselves to the amelioration and uplifting of humanity. How it broadens one's nature and brings one into kinship with the great, loving Over-Soul of the universe. Did you ever think, dear reader, that you cannot pluck a thorn from your neighbor's path without adding a rose to your own? That you cannot assuage a pang of a suffering soul, or pour the balm of sympathy upon a wounded heart without laying up pricelesss treasures of joy for your own spirit? But so indeed it is. Heaven is made up of generous, loving, noble spirits who vie in each other's welfare.

————‡o‡————

There is something sublimely beautiful in a serene and happy old age. The struggles of life—the rasping cares of business—the work and worry of earlier years, now are past, and in sweet content the aged sire, or white souled matron, now patiently wait for the change that will unite them with their loved ones on the other shore. To the man or woman who has lived their best old age brings joy, and not sadness.

.

Where is the man who would like to marry a woman who chews tobacco, drinks whisky, or uses profane or vulgar language? And yet many a man who indulges in all of these nastinesses and vices, will impose himself upon a pure and loveable woman as proper material for a decent husband. Does he not thereby commit a felony like that of obtaining goods under false pretenses, and ought he not to be arrested and punished as a fraud?

THE STRUGGLE OF LIFE.

"What is man that Thou art mindful of him?" Greedy, selfish and sinful, the great mass of humanity appears to the spiritual vision. Each for himself, struggling to overreach his fellows in aggregating to his own advantage the perishable things of this life. And yet, here is the soil for the growth and unfoldment of angels. Mortal life is so short, and man has so many needs, and is such a creature of environment, that we sometimes wonder that he is as far advanced, spiritally, as he is,—or rather, that so many noble examples of unfolded humanity exist in the world. There is hope for all when even one unselfish, gentle, loving nature is found, for are not all children of the one Father, and equally entitled to His care? Can God afford to be unjust? He certainly would be if any one soul in all His vast creation were suffered to grope forever in "outer darkness."

No cause founded on truth or justice can be ridiculed or argued down, or persecution successfully assail it. Did not paganism, with all its mighty enginery of power, do its utmost to crush out early Christianity? May not the Christian persecutors of Spiritualism profit by the lesson? Let them preach against it, and they but emphasize the fact of its existence, and pave the way to the investigation of its phenomena by many who would otherwise never have thought of it.

*_**

Mr. Colville thinks the time will come when man will be ashamed to be sick, and when his intuitions will be so developed as to enable him to be forewarned, and thereby able to avoid accidents. Then, in the fullness of time, will the laying off of the mortal be as simple and painless as the casting aside of an old and worn-out garment. There is no doubt that there is a perfection of physical life possible to man whereof he little dreams in his present undeveloped state.

Nature is ever striving for the best. She will have it at any cost. This is apparent in all forms of life below that of man. The strongest and best fitted to endure survives ; the weakest is crowded out. The struggle for supremacy is ever waging. In the world of moral and spiritual forces the same law prevails, though less apparent to the physical senses. Here, too, nature is persistent in developing the best. She is ever seeking for a better order of manhood—for a manhood akin to angelhood, and will be content with nothing less. Knowing her purposes in creation, how can man have the heart to disappoint her, by proving himself unworthy of her high expectations.

*
* *

Blessed indeed is the one upon whose life has fallen the sweet baptism of love and light from the spirit world, infusing the soul with thoughts of love divine for all mankind, and drawing it nearer and nearer to the heart of Infinite Goodness.

*
* *

Nature is a kind and gentle mother to all who live in harmony with her laws—who obey her mandates. To them she brings the sunshine of joy and gladness—in the bounding heart beats of youth, in the eager energies and pursuits of middle life, and in the calm restfulness of old age—and they find it good to live.

*
* *

" Progress " is the watchword of the age. We are improving our methods and our machinery in all directions of life and industry. Why should our religious creeds be an exception to the rule? Shall we arrange vast systems of rapid communication throughout the world, circumvent the globe with electric wires, and climb to cerulean hights of grandeur in all that affects man's physical welfare, and still continue to carry our religious grist to mill with the corn in one end of the bag and a stone in the other?

ARROGANCE OF OPINION.

The arrogance of opinion is the rock that has wrecked and broken in pieces whole argosies of happiness. Here is where many a society, organized for good work, has foundered and gone down. Some strongly magnetic man or woman asserts a proposition, authoritatively and reckless of the opinions of others. They draw around them their followers. Others, alike constituted, assert the opposite. Soon the society is divided in cliques and factions, all bitterly endeavoring to destroy each other; and then they all fly apart and chaos reigns. Men will respect the opinions of others, we care not what they may be, when presented in a modest and respectful manner. The "sledge hammer" style of argument never convinces, and generally shocks and disgusts those it is aimed to convince. Spiritualists should bear this thought in mind.

————‡o‡————

When will the world learn that there are higher and better uses for human energies than in their exclusive devotion to the acquisition of wealth. If the young man, of bright hopes and laudable ambition, could only realize how the eager pursuit of gain is apt to shrivel up the spirit, and encase it in an armor of selfishness—how like the sirocco of the desert it will dry out of his nature the sweet juices of benevolence, and the thought for the welfare of his fellow beings—we think he would see to it that other and higher objects in life should absorb a portion of his attention.

* *

It is not for man to question the wisdom of the Creator. If He sees fit to create venomous reptiles, or fan the soft airs of heaven into devastating cyclones, or rend the foundations of the earth itself with mighty convulsions, that is his business —ours to keep out of the way—if we can, and if we can't, to accept the situation in a manner that will produce the least disturbance to ourselves.

There is an old adage that "the good die young."—Because they are denied the time and opportunity to become bad! The real good are those who have struggled with life's temptations and have overcome them—who have conquered their own natures, and who live to bless others. That kind of "good" always "die old."

***

Self-reliance is a better legacy for a young man to begin business with than much gold. If to this be added habits of temperance and industry success in life is certain.

***

We are told that "God tempers the wind to the shorn lamb;" that is, provided the lamb be shorn in the right season. The truth is, Nature, of which wind and lamb are both parts, is as heartless as the avalanche. It kills or maims all who get in the way of her laws. She is kind only to those who have instinct enough, or sense enough to obey her laws.

***

There is no fact of nature of quite as much importance o the world as the fact of the continuance of human life beyond the gates of death. A thorough understanding and adaptation of this truth to mortal existence means everything of good to the race. It will eventually bring about an era of universal brotherhood wherein no one can do another wrong.

***

Spiritualism not only brings us a positive knowledge of a future life, enabling us to hold happy communion with our loved ones on the other side, but it brings to the world a clearer and better conception of human life and duty. It shows up, in a clear, white light, the misconceptions of theology concerning a future life, and indicates the proper unfoldment of man's spiritual nature in this life in order to attain true happiness in the next. Spiritualism and Calvanism! Light and darkness—Gabriel and Lucifer!

DON'T WORRY.

Don't worry; it only makes matters worse. Is rent day near? Have you bills to meet and nothing to meet them with? Do the best you can, leave no resource unexhausted; but don't worry. You will need a clear brain to-morrow to plan with. If you lay awake all night, worrying over your troubles, your nerves and brain will be in no condition for business—for cool, deliberate planning. And then some wise spirit friend, seeing a way out of your trouble, might come and impress you (they often do), if you will keep yourself in a passive condition. They cannot come to you when you are excited, or your nerves are all unstrung with worriment. Bear in mind that no one can do his best unless he keeps cool. The prize-fighter who loses his temper is lost. Many a bankrupt might have avoided disaster if he had only not given away to despair. Whoever does his best can do no more. Then if he fails he has no right to blame himself therefor. We are all human, and all liable to err in judgment.

UNSUNG HEROES.

The world has many heroes whose deeds are unsung. There is one now, across the street—that pale, delicate young girl, modestly going to her daily task, at the counter or the printer's case, where by eight, or perhaps ten hours of patient toil, she earns ten or twelve dollars a week. And this meager income she faithfully hands over to her mother for family expenses—to support an invalid father, perhaps, and two or three younger sisters. How her modest eyes droop as she *feels* the vulgar stare of the young roues at the street corner! How patiently she pursues her task, spurning the hourly temptation to a life of gilded sin— lifting her soul in prayer for help to be good and true, and bear up bravely under the crosses of life. Do we not all know of many such, of both sexes, and are they not angels of light and love to mark the way for human duty?

Do not, O sorrowing mortal,—O victim of disaster,—waste your precious hours in thinking perpetually of your own troubles ! Have you lost your fortune? Think of some poor fellow sojourner to the grave who has not only lost his fortune but his health also, and extend to him the blessing of a gentle word of sympathy. Have you lost an eye or a leg by some unfortunate disaster? Let your compassion go out to the one who has suffered the loss of both eyes, or legs. Most of the unhappiness in this world comes of brooding over our own troubles. It will mostly disappear when we turn our thoughts and sympathies to others.

***

It does no good to scold, or find fault with your neighbors. You cannot mend their faults in that way, while you will be apt to cloud your own spirit. There is a bright side to every human nature, no matter how undeveloped or befogged by vice or crime. It is by this bright side, where are located the open windows of the soul, we must always approach our fellow beings, if we would do them good. Try it, ye who would work the reformation of humanity. Reach forth a loving hand to the erring one ; it is only thus that you can become his savior.

TEACHING BY PRECEPT.

Teaching by precept has a double force when backed up by example. It is a very easy thing to tell others what to do and how to do it; not always so easy to practice what one preaches. We all know, or think we know, right from wrong. The *thought* of the right will help others, who are wavering in the balance, to a better life; but its moral force is lost upon our selves unless we square our lives by that thought. And us here is the lesson: All the helps in the universe will profit us nothing unless we help ourselves. And the very moment we determine to help ourselves, it is amazing how numerous and potent will be the friendly forces that will come to our assistance.

BE COMFORTED.

O hearts that ache from the loss of loved ones! Be comforted with the blessed thought that there is only a thin veil between you and them! And this knowledge is the glorious boon that Spiritualism has brought to the world. How it lifts the clouds of doubt and uncertainty, and takes that heavy weight of woe out of the heart. The saddest place in all this world is an orthodox funeral, with its hopeless, cheerless gloom of the grave. Not a ray of light, not a glimmer of hope, when your unconverted loved one dies! No escape from God's wrath! Lost, lost, eternally lost! Why, it is enough to make the corpse rise up in its coffin and rebuke the "minister of God" who dares thus to malign the All-loving Father!

A GRAND SOUL.

We know a grand unselfish soul—a man at the head of a large and profitable business, giving employment to many hands—a Spiritualist in the truest meaning of the word—who religiously gives away to charitable purposes, every dollar of his large income not otherwise needed for the proper support of his family. He helps every worthy cause to the extent of his last available dollar, and then regrets that he has not more to give. No poor or sick medium ever appealed to him in vain, and no hand of worthy want, outstretched to him, ever returned to its owner empty. He gives for the very love of giving. His sympathetic nature overflows with goodness, with kind and loving thoughts, with generous and noble impulses, towards all humanity. Riches! what does he care for worldly wealth. *His* riches are of a kind that never perish. Why, he could pile up a mint of money if he so desired; but he prefers to enjoy it in making others happy as he goes along. And so he fills the air all around him with sunshine. What a host of loving spirits will stand at the portals to bid him welcome to his beautiful home in the "sweet by and by!" What a host surround him here to bless and gladden his life!

SPIRITUAL CRIPPLES.

Let us be honest with ourselves. We can't afford to deal unfairly with our own spirits. In fact we can't do it and expect to escape the consequences. If we cramp our spiritual natures into a straight jacket, and take on the conditions of error incidental to such spiritual distortion, we can expect nothing else than that we shall enter the other life spiritual cripples, with our faculties for growth and unfoldment seriously impaired. It is with the spirit as with a dwelling house: Open the windows, and pure air and sunshine will flow in, bringing health and happiness to the inmates; close them and the pale shadow of disease and death will ere long make its presence felt.

AN EMPTY SHELL.

What an empty shell is life not lived to some good purpose! How barren and desolate it seems! How vastly more so when perverted by selfishness into corrupt and dishonest ways! If we could only see ourselves as we are seen by those shining ones who have fought the good fight over their lower natures and won the glad victory, how small and unworthy we would seem in our own eyes. Scavengers of earth, gathering up rags and rubbish for mortal junk shops. Bye-and-bye death comes along and breathes upon our possessions, and they all vanish, and we with them. The question which the angel of each individual conscience will ask its owner sometime, will not be, How much money did you make on earth? but, *How* did you make it, and what have you now to show for it? There, your bank deposit will go for naught, and your houses and lands also. What else have you? Ah, brother mortal, beware!

WHAT ARE WE HERE FOR?

Just in proportion as man lives unselfishly, and kindly assists in bearing the burdens of others—helping the weak over the rough places, and the foolish to better ways of life— will he be blessed in his own spirit. What are we here for? To fatten on the labor of others, and profit by our superior ability or opportunities? By no means. It is thus that we put away the day of our own truest unfoldment. We harden our natures to the gentle influences of the spirit world. We grow tough and resistant to the softening and moulding processes of the angel ones who would lead us upward into the light and glory of true manhood or womanhood, and mould us into the image of the divine. Life is at best but a brief day. It is so short, and there is really so little of it, that it doesn't pay to be mean, or unkind, or uncharitable. We were but boys and girls yesterday; to-day, with many of us, the shadows of evening are lengthing; to-morrow——

CONCLUSIVE EVIDENCE.

A message written betweem slates, locked and sealed— the slates prepared by one's self and not for a moment out of one's hands or sight, ought to be conclusive evidence to any fair mind of the existence of an independent intelligent, though unseen, power, capable of communicating with mortals. This evidence has come to thousands through our mediums for this phase of spirit manifestation, and may be witnessed by any reasonable person, who will take the trouble to investigate. When this message comes in the familiar hand-writing of some loved one who has passed to the other shore, and also bears internal evidence of its genuineness, what sense is there in attributing it to anything else than what it purports to be? " I am your mother, and I come to prove to you that I still live and love you," appears written between slates held in the hands of the son, in that mother's familiar hand, with her name in full, that the medium never knew. "Go away from me; you are the Devil," says our Adventist friend; "my mother is sleeping in the grave waiting for the resurrection!" This is a funny world. P. S.—We wish to add that we have had, many times, through that grand medium, Mr. Fred Evans, the most positive evidence of independent spirit writing.

The first thing a man or woman should do, after coming to a knowledge of the truth of continued existence, should be to adjust his life in harmony therewith. He should realize that only by the unfoldment of his own spirit can he expect to reach the highest rewards of happiness in this life or the next. He must lay aside the besetting evils of his lower nature—all jealousy, envy, and unkindness, and seek for the highest good in his own life, and of all with whom he comes in contact. Not to do this is to fail to profit by the glorious lesson of angel ministration.

IRRECONCILABLE CONTRADICTIONS.

Why is it that some men succeed in business in spite of themselves, while others fail, notwithstanding they put forth the best of efforts? James Lick was a type of the former class. Having lived near him for many years it was the writer's privilege to know something of this man's personal ways. He never undertook a business project that was not marked by almost sublime folly. He built a flouring mill, in the Santa Clara valley, the heavy timbers of which were polished mahogany imported from Central America, while the mountains, a few miles distant, abounded in the choicest redwood and fir. He spent a quarter of a million of money improving a portion of his property, which he afterward donated to the Paine Hall people of Boston, and which they sold for less than $20,000. And yet, notwithstanding these and many other like follies,

James Lick accumulated several millions of dollars, which hē wisely gave to noble uses ! Such financial contradictions are irreconcilable with all known business principles. Who can explain them ?

SCIENTIFIC CONDITIONS.

Spiritualists who insist upon scientific Spiritualism, or phenomena under scientific conditions, are often most unscientific in their methods. They impose on mediums conditions which are at utter variance with the laws of mediumship, and call their methods scientific. For instance, the occult telegraph will work best, if at all, when held in the lap of the medium, or very closely to his or her aura. It will work in a harmonious atmosphere when not in contact with the medium, but the results will not be as satisfactory. Here is a law not difficult to be understood—or perhaps we should say, a fact, that pertains alike to psychography and other phases of physical mediumship. Harmony is always essential to good manifestations. To challenge the genuineness of a manifestation upon the offer of money to produce it, or upon a wager, is to create a resistent force that will generally so disturb the conditions as to prevent the manifestation. In the light of this fact, what course would the true scientist naturally pursue in searching for the truth ?

The most sterling manhood is almost invariably self-made. It is the hard struggle with poverty, and other seemingly unfriendly conditions of life, that give keenness to one's faculties. This struggle has made a success of many a man who, with a fortune to start with, would have grown limp and good for nothing. In fact, there are but very few of our men of wealth or worth of to-day who did not start at the bottom of fortune's ladder.

FUNERAL CEREMONIES.

The Spiritualistic world is hardly yet prepared to accept cremation as a proper means for the disposal of the bodies of the dead. While many approve the theory as applied to other people's dead, but few are quite ready to adopt the practice as regards their own. Still there is a compromise ground on which all ought to be willing to stand. All Spiritualists will admit that our present expensive funeral system, with its showy hearse and casket, and its long procession of hired hacks, is not the proper manner to show our respect for the dead; it is, besides, not at all consistent with our belief. A much better way would be to consign the body to earth in an unexpensive way, privately and without the least ceremony, and then on the following Sunday, say, (as that day is more convenient for a public assemblage,) hold a memorial, or resurrection service, in honor of the departed. This service could be made most expressive and instructive. It should be free from all funeral trappings. The hall or home where it is held should be decorated with flowers and vines, and instead of one speaker, we would invite all who felt so disposed, to assist in making the occasion worthy of the risen spirit. This, it seems to us, would be a happy improvement on our present funeral system.

————‡o‡————

DON'T CROWD.

Don't crowd. The world is broad and wide. There is room for all, and enough for all, if those who already have more than their share will only stop crowding. Why should any one want more than he can wisely use? It only brings a burden of care that is anything but happiness. One of the richest men in this state, one who is devoting a large share of his many millions to a mighty educational enterprise, was recently asked his opinion upon the subject. He replied that his great wealth brought him anything but rest and comfort. On the other hand, it was a source of perpetual annoyance to him. It bound him a slave to the wheels of drudgery and hard, unceasing work. Far better for his own happiness if he possessed only a humble competency. Such, we doubt not, is the experience of all rich men; they are slaves to their possessions. But not all are so wisely decorating their chains with beautiful flowers of the spirit as he of whom we speak. My hard-working, wealth-seeking brother or sister, thank God, and take courage, that you are not rich.

————‡o‡————

A LITTLE WHILE.

A little while and the dream of life will be ended; the curtain will fall, the lights be turned out, and we shall go to our homes to sleep till the morning dawns. And what a morning that will be! Did its full significance ever occur to you, dear reader? As you wake to consciousness, you will find yourself surrounded, perhaps, by a circle of happy faces, of those near and dear to you, who went out from your mortal life and left you crushed and desolate. A fond mother, a precious child, a beloved wife or husband, all waiting to give you a glad greeting and welcome to your spirit home. Who talks to you now of woe, of pain or sorrow, as the roseate dawning of that first new day in the "land beyond the river," breaks upon your enraptured vision! A little while, aged brother, sister, and the Angel of Delieverance will invite you to lay your burden down and rest.

————‡o‡————

There is no one virtue that Spiritualists need to cultivate quite as much as that of forbearance with those who do not agree with them. Here, for instance, is some medium that scores of good, honest people believe in—whose genuineness they claim to *know*; while other scores are equally certain that said medium is a shameless trickster and cheat. Neither party is willing to tolerate the opinions of the other, and so they allow the serenity of their souls to become disturbed with unkind feeling toward each other.   Ah, friends, it is of far less consequence to you that said medium is dishonest, or otherwise, than it is that your own life is made sweet and beautiful.

"LET US PRAY."

Not to a personal God, for we have no evidence that there is any such being in the Universe.   Not for the purpose of changing any law of nature, or persuading the Infinite Energy, called by many names, to do what He or It would otherwise not do; but simply because prayer is a natural attribute of the unfolded spirit, and by it the spirit is brought into beautiful unison and harmony with the Spirit of Nature—with the magnetic currents of sympathetic thoughts of love, and goodness, that flow in and about all human life upon this planet, and connect it with the higher forms of life of all planets. True prayer is simply an aspiration for the best in one's own soul, and in all other souls.   The truly spiritual man is compelled to pray, in this sense, and he cannot help it.

There never was so much honor and virtue in the world as there is now—never so much charity, or goodness—never so much aspiration and striving for the higher life.   It is true that vice abounds,—so did it ever.   But never so little as now. The race is slowly but surely coming "up the steeps of time."

* *

Press on, O pilgrim, journeying through the valley and shadow of time.   There is a station just ahead where you can lay aside your burdens and rest for the night—the night that bridges the chasm between two eternities, the past and the future.   Beyond, you will find the journey easy and the burden light—if you so will it here.

DOGMATISM.

Suppose the universe is governed by law, as it doubtless is, then what is law, where did it come from, and who made it? May there not be a Something behind law that we know nothing about? The Spiritualist possesses a knowledge of spiritual things that the Materialist denies. Why should the former deny the possibility of the existence of far greater spiritual realities whereof *he* has no knowledge? It becomes us all, in our researches through Nature, to be humble and modest in our conclusions. Dogmatic theology has been the evil genius of humanity. Dogmatism in science is but little better. What most of us do not know about Nature, and its pulsating energies, would make many large volumes.

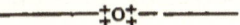

Ye shining ones, look down in tender pity upon the heart where nestles no brood of loving thoughts—no holy desire for another's welfare—no gentle promptings to a better life. If there is a being in the universe who, more than another, needs our deepest sympathy, it is that one.

The man who, from choice, would live the life of a celebate—going and coming from his solitary den through all the dreary years of his existence, until death claims him for his own,—with no gentle welcome home, nor parting blessing as he goes forth to mingle with the world,—with no loving hand to smooth the wrinkles of care from his brow,—and with no eye to shed a tear upon his grave,—is a——is unwise!

What better protection from evil associations can a young man or woman have than the thought that the eyes of a loving spirit mother are upon them, and her gentle presence ever near them when they would go astray? If Spiritualism is a good thing for the aged, affording them comfort and happiness as they near the dark river of death, is it not far better for the young as they move amid the temptations and vicissitudes of life?

**

Those good people, who, with their eyes set in the back of their heads, are forever prating of the "good old days," and drawing comparisons between the past and the present, highly unfavorable to the latter, should visit the ruined cities of Pompeii and Herculaneum, recently unearthed from the horrid nightmare of raging Vesuvius. They will there see evidences of moral degradation which would forever close their mouths to the superior excellence of the people of past ages.

**

Don't worry yourselves by disturbing the palpitant air with bewailings for your sins. That is a matter the remedy for which is in your own hands. If you are under the dominion of sin, why not throw off the yoke and step forth a free man? Salvation from sin is simply ceasing to do evil and learning to do well. If you know the wrong, why persist in doing it? And above all, do not lay the responsibility of your sinful acts upon the shoulders of another. There is enough of divinity in every soul to save it, if it but thinks so.

**

"O wad some power the giftie gie us,
To see oursels as ithers see us,"

So sang the Scottish bard; but the "giftie," are not, unfortunately, as far as heard from, able to bestow that power upon mortals. At least but very few of us seem to have the power of visional introspection to the extent desired by the poet. Some people are shocked at defects they see in others, when the same or greater defects constitute the most prominent features of their own lives and characters. They diagnose others' cases by their own prevailing symptoms, and prescribe accordingly; but they seldom take their own medicine.

THE DEAREST SPOT.

What are the dearest spots in one's memory, around which one most delights to linger? Are they not those occasions when some loving thought found expression, or some noble and generous action was done? Do we ever cherish the recollection of our meanness—of the things we would gladly forget? In some moment of anger, or thoughtlessness, who is there that has not said or done something he would gladly recall? And how such things will rankle in a sensitive memory, sometimes all through life. An unkind act will place a thorn in the pillow, which only sincere penitence and long suffering can remove. What though one may have suffered from kindness unworthily bestowed, the virtue is in the act, not in the abuse of it. If the memory of good deeds always brings happiness, and of evil deeds unhappiness, are we not cruel to ourselves whenever we indulge in the performance of the latter?

The best antidote for vice and crime of all kinds is work, and a plenty of it. If the young man who delights to hang around the saloons, or dance and dawdle attendance upon some pretty miss with a pretty hand, and nothing to do;—if the young woman whose head is "bequackled" with the "fellows," and who thinks of nothing but dress, and her many admirers—were both set at hard work—the former at some good trade, and the latter at good, honest housework, or at some other respectable employment, that required ten good hours of their time every day, they would both, in the coming years, be happier and wiser.

How like the refreshing raindrops upon the dry and parched earth, or the soft glow of the summer sun that falls upon the hearts of the opening flowers, falls the warmth and glow of a kind word and loving thought upon the tired heart, hungry for sympathy and kindness. How very easy it is to make one's self beloved by one's neighbors and friends; and just as easy to make one's self disliked. People who succeed in the latter respect often complain of what they alone are wholly responsible for, and do not actually know it. What a grand world this will be to live in when we all learn to practice the Golden Rule.

NOT THE ALL OF LIFE.

It is only when one's spirit soars above the material plane and into the realm of soul, that he really learns to live. It is then one comes to a recognition of the fact that the things of earth—wealth, fame, the pursuits of trade, and all that pertains to earthly affairs—are not the all of life; that in fact, there are spiritual delights infinitely above those of the physical senses, to which the mere worldling is a stranger. It may be thought by some that such spiritual unfoldment or exaltation would unfit one for the necessities and duties of life on the earth plane. On the other hand, it especially prepares and qualifies one for the true work of life in its better and higher sense. It makes one reasonable in his wants and desires, and takes out of his nature that narrow selfishness that would exalt one's self at the expense of the rights and needs of his fellow men. Instead of derogating from his usefulness as a citizen, it ennobles him and crowns his citizenship with the glory of an exalted manhood.

We should build our characters upon the Rock of Truth; for thereby we are building for the ages—for eternity. We surely do not want to go into the other life with our work half done,—wholly unprepared for the change. We should know something of the place whither we are going, and what we shall expect to do when we get there. And especially should we know what kind of preparation will best fit us for the new life upon which we all, sooner or later, must enter. We should not

encumber our spirits with any useless baggage. If we are wise we
will cut ourselves loose, and leave behind us all weights to the
spirit's advancement. And we cannot begin this grand work
any too soon.

IT DOESN'T PAY.

It doesn't pay to thrust spiritual facts upon the attention
of people not ready to receive them. We only get ourselves
suspected of lunacy, and accomplish no good. There is a
proper time and a place for all things. Wait till the heart
grows tender from some great sorrow—till death has taken
away some loved one—then they will listen to you, and you
can tell them of the priceless love of the angels ; that death is
but a change of conditions, and that the way has been opened
for communion with the precious one whose body they have
laid away in the grave. No one who has never had this
experience can realize the wonderful joy that the knowledge of
spirit communion brings to the stricken heart. Hope and
faith in the promises of Christianity—even the firm belief in a
resurrection to life everlasting, and a home in the fabled
heaven of the Church, brings no comfort like this—the
positive knowledge that your dear one lives, and comes to
gladden your heart with that knowledge.

The young woman of eighteen and young man of twenty-
one who haven't yet found out what they are here for, have
missed their reckoning in some way and got into the world by
mistake. This is no world for unsettled people—for people
who do not know exactly what ails them, or what was intended
in their coming here. The man who waits for circumstances
to adjust themselves to his convenience stands a poor show in
the competitive struggle with the one who makes his own c ir-
cumstances, and adjusts himself thereto, seizing the opportunity, as it were, before it is born.

WHENCE AND WHITHER.

Infinite heights of being! Beyond, above all thought of time or comprehension of soul encased in matter! Whence and whither? Onward and upward forever, through such sweeps of space and time as stagger thought and hold in suspense the breath of infinite being. What is the momentary sense of earth life compared with the illimitable beyond? A heart-beat to the life of the sun—a moment to an eternity of ages. And yet we live here as though this were the all of being—as though our physical needs were to last forever, and the heaps of rubbish we rake together were to benefit us in some way when our mortal bodies themselves become rubbish. Why not strike out for something higher and better in this life by making each moment a prophecy of the higher life to come.

MEDIUMSHIP AND MORALITY.

It is a generally accepted fact in spiritual circles that mediumship and morality are in nowise related to each other —that a good medium may be a deplorably dishonest man or woman. And this is one of the stumbling blocks in the way of the advancement of our Cause. Why it is that good spirits should seek to return to earth through corrupt channels, is a puzzling problem. That they do so is beyond question ; but that they would prefer to communicate through honest mediums is also no doubt true. And herein, perhaps, we may discover the key to the solution of the problem: Mediumship is a physical condition wholly depending upon a certain peculiar status of the material elements of the body. There can be no dishonesty in matter. Thus, the spirit who finds the way open, comes, without any thought of the moral qualities of the man or woman whose body furnishes the way. We go by railroad or steamboat to visit our friends in a distant city, but do we ever stop to consider the moral character of the engineer who runs the train, or the pilot who guides the vessel? No one would think of requiring credentials of good character from the postmaster or telegrapher through whom one would communicate with his friends. That is probably the way in which spirits look upon dishonest mediums. They take no note of their dishonesty, so long as the message goes through to its destination all right.

————‡o‡————

THE "KNOCK DOWN" ARGUMENT.

You cannot win souls by what is called "Knock down arguments." You may antagonize and disgust, but you cannot convince. Our teachers and speakers should ever bear this in mind. The thought that goes on its mission barbed and feathered with the spirit of love and good-will, will cleave its way through all barriers of opposition straight to the heart; while the same thought, sent forth in a harsh and uncharitable spirit, will simply embitter and disgust. There are those who delight in seeing the cherished opinions of others rudely assailed, who would repel as a personal insult, any rude assault upon their own cherished opinions. There can be but one wise rule of human action, and that is the Golden Rule.

————‡o‡————

The writer is thoroughly satisfied that there is only one way whereby man can be led to the truth—only one way to overcome the evil in human lives, and bring men into harmony with the Divine Life—and that is by the flower-strewn pathway of love. Nor abuse, nor ridicule, nor unkind thoughts, will accomplish this. "As ye sow so also shall ye reap." If you would make an undeveloped man hate you treat him unkindly; if you would make a religious bigot despise you ridicule his religion; if you would make the world skeptical of your facts as Spiritualists, and wish not to know you, throw mud at each other, and bedaub your own spirits with the slime of uncharitable thoughts.

The higher love is an unselfish love, a love that reaches out far beyond the confines of one's immediate kindred—a love that honors all life, and can do no harm. The she tiger will die for her cubs—could a human mother do more? Both are governed by the same law to that extent; but beyond that is a mighty realm of love whereof the brute knows nothing—a realm of eternal growth and everlasting delights. It is only the advanced spirit—the spirit that has risen superior to self—that has learned to explore this higher realm.

THINK KINDLY OF THE ERRING.

It is better to think kindly of the erring, even though they may persist in their evil ways, than unkindly or harshly. What right have those who are better organized and educated than their less fortunate fellows to think otherwise than kindly? Is it any particular credit to the one, or discredit to the other, that they are what they are? Is the fox to be blamed for being a fox, or the snake for being a snake? Is not all animal life—human life included—very much what it is made to be? If one, by virtue of better birth, and a better developed moral nature, lives wisely and righteously, ought not the fact of the possession of these superior qualities to fill his soul with tender sympathy towards all who are not thus favored? We cannot avoid the responsibility of a common brotherhood of the race, even though some of the family are not what they should be.

Whoever harbors an evil thought entertains a burglar and a thief—one who is sure to rob him in the end. To give expression to such a thought is to invite evil to one's self—is indeed to become evil. There is only one line of life to pursue to obtain true happiness, and that is the straight and narrow way of Good Will—to think kindly and act kindly towards all. Whoever departs from this way only prolongs the journey before him. It is as though one should leave the beaten path while journeying through a dense forest. The result would be garments and flesh torn with briars and thorns, and no great headway made.

————‡o‡————

A SUBLIME FALLACY.

" The world owes me a living," says one, not over-indus-trious or thrifty. It does, does it? Now, it owes you nothing that you do not earn by honest labor with head or hands. What right have you to eat the bread of idleness, earned by others' labor, and claim that the world owes it to you? Did it never occur to you that not even the elements of your physi-cal body—the lime in your bones, or the iron in your blood, are *your* property. They have only been loaned to you for a while by Mother Nature to enable you the better to obtain the experiences that your spirit stands in need of. You will have to deliver them up some day, when your spirit takes its depart-ure out and into the Beyond ; you will not be allowed to take with you a single atom. Don't make that dear old Mother ashamed of herself that she ever loaned you the ingredients for a man, and you made a worthless mess of it ! Don't make her feel sad to think, when you pass on, that she will get back her raw material for a man, and nothing more.

———•———

We shall never find any better heaven than that we carry around with us in our hearts. He who takes his own life to escape from trouble commits a stupendous folly. If he would get his spirit into harmony with the divine law of being, root out all evil and set up the throne of righteousness in himself, he would never do so unwise a thing, but would patiently endure all the ills of life to the end. And yet in the light (or darkness rather) of materialism, suicide is a natural and reason-ble escape from trouble. Ignorance of the consequences of he act will not atone for the mistake.

Perfection is found nowhere—all humanity is struggling up the heights, even though some portion of it may seem to be slipping backward. But it is with the latter only to get another and better start—if not in this life, then, perhaps, in the next. Man has come up out of an infinite past, and he has an infinite future before him. The present is his opportunity of growth and unfoldment. If he is wise, he will improve it to the utmost. The golden hours of this mortal day are swiftly speeding by. Behold the night cometh!

————‡o‡————

VENERATION.

The Materialist may ridicule the idea of veneration for, and worship of a Supreme Being, but can he do so except at the expense of his spiritual nature? The ox that grazes the field, and the swine that feeds upon the acorn, have no thought of the whence their maintenance comes, or the wherefore of their existence. Shall man imitate the swine and the ox in this respect, and glory therein? Shall he take delight in the thought that he is superior to the brute only in an intellectual sense? Would you build an arch and leave out the keystone? Would you create an angel without the unfoldment of the higher spiritual faculties, whereof reverence for the Infinite Something we name God is the chiefest? In the light of true spirituality what a puny, insignificant thing is man! How it becomes him to lay aside all vanity and pride—all sense of his own importance—and walk humbly as he grows into a better and truer manhood. In no other spirit is it possible for him to grow.

————‡o‡————

Come up higher, brother, sister—up and out from the mists and shadows of the valley—from the realm of unworthy thoughts and things—into the pure air and bright sunshine of God's eternal highlands. There, and there only, is peace, strength and lasting happiness.

IS SPIRITUALISM A RELIGION?

Is Spiritualism a religion? That depends upon how we take it and what it stands for with us. If we regard it simply as a demonstrated fact of nature, there can be nothing of what is understood to be religion in it. But if it means the bringing of the human spirit into harmony with the Divine Spirit, reacting upon the former in the unfoldment of all that is true and beautiful, and leading it onward and upward, into a better way of life, then is it indeed a religion in the highest sense. Man, as a spiritual, but not as an intellectual being, needs and must have a religion of some kind. Why may he not, as a Spiritualist, make his Spiritualism broad enough to embrace all that his nature may require of religion? He needs no vicarious atonement, no ecclesiasticism of any kind, but only to conform his life to the simple rules of right living taught by all advanced spirits. That is the best and truest religion. "To do good is my religion," said Thomas Paine. Can there be any better religion than this?

———————‡o‡———————

EMERGING INTO THE LIGHT.

From what a night of theological darkness the world is emerging! From the cruel, heart-crushing Calvinism of a half century ago, with its stern, revengeful, awful Being of infinite wrath and hate, who for his glory consigned all but a small portion of the human race to everlasting torment, to the gentle, loving Father, leading his children by ways they may not know into the light and likeness of himself. Although lacking the moral courage to modify their written creeds, which not one in ten actually believes, there is scarcely an intelligent clergyman in the evangelical churches to-day who pretends to preach or teach the doctrines of the church as taught fifty years ago. A few years hence they will be compelled to make an entire new statement of dogma or preach to empty pews.

FOR WHAT PURPOSE.

If a man has not a religious side to his nature, for what purpose was the organ of veneration placed in the brain? Phrenology teaches us that the frontal brain of man contains the organs of the intellect, the back brain those of the animal propensities, while the dome, or center of the arch, is the region of the spiritual faculties—veneration, hope, reverence, benevolence, etc. If there were no Supreme Intelligence—nothing in the universe worthy of adoration or worship, why were these faculties placed in the human brain? Admit that the universe is governed by law, has law intelligence? Can it design the pattern of a butterfly's wing? Can it plan a human eye or ear? Say, if you please, that this Mighty Mystery which we call God recedes as science advances, still there must ever be an infinite realm where science can never penetrate—a realm of the Unknown and the Unknowable—a something behind and before, and interblending with law, that is superior to law. Why ignore this thought, O Materialist! Is it not written in letters of living light in the constitution of man?

One of the first fruits of the " gift of the spirit" is that of being able to sense the spiritual status of those with whom one comes in contact. He reads his fellow-beings, whenever he chooses to do so, as from an open book. He cannot tell you how or why, but he *knows*, and that knowledge is almost infallible. In the higher unfoldment of this wonderful faculty one may ever know in whom to put his trust. Armed with this power how many of "the rocks and shoals of time" may be avoided.

*
* *

It is only when one comes to know and accept the fact of the psychic form manifestation that he is qualified or prepared to judge justly or wisely of this phase of mediumship. Until he can disabuse his mind of all unjust suspicion, and enter upon the investigation of the subject with a gentle, reverent and loving spirit, the forms of his spirit friends will not, indeed they can not, come to him, if at all, with any degree of positiveness. But once the way is broken, communion with the spirit world becomes a beautiful and ennobling fellowship, lifting the thoughts and aspirations into all goodness.

TEACHINGS OF JESUS.

What is there in the simple teachings of Jesus, as set forth in the Sermon on the Mount, and in his re-affirmation of the pagan doctrine of the Golden Rule, to warrant the pomp and mummery witnessed in the name of Christianity to-day? What is there in his simple statement of immortal principles to justify the Thirty-nine Articles and Confessions of Faith, held in some form by all branches of the Christian Church, from Rome to the Seventh Day Adventists? Is it not apparent to all thoughtful minds that the whole machinery of ecclesiasticism is a cunning devise of men intended to befog the minds of the people the better to command their consciences? The simple gospel of Jesus was free from all these strange devices. It was not until centuries after the death of the Nazarene that this fungus growth appeared upon the body of true Christianity, where it has remained ever since to obstruct the Way.

Ignorance is the cause of all discord. Those who know the truth should be patient and charitable with those who do not, ever remembering that they themselves were once in darkness and saw not the light.

*
* *

Don't waste your time trying to find the heart of a man or a woman who doesn't love children. There isn't enough of it to bother with when found. Wait till it grows, unless you can help it to grow, which is better still.

RELIGION OF LOVE.

The religion of love, of kind thoughts, of unselfish charity, of generous acts—this is all there is of it of any worth to the world. All else is useless rubbish. We pay vast sums of money for costly church edifices that are unoccupied six days out of seven, and vainly imagine that we are serving God thereby. There is no religion in that. Far better had we used the money to establish homes for the poor, or co-operative farms, shops and factories, where the humble toiler could be relieved of the fierce struggle for bread he is now compelled to endure. The strong will dominate the weak just so long as competition in the necessary work of the world endures. Give us the religion of good deeds, the religion of love, of temperance and charity, and the church may have its robes and mitres, its swinging censors, its catechisms, prayer-books and beads, its high steeples and higher priced ministers. We believe in bringing heaven down into this life, and not in leading man through a maze of superstitious obscurity in the hope that we may find it in the next.

Envy and Jealously are the two demons that sit on either hand at the gateway of men's souls, where they feed and thrive on the moral garbage from within. They are never seen where love abides in the soul, or where the spirit has grown into the likeness of the All Good. They are ungainly monsters, whose presence is always odious, and whose breath is malaria and death.

The Spiritualism that would under-estimate the importance of phenomena in the dissemination of our spiritual gospel, is quite as erratic as that which lives wholly upon phenomena. First the foundation (the phenomena), and then the super-structure (the religion and philosophy). Each is essential to the other.

SKIMMING THE SURFACE.

If we would get out of Spiritualism its purest joys and sweetest delights, we must bring its higher teachings home to our hearts, and practice them in our daily walk and conduct. There are heights upon heights, and depths upon depths, in our beautiful philosophy, that many a believer in our facts hasn't the slightest idea of. He skims the surface of Spiritualism without turning his gaze to the star-gemmed vault above, or ever sending a thought down into its crystal depths below. The truly spiritual soul drinks in those heavenly joys until his or her countenance (for it is woman more often that enjoys this divine beatitude) shines as with the light of heaven. There can be no better Christian, no better Pagan or Jew, no better man or angel than the *true* Spiritualist.

In presenting our spiritual facts and philosophy to the world, we must, to create a lively demand, show we have a better article of goods than are offered by our neighbors ; and this we can not do by crying down their wares, but by establishing the superiority of our own. If our lecturers, writers, and contemporaries of the spiritual press, would but act upon this suggestion—if they would seek for more of the spiritual in their own natures, and strive to excel each other in the exercise of all that conduces to nobility of character and true manliness, what a mighty impetus would it not give to our cause.

***

We wonder what our Adventist friends would have to say of the little four-year-old boy who, waking from his sleep one night, while his baby sister, lying in a crib near by, surrounded by anxious friends, was passing away, rose up in his bed exclaiming, "O, mamma, mamma, see the pretty ladies ! they are taking baby away !" an account of which appeared in a recent issue of the GOLDEN GATE. Would they say that the Lord had sent this delusion to that little child ?—that there were no "pretty ladies" there?—that the baby had no spirit separate from its body to be taken away, and that what seemed so was the work of Satan?

***

Many a man in this world begins to die before he is one-half grown. Instead of pushing onward and upward, as he should, gaining in wisdom and knowledge with his years, and evolving the grand possibilities of his nature, he reaches a point of stupid mediocrity, and there he stops and stagnates; and when he should be ripe and beautiful in soul he is found to be fossilized and covered with moss.

***

Age does not belong to the spirit. We have a jolly friend, now in his ninety-fourth year, whose heart is as young as ever it was, with all the added wisdom and beauty that years are supposed to bring. The moss and barnacles of mental and spiritual inaction have never stuck to him. The fact is he has never found time to stop growing, and never will, through all the countless ages of eternity.

***

What an empty bauble is fashionable society life. To live to dress, to shine, to flutter butterfly wings in the sunshine of worldly advantage, with never a heart-beat for the sorrow and suffering of others, for the overburdened lives, for the "spirits in prison," for the sin-sick, for the souls struggling for the light,—oh! is not this to live the life of utter misuse and worthlessness! Better far a daily struggle for bread, with longings all unsatisfied, if but the spirit be kept sweet and tender, and the affections and sympathies pure.

***

If, in the light of the truly developed spirit, we could look out upon the world of humanity with all its imperfections and undeveloped conditions—if we could see and understand the marvelous springs of action, the secret workings and motives that dominate human action—as we shall sometime,—what a tidal wave of sympathy for our erring fellow beings would sweep over our souls. How little we know the harm we do to the erring one, also to ourselves, when we harshly condemn. It would humble us all in our own conceit, if we knew as we are known.

--------◆●◆--------

CHRONIC FAULT FINDING.

Chronic fault-finding with the shortcomings of other religious systems is not the way to advance the cause of Spiritualism. We must show to the world that we have something more natural and philosophical than the old religious beliefs—something better to live by—something that, properly directed, calls into livelier action all the innate goodness of the undeveloped nature. Look, ye railers against the church, at the broad charities of the Christian world—its great universities, its vast missionary systems, its splendid churches, its asylums, publishing houses, kindergartens, and other mighty efforts for the uplifting of humanity, and then consider what Spiritualism is doing in like directions! Modesty should make us pause and reflect. In the infancy of this new revelation to the world, ere we have "won our spurs," we should be less aggressive toward other systems, and more zealous to impress upon the thought of the world the merits of our cause.

--------◀●▶--------

It is said that no man is wholly sane ; that is, each individual has some quirk or hobby not common with the rest. Indeed, a perfectly balanced mind—one equally developed in all directions of its nature—is something that does not exist. It is, perhaps, well that it does not, for therein only is found excellence. This would be a very tame world, a world of monotonous mediocrity, but for the exceptional insanity of some—or rather, the disposition of some to an abnormal development in special directions, which is but another name for insanity. It is only when this tendency becomes violent and hurtful that society finds it necessary to interpose restraints.

EYES TO THE FRONT.

All religions have been the outgrowth of the civilization of the age in which they existed ; and, if not the best products of their age, it was due to the undeveloped condition of the human race. Thus, to quarrel with the old systems is childish. One might as well find fault with his anthropoid ancestor for being an ape, or with his mother for having red hair. The question should not be, What of the religions of the past ? but What shall be religion of the future ? That is something for the present race to determine. The intolerance, cruelty, misconceptions of God, and persecution for opinion's sake, of the past, are all beyond our reach ; they have gone into history and cannot be changed. With eyes to the front, we should move forward in the pathway of progress, leaving the dead past to bury its dead.

SECRET SPRINGS OF POWER.

Did it never occur to you, dear reader, that power, wisely exercised, is the greatest of harmonizers? Now, property is one of the secret springs of power, and perhaps the most potent one. Take the cohesive element of property—of church edifices, universities, book concerns, etc.,—away from any of the religious sects, and what weight of influence would they have in the world? They agree because they can not well afford to disagree. Spiritualists, having none of this unifying element, agree to little or nothing, and that in so weak a way as to carry no weight with it. Give to the Cause fine temples erected for spiritual uses, with assembly and seance rooms, free library and reading rooms, a book depository and a live press, and a change like a new creation would come over the now somewhat chaotic elements of Spiritualism.

We do not agree with Chas. Dawbarn that morality is all there is either in Christianity or Spiritualism that is of any value; neither do we believe with him that there can be any religion without morality. An observance of the *forms* of Christianity or religion, merely, is not religion ; neither is the mere acceptance of the facts of Spiritualism religion. There is something more than morality, something broader and deep- er—an exercise of the higher spiritual faculties—reverence, aspiration, love, devotion—that constitutes what we term re- ligion. And this is the true gospel of Spiritualism, as it is of Christianity. It is the heart of all systems of religious belief.

MOVING FORWARD.

The spirit world is ever moving forward to a purpose. It takes no note of the things which do most disturb the serenity of mortal minds, in the presentation of spiritual truths; but presses into its service all who are able to bear arms—that is, all who can be used to bring its grand truths before the world of humanity. Its ministers and evangels may fall by the way- side, or follow the tempter of lust or gold into unbidden ways, and straightway it finds new recruits among young and old, in quiet Christian homes, in the abodes of skeptics and unbe- lievers, and the good work goes onward, ever onward, to the glorious end of man's spiritual unfoldment, and the conscious interblending of the two worlds. Spiritualism has a stronger hold upon the world to-day than ever before.

We are weary of this everlasting mouthing of the foolish conceit we so often hear, that "I am holier than thou." There are those who are so pure and lovely—in their own eyes—so far above their neighbors in moral excellence, that one natur- ally wonders how they manage to hold themselves down to earth. It would seem that they ought to be soaring in em- pyreal ether, with a pair of back-action, triple-jointed wings, leaving a streak of condensed glory in their wake. They are all too pure for earth.

If a rich man, dying, bestows his wealth upon some church, or for the endowment of some theological seminary, or to send the gospel to the heathen—if he even leaves a large sum for the senseless mummery of masses for the repose of his soul—he is a noble philanthropist; but if, being a Spiritualist, he bequeathes his property for the promotion of the cause of Spiritualism, he is insane! No matter how level-headed he may be upon all other subjects, his heirs immediately set about the task of proving him *non compus mentis* in the matter of disposing of his own; and judicial owls upon the bench and before the bar blink stupid assent to the proposition. It will not always be thus.

* *

There are many of the brightest minds in the lands—judges, journalists, politicians, poets, statesmen—who accept the facts upon which Spiritualists base their knowledge of a future life, and some of whom do not hesitate to acknowledge, in private, their belief in the philosophy of Spiritualism, but who are not classed as Spiritualists. They do not choose to pin their faith upon their sleeve, and it is not at all important, or necessary, that they should. They are doing a good work in a quiet way, among people whom, as out and out Spiritualists, they could not reach. Truth does not always require martyrdom of its votaries. There is sound wisdom, sometimes, in the exercise of a little policy.

* *

When some weak medium yields to temptation and goes astray, straightway the pharisees of the religious press, and the time servers and quidnuncs of the political, immediately elevate their muzzles, and howl in lugubrious concert. Just as though sin was any blacker, or wickedness more reprehensible, when practiced by a Spiritualist than by an orthodox minister. Why can't men be honest and just, if they do think differently on religious questions?

THE SUCCESSFUL MAN.

Who is the successful man? Is it the one with title-deeds to vast estates, with a large rent-roll and plethoric bank account? Or is it the man who has stored his mind with useful knowledge, and brought his spirit under the dominion of wisdom, love and truth? That life is the greatest success whose possessions afford the highest degree of happiness, and endure the longest. What is the brief span of human existence as compared with eternity—a drop of water to the ocean, an atom to the universe. Earthly possessions perish with our capacity to enjoy them; and we cannot surely enjoy them when we cease to control them; or, rather, when we pass beyond the conditions of earth wherein they alone exist. Look back over the lives of men—was Nero a more successful man than old John Brown, or William Sharon than the humblest toiler who labors faithfully to support his family and train up his children in ways of virtue and usefulness?

"It is all the world to me, the comfort I derive from my knowledge of a future life, and from my communion with my spirit friends," remarked a worthy lady to us the other day. This is the common experience of all who have entered the inner temple of our beautiful religion and have learned the better way of life. There is something in Spiritualism infinitely higher and better than a mere belief in its phenomenal facts,— and that is its religion. Until one experiences this religion he knows but very little of the real comfort, and serene satisfaction that may be derived from a knowledge of spiritual things.

* *

How barren and empty must seem the bauble of wealth or worldly fame to the spirit just awakened to consciousness upon the other shore. If the opportunities wealth affords for blessing the world have been neglected, then how doubly barren, and even harmful, it must appear.

WHAT WE NEED.

It is not what one really needs, but in what one thinks he needs, and cannot have, that consists the inharmonies and miseries of existence. If we could only school our spirits to be content with but few of the perishable treasures of earth, while ever seeking and aspiring for those riches of the spirit that endure forever, we should find a happiness and joy of which most of us but little dream. Man commits a terrible mistake in imagining that wealth, or fame, or worldly advantages of any kind, are essential to his true happiness. For do they not all fade away? And does not man himself, in time, come to regard them with utter indifference—that is, when the cold waves of dissolution break at his feet? There is no wealth like that of a soul rich in the graces of goodness.

My friend comes to me from the spirit side of life; he writes me a loving message between closed slates held in my own hand, and signs his name in his old familiar way; he entrances some medium and recalls familiar scenes, and awakens old memories, known only to us two; some clairvoyant sees and describes him accurately; he controls the elements and temporarily presents himself to me in tangible form, and I look into his face, and know of a verity that it is his own living self. "But that is not your friend," my Seventh Day Adventist brother presumes to tell me. Then who is it pray? "It is the Devil!" The Devil it is! God pity us for our ignorance!

What a dull, leaden thought is involved in the sad refrain, "It might have been." Ah, friends, there are fierce torments, raging hells untold, in spirit life—conditions which one would gladly exchange for annihilation, and from which there is no escape except by honest repentance and earnest endeavor. There is no one in the universe upon whose shoulders one can shift the burden of his own sins.

WORRYING GOD WITH ADVICE.

We are tired of that kind of religion that is perpetually worrying God with advice and coaxing him for favors. How often have we heard some wealthy and devout but stingy Christian, with his cribs full of corn, praying God to "remember the poor," when the thought of remembering them himself was the last thing that would ever enter his mind. And then again, how some people are perpetually worrying about the sins of their neighbors, while their own paths are beset with duties undone. The main and first question with each child of humanity is to bring himself into harmony with the true life, and not undertake to manage the entire universe, at least not until he has had more experience. He will generally have all he can attend to to manage himself, if he does the work wisely.

* *

A grave mistake, which even Spiritualists are slow to recognize, is the fact that spirits are by no means infallible, but are wise and otherwise, just like mortals. They may have opportunities for knowing many things that mortals do not ; in act they may possess, as doubtless many of them do, wisdom vastly superior to our own, and yet they are only fallible, with all a finite being's tendency to err. How often have we heard spirits questioned in matters that only a being of infinite intelligence could answer, and the questioner would be surprised to learn that his spirit friends were only human after all.

* *

How the vain and perishable things of this life—wealth, position, fame—all dwindle into utter insignificance as compared with the unfading treasures of the immortal spirit. We brought nothing into this world but a little pink lump of clay; that which we take out is of no more value than dust. All that we are, and all that we can possess forevermore must be of the spirit. How are we off for that? is a question we should consider just now.

With what marvelous precision and wisdom is the machinery of the universe managed and run ! In the mighty sweep around the sun of the most distant planet of our solar system, extending through years of our time, each revolution is the same in duration as every other revolution, though centuries apart, even to the fraction of a second. The same is true of all suns and systems, for all are sweeping onward in vast circles, all held and governed by the same unchanging law. In view of such inconceivable grandeur, well may the Psalmist exclaim, " What is man that Thou art mindful of him ! "

*
* *

How our cold-blooded competitive system of labor, with each man on a perpetual tension of ingenuity to out-trade and circumvent his neighbor, hardens our poor human nature, and dries up its springs of charity and humanity. Is it any wonder that men become indifferent to the needs of the suffering poor ? Is it not, indeed, a *seeming* necessity, at least, that they should come to regard selfishness as a sort of negative virtue? It takes a high order of spiritual unfoldment to enable one to rise superior to environment, and to be noble and grand notwithstanding the besetting errors of our earthly conditions.

*
* *

Alas ! how often is the cup of hope dashed from the spirit's lips, and we awaken to the dull, cold reality that our dream of joy is over. The fond anticipation of happy days to come—days of delight in plans and projects that give a roseate tinge to life, and make its cares and duties all the less irksome —is swept away as with a breath, and we take up the old burden and journey on, and on, till the sunset shall kiss our eyelids to sleep—the last sleep.

*
* *

Peace, like a mighty river, flows through the soul of him who has learned to think no ill. It is then he becomes one with the All Good, and is ready to mount, as on eagles' wings, to the infinite heights of being.

SPIRITUAL SIMPLETONS.

"The manly art!" That is what they call it when two thick-headed, beatle-browed bruisers batter each other's faces out of all semblance of humanity! They do not seem to realize, in thus placing themselves on a level with a beast, that a sway-backed, wind-broken mule can strike a harder blow with its heels than they, its human emulators, can with their fists! Business men, with respectable associations—with loving wives and innocent children—patronize the clubs where these disgusting exhibitions are held, and pious editors publish the sickening details, thus lending their influence to fostering and upholding human beastliness! O, ye spiritual simpletons, is it thus that ye would become god-like? Or, prefer ye to demonstrate in your own natures, the truthfulness of that despairing saying of Job that "Man hath no pre-eminence over the beast?"

**

How little we know of life and its possibilities—how little of the here or hereafter. We realize that we have come from an infinite past, and are moving on toward an infinite future; but wherefore? The countless millions of human beings who have lived their little day and passed on—for what purpose, or what uses in the economy of creation, who can imagine? We can only know that we are, God only can know the rest.

**

The world is wide enough for all. If you can not agree with your neighbor, and he will not go hence, *you* had better place a comfortable distance between you and him. You can not afford to have your peace of mind continually disturbed from any cause within your power to remedy.

**

Who would not rather leave the world with a tender memory in some grateful heart, and the thought of some life made happier by his living, than, without such memory or thought, to wear a costly monument above his worthless ashes?

AN ELEMENT MISSING.

How very little of the spirit of Christ there is in the churches of to-day. There are millions of dollars worth of church edifices in any of our great cities, and yet crime, and drunkenness, and poverty abound, seemingly, as never before. In most of them the worshiping of Christ is made paramount to love for humanity. The Roman Catholic saloon keeper spends the hour devoted to religious service on Sunday, in counting his beads, and stupid adoration of the Host, and then hurries back to his whisky-selling! The Protestant Christian takes all manner of advantage in trade throughout the week, driving hard bargains with the poor, selling fourteen ounces of butter for a pound, and the like, and then eases his conscience by listening to an unctuous sermon on Sunday by a ten thousand dollar preacher! And all the while there are poor women making shirts for ten cents a day, and homes all around where squalor, and rags, and ignorance abound. The money invested in the churches of San Francisco alone, if properly applied to some practical plan of co-operative labor, would give to every poor man and woman in the State a home and the means of a decent livelihood. And yet we would not do away with the churches until we are prepared to put something better in their place. The people had better be taught to give for a lesser good than to give nothing for a higher good.

———‡o‡———

Evil thoughts poison the blood, and thus invite all manner of physical ailments. The anger of the mother will sometimes throw her nursing babe into spasms. So closely is the body in sympathy with the soul that whatever disturbs the harmony of the latter also deranges the secretions of the body—breaks down its defenses, as it were, and opens its gate to the enemy.

**

He who seeks for the best in his own life has no time to spare to search for the evil in other lives.

THE YEARS WEAR ON.

The years wear on, and to the wiser, life, in its highest significance, broadens as we near the goal of its earthly expression. We begin to realize, with the great bard, "What a wonderful thing is man." A spark from the Infinite sent out from the great source of life, to glow and blazon through space forever? Here but a day, then comes the morrow! And it is how to make that morrow brightest and happiest that we should devote to-day. Here comes in the beautiful teachings of Spiritualism. It can only be by making the best use of ourselves and our opportunities here. We need not expect to wear a frown to-day with the hope that it will turn into a smile to-morrow. Fill this life with sunshine and the next will catch its glow. And how can we fill it so completely full of sunshine as by doing good to others? The tears we wipe from the eyes of suffering and sorrow will, in the coming time, blossom into peerless gems for our own brows. The burdens we help to lift from the shoulders of the struggling ones of earth, the cares we help to lighten, the griefs we assuage, the kindness we bestow, will all return to us in the shape of unfading joys in the beautiful hereafter. All this they tell us who have passed on to the other life. Shall we not believe them, and put into practice their holy teachings?

Is there anything in the Universe more beautiful than a beautiful soul? To have the companionship and friendship of such a soul—of a man or woman who has purged away the dross of his or her earthly nature by the refining fires of experience, and ascended the upper levels of life—is to walk arm and arm with God. Ah, there are many noble natures we know, who are our ideals of manly or womanly worth, who are as true to principle and duty as the magnet is to the pole. We are proud of their friendship, proud to realize that they have confidence in us, as we in them.

VIRTUE OF GIVING.

It isn't the amount one gives to a worthy cause that does one's spirit so much good as the sacrifice one makes in giving it. The young lady who, on experiencing a severe case of religion, gave her ear-rings to her unconverted sister, was entitled to no credit therefor. There was not the slightest virtue in the gift. Neither is there virtue in any gift of what one can dispense with without sacrifice. The gifts that exalt one are those like the "widow's mite" that go down into the soul, and mean some unselfish deprivation of enjoyment. That in the widow's case meant something more then that, it meant deprivation of comfort, if not of the actual necessaries of life. We should all learn that to be generous in giving in a good cause, is the true way to "lay up treasures in heaven."

* * *

"I do not know," says the scientist, "of any future life— at least, of no individualized, conscious existence for man after death." Therefore, why should we ask for proof of continued existence from that source? Shall we ask of science what it has not to give? Better seek for the evidence from some one who *knows*.

* * *

Give to woman the ballot, and how long do you suppose it would be before that hydra-headed monster, the rum.traffic, would receive its quietus? There are none who feel the terrible curse so keenly as the wives and mothers of the land. Spiritualists should stand solid in favor of temperance reform, and thereby set a worthy example to political Christians.

* * *

It costs nothing to be civil. One can say "no," in so gentle and pleasing a way as to make a lasting friend of the one whose request is thus denied. While, on the other hand, a favor grudgingly rendered, will win no esteem from the recipient for the one who bestows it.

THE SPREAD OF TRUTH.

One has but to make inquiry among one's acquaintances to learn how very widely and generally the belief in spiritual manifestations is spreading and taking root in the world. Many do not care for it to be known, others do not accept all the facts ; but the fact that the great truth is spreading, especially among thoughtful minds, at a rapid rate, can not be refuted. Our modern literature is full of Spiritualism ; orthodox ministers of the gospel,—those whose backs are not covered with theological moss,—do not hesitate to preach its central truths. It is interpenetrating, in some form or other, all enlightened thought. And while thousands of believers in these truths would rebel at the idea of being called Spiritualists, yet they are such all the same, and they do not know it. May the blessed truth run and be glorified among men. May it help the world to broader and better views of religion, and to a better quality of humanity — as it surely will, as it enters more and more into the spirit as well as into the understanding of men.

Some men, who are genial and affable in public, are the worst of tyrants in their own families. They seem to save all their meanness for their homes. They always have a kind word and a pleasant smile for their neighbor's wife, while for their own they have only sullen looks and unkind speech. Such men need a baptism of the Holy Ghost, and they need a hot one !

Is there a depth of woe more profound than that which overshadows the heart of the mother bending over the form of her dying babe ? The little pale face, the fluttering pulse, the short, quick breath—" Doctor, O, is there no hope ? Could the mother only see, as some can, the beautiful spirit form standing by her side, ready to receive to her loving arms the spirit

of that precious babe—could she but realize that in the spirit
world her heart's treasure will be trained in every perfect way
of life, and grow up into all grace and beauty, with no loving
tie sundered—would not that knowledge be to her a boon
above all price? This is the balm Spiritualism brings to the
stricken heart.

***

How little the multitude realize the responsibilities of life.
They live for the present hour, and its selfish enjoyments.
They buy and sell, and seek to circumvent each other in trade,
as though true happiness was to be found in securing something of earthly riches or fame to themselves that their fellows
do not possess.   And just when they have secured their prize
Death tears it from their grasp and sends them out into a
world where wealth and worldly honors count for naught.

***

How often we sing at our seances and in our public meetings the dear old words, "Nearer, my God to Thee—nearer to
Thee."   Would that all Spiritualists could sing these words in
the spirit and with the understanding also.   That is, that all
could feel as they sing that they are drawing nearer and nearer
to the Great Central Good of the universe—to the divine life
of the soul.   It is only thus we can derive from this earth experience its highest and truest meaning.

***

No man can lose his temper without injury to his own
spiritual nature, to say nothing of the harm and wrong he may
do to others.   The horse that becomes frightened and runs
away is never quite as safe or trustworthy afterwards.   There
are occasions, do you say, when you cannot help becoming
angry?   Those are just the occasions when you most need to
hold yourself under control, and which best show the metal of
which you are made.   It is only the spiritual weakling that flies
into a passion for trivial causes; the moral hero is he who can
hold himself level under great provocation.

THE COMING CENTURY.

What mind can grasp the wonderful possibilities of the coming century? Is it not possible that Bellamy's speculative literary creation, "Looking Backward," will be more than realized by the year 2000? Scan the achievements of the past century—its marvelous inventions and unfoldments in all directions of art, science and ethics,—its spiritual revelations—its idol-breaking and myth-destroying processes—its new revelations of truth—its disenthralment of the mind from old superstitions,—and who shall say to what heights of knowledge the world may not advance during the coming century. To the prophetic soul, it is evident that enlightened man is standing upon the threshold of the chamber of knowledge, within whose secret recesses are wonders that eclipse conception with their mighty meanings. The lightning express train of progress is sweeping onward. It is bearing us away from the old and out into the new. Unwise are they who wait for the slow freight.

* * *

The power of thought! Who can realize its potency? We are not only subject to the psychological power of thought of others, but we psychologize ourselves into wrong ways of thinking, until we come in time to reconcile ourselves to the commission of wrongful acts. Pope never uttered a truer sentiment than when he said :

> " Vice is a monster of such hideous mien
> That to be hated needs but to be seen ;
> But seen too oft, familiar with her face,
> We first endure, then pity, then embrace."

* * *

A thoroughly good, intelligent, high-minded, spiritual woman, what is there in the universe below the rank of archangel that can compare with her? How the aura of her presence makes everybody who comes within its influence better and happier! Such a woman never grows old. She is always young, and fair, and beautiful, and becomes more so with the years, until at last she steps across the border, an angel of light and love forevermore.

A SUNNY SOUL.

One of the happiest and sunniest souls we ever knew is that of a dear old lady now nearing the border land of time, whose last dollar, with the kind help of others, was spent to secure a stopping place in one of those loveless and barren shelters, known as an "Old Ladies' Home." This lady is a great reader, a devout Spiritualist, and not an unfrequent visitor to our Free Reading Room. A few years ago her only son and support in her old age was killed in a railroad accident. Coupled with this is a personal affliction of absolute deafness. Most women, and all men, in such sore straits, would sit down in the everlasting dumps. Not so, our heroine. Misfortune and poverty seem but to have brightened her spirit. She radiates sunshine and happiness all around her. She lives close to the heart of Infinite Love. She knows that there is no death, and is looking forward with rapturous delight to the time when she shall cast aside the form and step forth a white-robed angel into the new and higher life. As a model of patient, gentle and abiding trust in the All Good we thank her for this fragment.

REMEDY FOR CRIME.

When we come to learn that crime is the result of ignorance and undeveloped spiritual conditions, we shall cease to *punish* the criminal for his offenses against society, but rather seek his reformation by kind and humane methods, and by appealing to the better side of his nature. Our prisons will then become schools of reform, and the criminal tendency be treated as a moral disease. The wrong-doer will be restrained of his liberty just as we restrain the insane, for his own good, as well as for the protection of society. And when the moral health of the prisoner is restored, he will be permitted to go hence without reproach. There was a time when our ancestors had but little respect for the rights of their fellows. The strongest and shrewdest anthropoid robbed his weaker brother without the slightest compunction of conscience. The reason all do not do so now is because some are more advanced spiritually than others.

BELIEF VS. KNOWLEDGE.

Belief without knowledge, is nothing but a thread of gossamer—an idle fancy—a something, nothing. The world has been cursed with too much belief and too little knowledge. Belief belongs to the childhood of the race. It is full of a child's fancies. It takes all shapes, and makes real all manner of grotesque things. But the time comes when knowledge relegates belief to its proper place among the shadows. The religions of the past have been mainly religions of belief, unfounded in the constitution of man. · The Christian world, for centuries, has believed in a conglomeration of absurdities unworthy the intellect of a child. In what a nightmare of the brain must have been conceived the idea of a lost world, and in fact, the whole orthodox plan of man's creation and redemption. To imagine an Omnipotent Being creating a Devil with power to frustrate his plans and undo the work he had done, and the necessity of killing a part of himself (which part was his entire self!) in order to prevent the Devil from getting possession of *all* the souls of the Father's creation—can the fruitful fancy of childhood excel in absurdity this idea? And yet from thrice ten thousand pulpits throughout the civilized world is this amazing fable taught. In the light, or darkness rather, of such teachings, did Modern Spiritualism dawn upon the world any too soon?

The light is breaking upon the hill tops—the light of a new day. The hideous phantoms of the night of a false the-

-ology that has stood throughout all the ages, as a fearful spec-
tre by the bedside of the race—is melting away into an unpleasant memory, before the advancing effulgence of the coming day.   We are just beginning to learn that Good, and not
Evil, dominates the universe—that Omnipotent Law is man's
best friend.   How hard has been the struggle with the shapes
of wrong, with the childish imperfections of our undeveloped
spiritual and moral natures, to attain this end.   But the race
is won at last, thank the good angels, and humanity is steadily
moving forward to vastly mightier ends and purposes.

SPIRITUALISM MADE PRACTICAL.

We believe in making Spiritualism a practical means for
the betterment of the race, and that by methods of its own.
Shall we have our theories of life and duty, and then indifferently permit other theories to dominate the world?   Shall we
have no schools of our own, no public charities, no schemes of
co-operative labor, or finance, or trade?   Shall we spend the
day in open-eyed wonderment of the "manifestations of the
spirit," until the night cometh on and finds us with our tasks
all unperformed?   Spiritualism is no longer a mere question
of phenomena.   It has outgrown its baby clothes.   The sensible world concedes that it is not all a trick—that there is some
good reason for the belief of its millions of votaries.   It is
high time that we did something more than talk—that we
garnered our sheaves, and reaped the reward of the harvest.
What can we—what should we of the Pacific Coast do?   We
can erect a temple in San Francisco, with lecture halls, a college of psychical research, a publishing house, etc., for the
dissemination of our truths.   To do less than this is to blazon
our weakness and indifference to the world.   Come, friends—
ye who have learned there is no death—let us wake up to a
realization that we owe a duty to our Cause.

OUR THANKSGIVING.

The appointing by the State of a day of general thanks-giving, (formerly of fasting and prayer), to the Supreme Ruler of the Universe, for the blessings of health and prosperity as a people, in compliance with a religious custom, is looked upon with much disfavor by atheistic persons. Like the institution of Sunday, such persons are not compelled to observe Thanks-giving day, any more than they are our other legalized holidays, —or even the exclusively holy days recognized by the Church. But surely there is no one, however deficient in the organ of vener-ation, who can seriously object to a recognition of the day as a day of rest and recreation, for the enjoyment of such social festivities as that to which it is now generally devoted. And surely all should be magnanimous enough, in the enjoyment of their own freedom, to permit, without cavil, those who may so prefer, to devote the day to fasting and prayer. If any should choose to clothe themselves in sackcloth and ashes, in token of their humiliation of spirit, on that day, for the crimes and wrongs committed in the name of liberty, they ought to be permitted to do so, and no one should say them nay, or ques-tion their right in the matter.

But there is a spiritual side to this question, which should commend it to the consideration of all who are seeking for the higher life : and that is the importance of developing a spirit of thankfulness as essential to true growth. "Thankful for what?" do we hear some one ask? Thankfulness for everything —thankfulness that we were not overlooked in the construction of the universe—that we live, and will live forever. Again our questioner : "Is a future life desirable at the price many of "us are compelled to pay for it in this life—of poverty, sickness, "misfortune, etc.?" What are the brief moments of mortal existence, compared to an existence of infinite duration, and the advantage of infinite growth in all the higher capacities of the soul? Of what stuff can any one be made that he should be unwilling to take the chances of a few earthly ills and discomforts for an unfoldment of spiritual powers and possibilities that eclipse conception in their mighty reach?

Some of our atheist friends seem so apprehensive that they may be betrayed into doing something that may squint at the recognition of an Infinite, Overruling Intelligence, that they will hardly allow themselves to be properly appreciative of the real joys and blessings of life, lest such appreciation might be construed to the disadvantage of their materialistic claims. The unhappiness of all such persons should forever stand as a warning to the more spiritually inclined to shun the rocks of pessimism upon which their life barks have been wrecked. He must be spiritually blind indeed, who cannot see a Divine purpose in human life, and in the varied and marvelous forms of matter with which we are surrounded, and of which we are, physically, a part.

How can we know what is best for us—the discipline, moulding and annealing, that may be necessary to adjust us to our proper place in the mechanism of the universe. The pain we suffer; the tears that are wrung from our very hearts at times —are all, for aught we know, Nature's processes for forging us into shape and harmony with the Eternal Plan. At any rate, isn't it better for us to accept them as such, than to rebel, like truant school-boys, from the discipline necessary to hold us to our tasks? If we accept our sorrows and sufferings in a spirit of thankfulness we rob them of half their hurt.

But there is so much of good in the world to be thankful for—so much of beauty and joy—so much to gladden the soul and thrill it with a sense of true thankfulness, that it would seem that we would hardly need to be reminded thereof by the setting apart of any one day in the year as a fitting time to give

expression to our thanks.   We should be thankful every day ;
our lives should be a benison of thankfulness perpetually to
that Infinite Mystery of spirit that has given us eyes to enjoy
the beautiful pictures of nature—its grandeur of mountain and
ocean ; ears to drink in the melody of sounds ; and other
faculties for sensing the delights of being.   For the pleasures
of friendship, for the gentle hearts that love us, for the sweet
intercourse of soul with soul, for the uplifting hands reaching
down to us from the bending skies, for the bright hope of a life
of happy usefulness beyond the gates of death, and for the
infinite possibilities opening out before us, let us give thanks.

Aye, indeed ! What though your lot may be cast in
poverty, and many misfortunes and ills attend you even al
through your earthly pilgrimage ; are ye not journeying towards
home—to the better land? See ye not "the light in the
window" to some of those "many mansions" that shall yet be
your abode in the land of souls? Take heart of hope, ye
sorrowing ones. With eyes fixed upon the shimmering summit
of the Mount Delectable, take up your staff and scrip and journey on. And so we will all give thanks.

" WHAT CAN I DO?"

"What can I do for a living?" we think we hear some
one say, some one who is passively waiting and waiting for
something to "turn up." Well, let us see, what are you good
for ? Workers are needed everywhere and in all departments of
life ; now what can you do? Have you a trade or profession?
No? That's bad ; but there is much work to be done that does
not require any great amount of skill—nothing more than
patient application and good practical sense. With a good
stock of the latter, and a reasonable amount of energy to push
it to the front, no man or woman need long remain idle. But
a great mistake of the unemployed is that they can sit down

idly, like young robins in the nest, and expect the fat morsel to drop into their open mouths without any effort of their own. It is better for a poor man to earn his board merely, than to eat the food of charity in idleness. All labor, if worthy, is honorable, and no man or woman should hesitate to accept any respectable employment, the best that can be had, of course, rather than be a burden upon his friends, or the charity of the world.

"Heaven is not reached by a single bound ;
We must build the ladder by which we rise,
From the lowly earth to the vaulted skies,
And we mount to the summit round by round."

Thus wrote that grand spiritual soul, James G. Holland. How true it is, and how suggestive of the necessity of steady, persistent effort to overcome the imperfections of our natures, and enable us to attain to those graces and glories of being that make us fit for the enjoyment of the pure spiritual delights of the higher life. The appetites and practices that drag one down to earth must be overcome, and the wisdom principle, sanctified by love, enthroned in the citadel of the soul. What a work is this, O Mortal, the All-Father has set you to perform ? And how important that you perform it well, that you may re-. ceive the welcome plaudit of the God within, "Well done, good and faithful servant, enter thou into the joy of the life divine."

LEVEL HEADS.

The world wants level heads in religion as well as in the business affairs of life. Fanaticism and bigotry are as much out of place in the one as in the other. It wants a religion of honesty in trade, and gentleness of conduct in all the relations of life. It wants a religion that will "sit down" on all manner of gossip and scandal, and make the good name of a brother or sister as sacred in their absence as in their presence. It wants a religion of generous impulses and good will; one that will not hesitate to do a kind act to an enemy; one that will never betray a friend! It wants a religion of cleanliness, inside and out—a religion of health, and pure air, and wholesome dress and diet. It wants a religion of sunshine and good cheer—a religion of love, in its broadest, holiest and purest sense. In short, it wants a religion of common sense. With a good supply of this kind of religion on hand no one need borrow trouble of the future, and lay awake nights mourning over his sins.

"IF I WERE ONLY RICH."

"O, if I were only rich!" sighs an over-burdened soul at our elbow—over-burdened with poor health and physical inability to struggle with the great competitive world, where the strongest come off victorious, and the weakest go to the wall. Have you counted the cost of riches, dear lady—the care, anxiety, and above all, their crystalizing influence upon all the finer qualities of the spirit? Why, there are rich men and women in this great world, whose hearts are as barren of generous impulses, and whose lives are as empty of noble purpose, as though they had been made of brass. Would you exchange your own warm, generous nature, though humble and empty it may be of this world's wealth, for the possibility of becoming like one of these? But we know it is not riches your heart pines for, so much as for a reasonable competence. How to be happy without even a competence, is the spiritual problem you should seek to solve. And one may be very happy in poverty if one only knows how. We read of one of old who "had not where to lay his head," yet he could teach us all lessons of contentment and true happiness.

Some people seem to take a sort of delight in being miserable. They will hide themselves away in the shadows when the sun shines brightly all around, inviting them to bask in its delicious, health-inspiring beams. Their pains and aches, their griefs and sorrows, they roll as it were "a sweet morsel under the tongue"—live them over and over again, as though they were memories to be cherished. Now, the true way of life is to put the unpleasant things of this world under foot—to forget them. When once a trouble is over, let it go, and think no more about it forever. Think only of the heights you have climbed, and others to be attained, and not of the thorny way you have passed, and must pass to reach them.

*
* *

It is a law of the universe that God helps him who helps himself, and just in proportion as he helps himself. The effort that one makes in the direction of the accomplishment of any worthy purpose calls moral forces to his aid that he little dreams of to fight his battles for him. Man is not left to make his way through life alone. He is, if his purposes are worthy, surrounded by a mighty cohort of invisible friends, who stand ready at his beck to further his interests. But he must not sit down in indifference, trusting to these aids to do his work for him. They come only at the call of his own persistent efforts; they yoke themselves with his own determined thought, and clear the way of all obstacles to his success.

*
* *

It is the height of folly to quarrel with Nature or find fault with her laws. To do so indicates a low order of spiritual unfoldment; besides, Nature takes not the slightest notice of your complaints, but marches straight forward in her undeviating course forever. Whoever stands in the way of her laws must suffer the consequences. There is no sentiment in the cyclone. It hurls to destruction the Christian mother, and the babe crooning in her arms, with no more compunction, or scruples, than it would the meanest of her creations. But then what if it does! Who knows that the mother or babe has received the slightest injury?

HOW DOES HE KNOW ?

It is a favorite expression of a dear old friend of ours, that " man is pushed into the world without his knowledge or "consent, that he is pushed through it and out of it, and he "cannot help himself." He will excuse our inquisitiveness when we ask him how he knows that he did not come here entirely with his own knowledge and consent, and for the purpose of obtaining the experience that this life affords. If man is a spark from the Infinite Life—a fraction of God — he certainly must have possessed a previous intelligent existence of some kind ; and if so, he must have known something of the purpose and object he had in view in embodying himself in matter. How does our friend *know* that he did not push himself into the world? Concerning things whereof we do not know, it is not wise to be too positive. .

HIGHEST IDEAL.

"He that ruleth his own spirit is better than he that taketh a city." That is, it is of more consequence to a man, a truer indication of worth and greatness, that he be able to rule himself wisely, than that he rank high in the world as a ruler of others. This is a rarer test of true excellence, than, at first thought, one might suppose. How is it with you, dear reader? Are all the appetites, passions and weaknesses of your nature dominated by an enlightened will? Have you the animal man "well in hand,"· with a taut rein, and are you sure of your ability to "hold him level," in the great race of life? Can you withstand temptations? Are you living up to· your highest ideals of right and duty? If you are, then pray for us that we may be like unto you.

"One world at a time," says the Materialist. That is good advice, provided one makes the right use of the "one world" he now lives in. But the trouble with most people who give no thought to a future life, or to another world, is, that their spirits become so incrusted with material things, and so oblivious to things spiritual, that when they enter upon the other life they are as illy fitted for its duties and responsibilities as babes. If one was going to a new country to reside it would certainly be a great advantage to him to know what was necessary to take with him to secure the best conditions and highest enjoyments of the place.

EMPTINESS OF RICHES.

How empty and vain must seem all the pomp and circumstance of life—stocks, bonds and bank accounts, houses and lands—to the man with the death rattle in his throat. A passenger upon a sinking ship, cast aside his belt, weighted with gold, preparatory to committing himself to the waves. His neighbor picked it up and buckled it around his own waist. One sank beneath the waves, the other floated upon the surface, and was rescued. Men who know better, sink into the grave daily, weighted down with that which will encumber their spirits perhaps for ages, and bind them down to the earth plane. Live, if you will, O ye favored ones of earth, in the enjoyment of your wealth while ye may, but for your own soul's sake, and for God's sake, do some good with it when you die.

We bring nothing into the world but the germs of body and spirit; we take nothing out but spirit. The body having done its work is resolved into its original elements. But what of the spirit? In this is centered the fruition of our years—of our experiences—of our joys and sorrows—of our good or bad thoughts and deeds—all of which may be summed up in one word, "character." This, and this only, we carry with us to the other life. Put this question to yourself, dear reader, "Stripped of everything else but character, what have I to commence business with in the other life?"

THE STILL SMALL VOICE.

The higher we ascend the scale of being, in our spiritual natures, the more susceptible do we become to the thought atmosphere all around us, and to the spiritual forces and currents ever descending to the children of earth from the shining ones of the higher life. No one can err who listens to the "still small voice" of the spirit within his own soul and follows its teachings. The trouble with most of us is that we either stop our ears and refuse to listen, or, hearing, refuse to obey. No mortal yet ever earnestly and sincerely sought for the path who did not find it, sooner or later. Help comes to him from sources he little imagined, clearing away the thick underbrush of doubt and uncertainty, and leading him forth into the light. All roads lead to happiness; but some are much longer than others. All travelers through the valley of shadows will get there, sometime.

ONLY FOR THE FEW.

As yet spiritual truth is only for the few. The multitude are not yet ready for it. Step by step and little by little the sunlight of the new dispensation breaks upon the world. The new convert to the stupendous facts of spirit existence and communion, is apt to be enthusiastic. He is naturally anxious that his friends should be brought face to face with such facts and phenomena as have convinced him of the central truths of Spiritualism. The result, in many instances, has been disastrous to the medium and of no benefit to the investigator. It is not the conviction of a great truth that men like Prof. Huxley seek for in their investigation of spirit mediumship, but to prove to their own satisfaction that there is no truth in it, an that what they do not know about nature's ways isn't worth knowing! The truth comes only to those who are ready and willing to receive it.

OUR GOOD OLD MOTHER.

How soft and beautiful on this glad Sunday morning (the hour we give to these fragments), the sunlight gilds the green hills and fertile plains with its golden glory. The air is soft and balmy as the breath of love, and the sky, with its gentle wings, seems to brood the earth with infinite tenderness. What an impartial friend is our good old Mother Nature. She has the same smile for the just as the unjust: Her soft air kisses the feverish brow of the misguided one just the same as it does the roseate cheek of innocence. She never scolds, or complains, or condemns ; but is ever inviting her children into the better ways of life. See ye not, O mortal, the loving hands down-reaching from the bending skies, to draw you closer to the heart of Infinite Love ? Heed ye not the "line upon line and precept upon precept" of her many teachings? She does not tell you that by any vicarious process you can escape the consequences of your sins, but she would have you live the true life, that your spirit may be clear from the scars of sin. Who can not draw from earth, air and sky, on such a glorious morning as this, an inspiration prompting to a better and higher life.

ACQUISITIVENESS.

The acquisitive faculty in human nature, though not the highest faculty, nevertheless has its uses in the world's unfoldment. It is through this that the Infinite Spirit works to mighty ends. The rich man whose heart has not been corrupted by his riches—and there are many such — becomes a vast storehouse of golden opportunities for the uplifting of humanity. It is through such means that universities are founded, great libraries established, and noble charities upheld. It is also by the aggregation and disbursement of the world's surplus wealth that mighty enterprises for the advancement of civilization are founded and fostered—railroads spanning continents; lines of steamships crossing every sea. Not ours to condemn the acquisition of wealth, except when perverted to ignoble uses. The pressure of modern thought in the direction of the brotherhood of man, and the common needs of an undeveloped humanity, is telling in this as in all other human affairs. The time is coming when a man will be ashamed to die possessed of great riches.

————ֿ:o:————

A WEAK CHARGE.

One of the weakest charges ever made against Spiritualism by the Christian world is that it is not respectable. True, it has no elegant churches, with softly cushioned pews, inviting the worshiper to dreamy devotion. It is wanting in most of the appliances of ecclesiasticism,—in theological seminaries, in orders of divinity, in conferences, and general synods. But then, in its earlier history, Christianity was entirely devoid of such things. It wasn't even respectable ! Jesus himself was looked upon by the Jews as a vagabond sort of a character, who fellowshiped publicans and sinners, and made himself very obnoxious to the prevailing respectability of his day. And so we ought not to shrink from the charge, but we should meet it by showing that we have a higher standard of respectability than that which judges a man by outward appearances. If a belief in Spiritualism brings comfort to the sorrowing wife or mother in the hour of her despair, when death has sealed the lips of her idol,—as we know it does, we will not trouble ourselves about its lack of respectability.

————•◆•————

Like rain to the parched and thirsty earth are the crystal drops of spiritual truth to the soul whose inner consciousness has been awakened to its divine origin and mission. In the light of its new day it mounts as on eagle wings to the upper air, where serene splendor and undiminished glory environ it forever more.

THEOSOPHY.

"We want you to come up a little higher," said a good Theosophist friend to us the other day.   Ah, but, we replied, there is such a thing as getting above and beyond the reach of the great pleading, plodding heart of humanity.   There are all grades in life's great school.   The primary is the basis of all education, all culture.   We cannot ignore that.   We print and preach for the many — not alone for the few.   Already some complain that they cannot comprehend the teachings and claims of our Theosophical correspondents.   We spread a table of choice viands, — of "milk for babes," and stronger food for the older grown— of "signs and wonders" for those who require it, of fragments of philosophy for speculative minds, of grains of golden wisdom for the highly unfolded. Reach forth, dear reader, and help yourself.   Select that best suited to your taste, and don't complain.   You cannot convert a skeptic to the truths of Spiritualism without first demonstrating the fact of spirit existence.   But once converted, we would lead him onward and upward into the higher and brighter realms of our beautiful philosophy.

Down from the bending skies, out from the infinite energies of space, around and about us everywhere, helping hands and friendly influences are ever reaching to guide us in the better way of life.   It is when our intuitions are dull to these influences, and our ears deaf to the gentle pleadings of the spirit, that we lose our way amid the fogs and brambles of unworthy things, and our footsteps are beguiled toward many a dangerous pitfall.

Spiritualists who denounce others for believing in phases of spiritual phenomena with which they themselves are not familiar, have no right to complain of skeptics who deride *their* claim to the possession of spiritual facts which are not the common property of humanity.

OUR FUNERAL CUSTOMS.

Day after day the funeral cortege moves slowly toward the city of the dead. There are the same sable trappings of woe, the same funeral aspect of the pall-bearers, the same solemn visaged neighbors and friends. And thus we lay away our dead—the young and the aged—the tender blades and the ripened ears. And then we erect monuments to their memories, which, a century hence, will be regarded by the living as a precious waste of marble. Why seek thus to perpetuate the memory of the mortal body, which, a few years hence will be but a handful of dust? Nothing lives but the spirit, and naught in the memory of that should be perpetuated save its generous promptings to noble deeds. The most elegant monument is seldom for the most worthy, but rather for the one whose mortal representatives possess the longest purse. After all, are not our funeral customs the outgrowth of paganism, the same as that which filled the rocky cliffs that border the valley of the Nile with mummies, and for the same object—the possible ressurection of the mortal body to a renewed life? As we bring ourselves more and more into the life of the spirit, the less regard will we have for the preservation of the decaying mass from whence the vital spark has flown; but rather shall we not hasten its restoration, by refining fires, to the elements whence it was taken?

————◆————

Who can account for the infidelity of those who call themselves Christians, concerning the demonstrations of a future life through the phenomena of Spiritualism? One would naturally think they would be glad to prove what they can only hope for. They not only deny, but will even ridicule facts occurring to-day, the counterpart of which occurring in ancient times, whereof their Scriptures abound, they place implicit confidence in. Who can explain the strange inconsistency?

WHAT OF IT?

Well, what of it? What if some one has wronged you—has abused your confidence—has borne false witness against you—has robbed you of your earthly possessions? Can you not realize that the perpetrator of these unjust deeds has wronged himself far more than he has you? All that there is of the real *you* is the soul that expresses itself through your physical organism; and that is beyond the reach of harm. It is helmeted and casemated in an impregnable fortress of divinity, where it can "smile at the drawn dagger and defy its point." Whoever lays siege to this fortress beats his breast against the Rock of Ages, and can harm or wound no one but himself. The injury your enemy may do you can only affect you in outward and transitory things, never in the interior and real self—if you so will it.

DON'T COMPLAIN.

Don't complain of your lot in life; you are not nearly as poorly off as you think you are, however deficient of this world's goods you may be. The real treasures of earth and heaven are all yours, if you want them. Love and honor are yours; so also are the beautiful stars, the bright sunshine, the golden glory of the evening sky, the breath of the rose, the song of the birds, and the laughter of children. Can you look into the eyes of the woman who loves you—your heart's idol—or the face of the babe crooning and crowing on your knee, and say that you are not among the favored ones of earth? Accept your lot and be glad. A few days hence the beggar and the king shall lie down together. What will be their relation to each other "over there?"

"Once upon a time" there was a rich man who fared sumptuously and riotously. He had many mistresses, and openly boasted of his shamé. In this direction there was no depth of dishonor he had not reached. At last he sickened and died, long before his allotted years. He passed on to spirit life, leaving all his millions, with the exception of a beggarly trifle, with instructions to spend the last dollar, if necessary, to defend him in his infamy. Oh, the long years of retribution! the agony and humility of spirit! the deep and bitter remorse! that must come to that erring spirit before it can mount the celestial hights.

THE THANKFUL WORM.

We know a man worth many millions of dollars, whose boast it is that he never gave a dollar to any charitable purpose in all his life. The time will come when in all God's universe there will be no spirit in such great need of charity as he. He is now nearing the border line that separates him from the world of eternal verities. A few years hence, and the only living thing to thank him for a square meal will be the worm that banquets on his body. But his spirit, O pitying heavens! in what darkness must it grope for ages! How strange it is that any man can be found who will take no heed of the future by glorifying the present. Here we must do our work and now, for this is the only moment we can call our own.

How little the world, or even the average Spiritualist, understands the requisite conditions for good spirit manifestations. A member of an eastern band organized to raid materializing mediums, who claims to be a Spiritualist, although a disbeliever in spirit materialization, writes us that he, with others, has offered $1,000 to any materializing medium who will submit to such conditions as he and his band may direct; and, with no one present but themselves, produce a separate and distinct form! Why not take a Swiss watch-maker, turn him loose with a sledge hammer in a pig iron factory, and insist that he shall make a fine chronometer in five minutes!

The wise man climbs to the higher levels of life by his mistakes. He who falls and rises again thereby gives evidence that he possesses the metal of true manhood. Why should we continue to condemn one who has recovered his missteps? Jesus did not condemn, but simply admonished the fallen one to "go and sin no more." There are too many people in the world puffed up with the pharisaical idea that they are better than their neighbors, and that their superior goodness is due to some superior excellence of their own. It will be as humiliating to their pride, as it was to that of their illustrious self-righteous prototypes, when the Master shall say unto them, "Let him that is without sin cast the first stone."

*
* *

"Did he leave anything?" That is the inquiry the world often makes concerning one who has passed on to spirit life. It is the question which oftentimes most interests surviving kindred. But the question which most concerns the departed is, "Did he take anything with him?" Some there are who, dying, leave everything. They are to be pitied. Those who leave most, in a worldly sense, are usually those who take the least along with them. It all depends upon the nature of our opportunities, and the use we make of them.

*
* *

There is a wide difference between the mere acceptance of the phenomenal facts of Spiritualism and the adaptation of one's physical and spiritual nature to the higher teachings of its beautiful philosophy. There are many who never get beyond the first or phenominal stage; they have become convinced of the truth of spirit return, and there they remain. The lessons of charity, temperance, benevolence, brotherly love, purity of life and conduct, etc., that come from the spirit world, make but little impression upon their lives. This is not the fault of the fact, but of the nature that lacks the disposition to adjust itself to the fact.

DOES PROHIBITION PROHIBIT?

"Does prohibition prohibit?" is one of the mooted questions that come uppermost in all communities where the temperance agitation has obtained a foothold. We should naturally answer that prohibition does prohibit. If it does not, then it is not prohibition. We would that we could always give the same affirmative answer to that other question, Does Spiritualism spiritualize? The fact that in very many instances a belief in the facts and philosophy of Spiritualism does *not* spiritualize to any considerable extent, is evident from the wrangling and inharmony so common among Spiritualists, or those who call themselves such. With the beautiful teachings of bright and enlightened spirits constantly before them, Spiritualists ought really to be the most kind hearted, charitable and forgiving people in the world. While we are glad to know that some of them are thus, yet many, to our humiliation, be it spoken, are not. We would that all possessed more of the Christ spirit.

———‡o‡———

We have no time to waste in unprofitable bickerings, or useless explanations. We should ever strive to live in a realm of thought currents that lead only to the All Good. Though clouds and shadows hover over the valleys, the sun shines bright and clear at the mountain top. Thither our pathway leads, and the angels of the bending skies ever invite us upward.

*
* *

The worm is no respecter of persons, neither is it particularly æsthetic in its tastes. The cheek of innocent maidenhood furnishes no daintier morsel than the hardened sinews of age. All is corruption, when once the spirit steps forth disenthralled. There is nothing permanent in matter—all is change and decay. The spirit only shall live forever—in light or darkness, as we will.

The theology of the past, that robbed life of all its sunshine, and filled the world with sadness and tears, is giving way, in the light of the Spiritual Philosophy, to a brighter and more cheerful outlook upon existence. The good Father, surely, does not want his children to go "mourning all their days." He cannot wish that they should be willing to be damned for His glory, but rather that they should endeavor to gather into their lives all the grandeur and beauty of creation. For what has He clad the earth with verdure, and surrounded it with the breath of His love, but to lead the children of His creation into ways of pleasantness. If we make this life full of joy there will be no room for sorrow here, or hereafter.

It may be asked, if none but initiates, or experienced investigators in the higher physical manifestations of psychic phenomena are to be admitted to seances for the development of the psychic form, how is any one to be convinced of the truth thereof? Conviction will come with spiritual unfoldment, and experience in the less startling phases of the phenomena. The seeker after psychical knowledge should not be too eager to grasp all truth at once. He should at least learn his alphabet before endeavoring to branch out in logic or the higher mathematics. It is well to study the philosophy of the spirit rap, or the nature of the trance, before endeavoring to take in the psychic form.

*
* *

After all that may be said or written upon the subject of psychic phenomena—accounts of wonderful individual experiences, etc.,—every one must settle the matter for himself. No revelation to A can quite satisfy B, however much confidence the latter may have in the honesty or powers of discernment of the former. He must know for himself. The mind is so constituted that it cannot accept the evidence of others in aught that relates to the seemingly incredible.

DISCIPLINE OF EVIL.

How many events and circumstances in this world which
we look upon at the time of their occurence as serious evils—
sickness, the loss of loved ones, business reverses, etc.,—do
we not come in time to regard as blessings in disguise? From
this fact may we not reasonaby conclude that all seeming evils
and misfortunes that come to us are wisely intended for our
good ; in other words, that behind and through all evil there
shines and permeates the rays of a Divine Good? Man needs
the discipline of temptation and misfortune more than he can
know. He needs the lash of the results of his own follies,
often, to teach him wisdom. What kind of limp and nerve-
less clods we should be without the hard experiences this life
affords. Let us then accept the cup, though bitter it be. We
shall be all the better for it some time.

Evil disappears from the undeveloped human nature just
in proportion as the good predominates therein. Then the true
way to uplift humanity is not by fighting the evil, but by
encouraging and developing the good. No man was ever made
better by abuse, or unkindness of any kind, and none was ever
made to see the error of his way by ridicule. When, O when,
ye would-be educators and reformers of the race, will ye learn
this fact !

* *
*

The higher phenomenal phases of Spiritualism should be
reserved exclusively for the initiate—that is, for those whose
perception of truth has been so far unfolded as to enable them
to discern "the things of the spirit." The pyschic form is
not for those who can not accept it. In fact, the presence of
one inharmonious person in a seance room, unless largely
counterbalanced by harmonious elements, will cause a vibra-
tion, or disturbance of the nice conditions essential to good results, and perhaps prevent the manifestations altogether.

There is no more independent class of thinkers in existence than Spiritualists. To some, it makes no sort of difference what others claim to know, they will argue with the knowing ones as persistently as will the skeptic against what *they* themselves claim to know, to convince the former that they are mistaken. For instance, some one claims to have had positive evidence of a certain phase of psychic phenomena with which some one else is not familiar. Straightway the latter denies that any such phenomena could possibly occur, wholly forgetting that his own claims to knowledge upon other phases of the same class of phenomena appear just as unreasonable to the skeptic. And so we go!

It is utterly useless to thrust our facts or philosophy upon persons not ready to receive them. The fallow ground of the heart must be ready to receive the seed before there can be any prospect of fruition. "But," you may ask, "would you hide your light under a bushel?" By no means. There are hearts everywhere hungry for the truth. All such are ready to be fed. "Feed my *lambs*," said Jesus. He did not say, "Go catch my goats and force them to eat of the bread of life." "*Ask*, and ye shall receive." There must first come the condition of mind that prompts one to *ask*, then will he receive.

Can the man who doles out to his wife, with reprimands for her extravagance, a moity of what is her just due as an equal partner in the firm, or of what he spends for his own personal gratification, have anyone but himself to blame when his children grow up to be thieves—made so by the pre-natal impulse of the mother to help herself to a little needed change from her husband's pockets, while he is asleep? The child born in an atmosphere of just, generous, and loving thoughts, starts out with a heaven in this life accomplished, and not with a hell to overcome.

NATURE'S WORKS.

How exquisite in design are all of Nature's works ! None of them are too insignificant for the display of infinite skill and wisdom in their construction. In all her marvellous methods and varieties she slights nothing, leaves nothing unfinished or incomplete in this life, save and except man himself, and she will make a perfect job of him before she is through with him. She weaves into the butterfly's wing the azure and the gold of her sunsets, and she paints the lily and the rose with the glory of her blushing dawns. And then how nicely she adapts means to ends. The mole blindly burrowing beneath the sod, the sea bird skimming the mighty wastes of ocean, the cricket drumming its love notes at the hush of day—all are cared for as fondly and tenderly as the mother cares for her babe. What a field for study—what suggestions of Masterly Purpose in the plan of the universe ! How can man grovel in lowly thoughts and things, in a world of such matchless splendor and possibilities as this !

There is a nameless force that goes out at times with human utterance, that gives to the spoken word a persuasive power never dreamed of at other times and under other conditions. This subtle force may be regarded as the "sword of the spirit." It is not always so much *what* one says that touches the heart and the understanding, but *how* it is said, and the spirit force that goes with it. This is well illustrated in the senseless exhortations formerly indulged in at old style religious revival meetings, urging sinners to the "mourners' seat."

* *

The Spiritualist who earnestly and industriously sets himself at the task of developing his own spiritual powers, and thereby bringing the spirit world into his own life, has begun to learn what true Spiritualism means.

No criminal was ever made better by punishment, and no wrong-doer by abuse. We can benefit the erring only by strengthening their moral natures—by building them up in good purposes, and calling them out on the higher planes of their being. This can be accomplished only as a labor of love. Whoever seeks to *drive* men into better ways of life has his labor for his pains ; not only that, he hardens his own nature, filling his spirit with all unkindness and bitterness.

"I don't know," is the language of honest doubt; "I know you don't know," that of intolerant bigotry. Why can't we respect each other in all matters of opinion, even remembering that what none of us know is to the sum of our absolute knowledge, as the big, blazing sun to the mote basking in its rays. Let us delight to differ, and love each other in our differences. If we all thought precisely alike, life would be too flat and insipid for healthy growth.

Someone has wisely said : "The, danger of riches increas- "es with their increase. Abundance serves not as water to "quench, but as fuel to augment the fire of covetousness." And so the acquisitive man comes in time to think that the more he has, the more he needs ; and this thought is apt to cling to him long after he has accumulated vastly more than he can wisely use for his own needs, even down to the last hour of mortal existence. But is it the best thought to carry into the other life ?

"The light on the path," is the light that shines down into one's own spirit from the source of all light, and radiates outward to illumine other souls, and mark the way that they should go. Who walks by this light, can not stumble or go astray. It will guide him safely to his Father's house, "where the many mansions be."

THE LEAVEN WORKING.

We apprehend the time is not distant when the fundamental truths of Spiritualism will be generally accepted by the
churches—when the evidences of spirit existence and return
will be as familiar to church members and to Christian preachers, even, as they now are to thousands outside the pale of the
Church. Then the churches will be compelled to remodel
their creeds to fit the higher order of truth, as presented from
the spirit world, or else to drop out of existence altogether.
Already the leaven of this new and brighter gospel is working,
even to the rendering and tearing assunder of all old notions
and ideas whose claim to veneration depends mainly upon their
antiquity.   Evangelical Christianity is nothing like as tyrannical
or intolerant as it was a quarter of a century ago; at least, its hold
upon the public conscience is nothing like as binding.   Even
the Church of Rome, that not long ago placed its foot upon
the necks of kings, and gave its adherents the choice of absolute
obedience or the stake, can not now coerce one poor priest,
who, like Father McGlynn, chooses to defy its power.

Happiness is a condition of the spirit — a something that
belongs within,—and is dependent only to a very limited extent, if at all, upon externals.   Martyrs have gone to the stake
with their souls aflame with gladness, while kings, with the
plentitude of earth at their command, have moped in melancholy misery.   There is more solid comfort in an ounce of
contentment, than in all the wealth of the Rothschilds.   The
happiness that is dependent upon wealth, can last only while
the wealth lasts.   There will come a time when the check
of the millionaire will not purchase the handles to his coffin.
Then what?

When you wake up, dear reader, in the morning of that
new day, to a consciousness that you have crossed the river

of death, and that all of your earth life, with its accomplished good or ill, is behind you forevermore, what condition of the spirit do you imagine will then afford you the largest measure of satisfaction? Will it be, do you think, the realization of the good you might have done to your fellow beings, but did not? How empty and vain will then appear the "pomp and circumstance" of earth, the bauble of wealth—the tinsel and sham of fashion, and the mockery of fame! Only the pure gold of character will be current "over there."

———— —·—●—·————

No man should boast of his superior powers of body or intellect. Neither his strength nor his greatness may be due to any virtue of his own. His very superiority should teach him modesty, and make him graciously careful not to wound the feelings of his inferiors. We should accept our lot and be thankful, ever seeking to make the best possible use of all our God-given faculties.

*
* *

If the man who imagines that he has a "call" to make light of the honest opinions and convictions of others, or to set himself up in judgment of the faults and failings of others, could only see himself as he is seen by the wise ones on the other side of life, he would blush with humility and shame at his own vaunting temerity. "Physician, heal thyself," is an old adage that all who start out to correct the faults of others should ever consider. A noble example is the best teacher!

*
* *

Wealth builds its palaces as though its tenants would occupy them forever. It shuts itself in from the great world of humanity, of which, in the order of nature, it is a part, and to which it owes its very existence. And for what, and for how long? An empty shadow and a day. Death laughs at all human distinction. The worm finds no daintier food in the king than in the beggar. There is no monopoly of sweetness in corruption.

PASSING ON.

Ten years ago we knew a sweet young girl, beautiful, gentle and graceful, just launching out on the sea of married life. The home of her parents and our own joined, and we had seen her almost daily from infancy. She was the idol of her home, and a great favorite among all her acquaintances. At her marriage she moved to a distant town, and we henceforth heard of her only occasionally. Children came to her,—one, two, three, four,—and the bearing of these, with other of life's vicissitudes, wrought sad havoc with her health. A few days ago we stood by the bedside of a pale, delicate little woman, rapidly fading away. She stood on the very verge of the river's brink, conscious that only a few days more of mortal existence remained for her. We could hardly realize that the bright, young girl of ten years ago and the fragile woman before us were one and the same person. We talked to her of the beautiful spirit world just before her, and assured her that death was only a gentle sleep from which her spirit, removed from the poor sick body, would awaken with rapturous delight, in the arms of a loving father, who had passed on before her, and whose spirit we both felt to be present. Ah! what a comfort is the knowledge of the glorious truths of Spiritualism to those who are nearing the great change.

———:o:———

One whose desire is ever for the highest good in his own life—whose aspirations are ever upreaching—never has to rely wholly upon his own powers. He will be met half way by some down-reaching spirit from the higher spheres to aid him onward and upward. There are always those ready to respond to the spirit's needs, when earnestly sought for.

* *

There is but little difference between the teachings and practices of the early Christians and the teachings and practices of modern Spiritualism. The former taught a gospel of love to God and good will to man. The latter teach the loving fellowship of all humanity, believing that in the practice of that virtue they can render to their Creator the highest possible service. The former healed the sick by the laying on of hands. Wherein does the treatment of the sick in these days by animal or spirit magnetism differ from that of Christ and his disciples? "Greater things shall ye do," said the Master; and surely the time is rapidly coming when these "greater things" shall appear—if they have not already.

"If you could see the dark aura that envelops some persons," says a faithful spirit worker in our own home, "you would feel like fleeing from their presence." It is well we can not see, for then we might shrink from the performance of duties where they were most needed. Spirits see and feel this aura, and are attracted toward, or repelled by mortals in proportion as their own spiritual natures are pure or impure, or correspond with those into whose atmosphere they come.

The exercise of brotherly love, charity for all, and good will towards the most undeveloped fellow-spirit, is the only means of subduing the baser promptings of one's own nature. Unkindness, jealousy, envy, selfishness, and unjust suspicion, constitute the deadly nightshade of the heart, which, if allowed to live and grow, will so poison the springs of happiness in one's own soul that all of its future will be saddened thereby. Overcome these evils, O brother, and refresh thy soul with the beautiful sunlight of Divine Goodness.

The fraud or dishonesty that injures only its perpetrator is far less to be deplored than the thought or act that seeks another's injury. While the first should never be condoned, the latter cannot be too earnestly condemned. He who would commit either needs the uplifting light of truth in his soul.

COMFORT OF SPIRIT COMMUNION.

No one can appreciate the value and comfort of spirit communion so well as the man or woman whose spiritual eyes have been opened to the light, and who can see and know for themselves. Who would close the doors of the heart to the wise and loving teacher and friend from the spirit side of life, who can make his presence known in the home circle, and who comes to inspire, to heal, to encourage, and in every helpful way to assist each member of that home in bearing the burdens of life? There is many a home in this great city, and throughout the land, that is blessed with such a faithful companion and guide. The shining ones are ever knocking at the doors of mortal hearts, but as yet there are but few to bid them enter in, and they go away grieved.

————‡o‡————

The great mistake of all churchmen, of whatever sect, is in imagining that they possess, in their religious systems, a monopoly of all spiritual truth. As though the revelation of spiritual truths to the world ceased with the advent of Jesus, and that henceforth and forevermore, man must take his gospel knowledge at second hand. The discovery of this mistake, and the adjustment of multitudes of the race to the new order of things, is what disturbs the little souls of an effete ecclesiasticism, and causes the "heathen to rage" against Spiritualism.

————◆————

"Words, idle words!" are all discussions with those who, not wishing the truth for themselves, seek to convince *you* of your error! We have no time to waste with such. It is not the skeptic who does not care to be convinced, but the heart athirst for the living waters of Spiritualism, that we care to bother with.

* ***

Life is barren or fruitful just in proportion as it is made a help and blessing to others. No one can live wholly to himself without dwarfing his own nature.

It is the disposition of writers for the spiritualistic press to be forever criticising each other's opinions, that keeps our cause in such a constant state of ferment. What is a writer's opinion upon any subject but simply his or her own opinion? —nothing more. No one is bound to accept it, and no one is specially called to refute it. If A wants to believe in re-embodiment, or the doctrine of Karma, and B in the evolutionary theory of creation, or the divinity of Christ, why make a fuss about it, and question their honesty or sanity? The main thing with every Spiritualist is to be sure of the soundness of his own opinion. He will then borrow less trouble concerning those of his neighbor.

**
*

If we would come into full possession of the truth—enjoy to our best the beautiful teachings of Spiritualism—we must place ourselves in a proper spiritual attitude. By aspiration, by the practice of generous deeds, and by the exercise of that God-given grace of all graces, charity, we can attune our lives to the divine harmony, and prepare our souls to enjoy the angelic melody and harmony that come of a well ordered life.

**
*

Love is the nimbus of the spirit, the white light in which every flower of virtue and goodness unfolds and exhales its sweetest fragrance. The clairvoyant can discern this light and therein read the character of those within whose atmosphere they may come. Spiritualists should seek to develop this light in their own spirits. It is not a difficult task to whoever earnestly seeks for it. It comes with the exercise of kind thoughts and the practice of generous deeds.

**
*

He who would start out on the search for evil should first turn his lantern fairly upon himself. After he has exhausted the subject in that direction, he will be apt to have no heart for pursuing the search further.

HOW LITTLE WE KNOW.

How very little we know of ourselves, or of the universe of matter and spirit around us. We are in the midst of an eternity of mysterious forces and laws, of which we can scarcely know the alphabet. Our very littleness and insignificance should make us humble and teachable. We cannot explain the marvellous force that holds us to this planet, rolling as it does, forever through the mighty voids of space. We cannot tell why we exist, or why we love or hate. We know not whence we came, or whither we go. Only here and there do we catch a glimmer of light in the eternal dark that well nigh overwhelms us. Let us keep the eyes of our spirits open for the faintest ray, ever believing it will show us the way to safe anchorage in the haven of rest.

What grand lessons of life and duty, what sublime principles of enriched manhood, of abiding trust, of upright and noble living, do we not hear continually from our spirit helpers and friends, through lips touched with their inspiration. Who lives up to their teachings will live as close to the heart of God as it is well possible to get. The fault is not in Spiritualism, but in ourselves, that Spiritualists are not always exactly what they should be.

The infinite tenderness of a mother's love ! What is there in all God's universe of soul so beautiful and pure? And yet there are children who treat it so lightly and indifferently that they would prefer to follow the dark ways of life to their sad ending, than to be guided by its pure rays to a heaven of rest and happiness. Such is one of the strange mysteries of human nature.

Until one's own nature becomes dominated by the spirit of love and good will for his fellow-beings—until he becomes thoroughly imbued with the Christ principle—he is unfit to teach others in the better way of life. He may denounce the wrong-doer, and receive the plaudits of his kind therefor, but he only hardens the former in his evil course, and does himself a serious injury.

"What shall the harvest be?" What shall it be, young man, with you, who are sowing the seeds of dissipation in the fruitful soil of your life? Will it be a harvest of tares, or of precious corn? In every life there comes a reckoning sometime; it is the harvest time—the gathering in of the sheaves. What empty granaries of character we see on every hand—men and woman "going home" from their life labor, with no song of gladness upon their lips. They have sown to the wind; they will now reap the whirlwind of everlasting regret. Let it not be said of you, O mortal, with the wealth of golden opportunity in your possession.

*
* *

We are inclined to the opinion that if there was less liberty in this country, there would be much more honesty. Then the grocer would not sand his sugar, or sell his butter thirteen ounces for a pound. The coal dealer would hardly presume to sell eighteen hundred-weight of coal for a ton, and the merchant would at least approximate the truth, because he would be compelled to. It is hardly safe to entrust the average American citizen with the liberty he is permitted to enjoy in this country; and yet we ought to give the "experiment" a fair trial before we concede the mistake.

*
* *

What matters it to the one who knows better—to him whose communion with the spirit world brings sweetest happiness and purest thoughts and aspirations—how much the skeptic may doubt, or the ignorant may ridicule! He is anchored to a mighty truth that will hold him steadfast to duty in this life, and give him peace and happiness.

SURER ROADS TO EMINENCE.

Brainy young men do not take to the cloth now as they did forty years ago. They find surer roads to eminence in law or literature. Nearly all of our bright preachers now-a-days are past the meridian of life. Modern skepticism, enforced by enlightened science, is too great a stumbling block for a thinking young man to venture to overcome. He naturally drifts with the skeptics, and leaves the evangelical ministry to an inferior order of minds. The average theological student of to-day is not calculated to "set the world on fire." He must be dumb to the voice of Progress to imagine that the world will longer subscribe to the dogmas of the church, founded as most of them are on fables no more substantial than those of the Arabian Nights.

————‡o‡————

A gentle, white-souled, loving woman—what is there in all the universe to compare with her, unless it be the very angels who walk the flower-decked ways of eternal glory. Her presence in the home of poverty and want, by the sick bed, in all the walks of life, is ever an inspiration and a benediction. She leaves a trail of light behind her, and fills the air with the aroma of heaven. As a wife, a mother, a friend, a comforter in sorrow, she is all perfect. She wears on her white brow the royal insignia of angelhood, "and of such is the kingdom of Heaven."

*
* *

Notwithstanding all the hindrances to the advancement of Spiritualism, it is, nevertheless, rapidly and steadily making its way to hearts hungering for the evidence of immortal life. It gives a silver lining to the cloud of sorrow that hovers over the living in the hour of their mortal bereavement. It dries their tears, and bids them to wait patiently the last change that shall open the gate to the heavenly mansions where their loved ones dwell.

There is a wonderful spiritual force in the universe working to the uplifting of the human race. Those only who place themselves in the current of this force, and come in rapport with the pulsating intelligence behind it, can realize to any extent its mighty energy. Armed with this power, (which is something akin to the *vril* spoken of by Bulwer in his "Coming Race,") one man becomes a host in the struggle between right and wrong, or in the accomplishment of any worthy end. It is thus he becomes "one with God," which is always a majority, and always victorious. Reformers should strive for this power, if they would dominate the world and lift man to a higher plane.

Shakespeare makes that strange puzzle, Hamlet, say to his bosom friend, Horatio: "Give me that man that is not "passion's slave and I will wear him in my heart's core, ay, in "my heart of heart, as I do thee." Indeed, what is there more grand in all the universe than a self-poised, clean-souled man—one that has complete mastery over himself—of his appetites, passions, and all hurtful habits—one who can look his fellow man square in the eye, and whose nature at all times bubbles over with generous impulses and kind thoughts. "Are there such men," do you ask? Aye, many; and grand and noble women, too, whose goodness makes them but little less than angels. Indeed, they *are* angels.

It is said that to a person drowning all the events of his life pass in panoramic array before his vision—no sin that he has covered up, no wrong that he has ever done, is withheld,—and he sees himself just as he is, in the light of his quickened faculties. Such, no doubt, is the case with the risen spirit. In the clearer perceptions of the spirit, disentangled from the mortal body, he sees himself as he really is—is brought face to face with every wrong act of his life, with every unkind word he ever uttered, and is thus made to understand his responsibility therefor, and the course he must pursue to put himself in harmony with the law of progression, and undo the mischief he has wrought.

———‡o‡———

PRAYER.

There is a sense of helplessness and weakness that comes over the soul, in times of great sorrow and desolation, that naturally prompts one to pray for comfort and strength to that Unknown Mystery we call God. And atheists and skeptics may say what they will, it is within the experience of millions of souls, that there comes, in answer to such prayers, earnestly offered in times of great depression, a rest and peace that the world knows not of. We do not care to theorize upon this fact, as to whether such rest and peace is the result of any changing purpose of Omnipotence ; or whether it follows from a changed attitude of mind which brings the suppliant into a truer harmony with the laws of his being ; or whether, still, it comes from the drawing nearer of gentle and loving spirits to minister to the distressed soul—the fact that through prayer the blessing comes is the main point of interest to the world. The man or woman who never honestly and earnestly prays misses some of the sweetest joys of life.

———‡o‡———

Love is the panacea for all ills. It is more potent than gold, more binding than human law. In it lies the solution of all problems of right, and of justice, of man's relation to property and to his fellow men. It is the only ruler in the universe that can be safely trusted with absolute power. The greater and more perfect its dominion, the more will justice prevail among men. Then all hail, Omnipotent Love! We will gladly bow our necks to thy yoke and worship at thy shrine, well knowing that thereby he who humbleth himself shall be exalted.

THE DOWN GRADE.

The down grade—how easy it is. How like the swift current leading to the fatal falls. It requires great moral courage to turn back when once entered upon; but it must be retraced sometime—every step of the way. Did you never think of it, young man—you that are drifting into vicious ways —you, frequenter of the drinking saloon, and the haunts of her "whose feet take hold of death?" Young woman—you that prefer a life of indolent ease to humble, but virtuous toil? The time will come when you will hear the call to turn back, and then, the steep ascent you must climb, the path beset with thorns that you must tread! But it is your only way to the light—the higher life of the soul. How much easier to conquer self in its first wandering from the path, and bring it into harmony with divine truth. O, erring ones, Infinite Compassion and Love ever brood over you, even in your wanderings.

———‡o‡———

" Bear ye one another's burdens," was enjoined by the Great Teacher. Therein is found one of the sweetest lessons of life and duty. To go selfishly along through life, strong and empty-handed, while the poor wayfarer at your side is plodding along borne down with a heavy load of sorrow, or poverty, or sickness, is not the way to "call the blessing down" upon your own spirit. The way to bless others is first to radiate your own spirit with the light and warmth of a loving purpose, and then to let them feel the glow of your own soul. There is a joy that the selfish heart never knew, in helping the weary and faint-hearted along in the journey of life.

***

The excessive "smartness" manifested by some of our alleged scientists in their treatment of spirit phenomena is paralleled only by their profound ignorance thereof. Where is the enlightened Spiritualist who has not seen mere babes who could confound them in their wisdom?

THINK OF IT.

The happiest time of a mother's life, hardworked and care-worn though she may be, is when her children are all at home from their tasks, and tucked away in their beds to sleep. It is then she feels that her little brood is under her wing, and that no danger can come to any. But by and by the children grow up and go out into the great world, some to fill a mother's heart with joy, and some, perhaps, with bitter tears. It is then anxiety comes to the mother's heart, and she realizes, as never before, the responsibility of motherhood. How noble and sublime the task of training into useful ways of life the children we bring into the world. Think of it, profane, smoking, intemperate, carousing fathers! Think of it, frivolous, fashion-able, gossipping, street-gadding mothers! The group of boys at the street corner, with cigarettes in their mouths, bravely exhaling the smoke through their noses, know ye not that they are *your* boys, and that they are taking their first lessons in vice? We shall next see them stoning Chinamen, and soon they will be found in the dives and saloons, from whence it is only a step to the lock-up, and one more to the grave. With what firmness of moral purpose should men and women assume the duties and responsibilities of parentage.

LAW.

This is a universe of law. Law stands personified at the helm of the great ship of Being. Nothing exists or transpires in contravention of law. All nature is subject to law—un-changing, irrevocable law. Ascending from the plane of physi-cal nature, we enter the realm of spirit. Here, too, we find the same governing purpose, as unalterable as the will of God. We call it Law; why not name it God, which indeed it is or else endow Law with the moral attributes of Deity, and as such enthrone it in our veneration? How little a thing is man that he should presume to consider himself capable of understanding Who or What it is that guides all things to a definite purpose—that holds myriads of worlds suspended in the infinity of space, with systems of unvarying motion extending through periods of time too vast for human calculation—that encompasseth man, as it were, in the hollow of a mighty hand, where if not inflated with a sense of his own greatness, he will naturally and reverently bend low in humble adoration.

"OUR" PROPERTY.

My friend owns a beautiful flower garden; at least, he thinks he does! He pays the taxes on it, and employs a gardener to care for it. He claims that privilege, and we shall not contest the claim. But are those flowers really any more his than they are ours, or yours, reader, if you please? His eyes can take in no more of their beauty than can ours. He can enjoy no more of their exquisite fragrance than can we. Is he not rather our steward in caring for our common property? So we might extend this idea of property rights until the humblest child of humanity becomes a very Crœsus. Are not the air and the sunshine, the songs of the birds and the rippling of the brooks, the mighty expanse of ocean, the majesty and grandeur of the universe, the joy of friendship, the glory of life and love, —are not all these ours? What more, O mortal, would you have?

THROUGH THE GATES OF IGNORANCE.

If we would have good and true men and women we should raise them, as we do superior grades of fruit or animals, by scientific methods, dominated by the combined love and wisdom principles of our natures. We apply method to the improvement of all things in nature except man, and him we leave largely to blind chance—first to find his way here through the gates of ignorance, or misguided physical impulse, and next to grow up amidst the rank weeds of indifference. Is it any wonder that California requires three great insane asylums, two state prisons, and any number of jails, hospitals, poor-houses, magdalen asylums, industrial and reform schools, expensive judicial and penal systems, and an army of petty officers, to lick into shape the miserable fruits of our ignorance and indifference? Shall we never learn wisdom from experience? Shall we never learn that if we would save the world from sin we must quit raising sinners?

LOVE NEVER DIES.

Love never dies ; it is a part of the universe—an attribute of the Infinite Soul. Hatred, ill-will, revenge, selfishness, these all belong to the undeveloped condition of the spirit, and must necessarily perish and pass away. Man must live on the earth as a mortal, or on or near it as a spirit, until he is purged of all evil propensities and passions, all unkindness and ill-will. He must learn the better way of life here, sooner or later, and he cannot learn too soon for his own happiness. Steeped in the errors of the mortal mind, he may think now he would be content to live forever on the lower level of his. nature ; but the time will come when he will awaken to a knowledge of his true self, and then his misspent years and lost opportunities will rise up before him as stern monitors to point him the way of duty. There is no rest or peace in evil —no true happiness save in the consciousness of right and truth.

Not to envy your neighbor the enjoyment of what you can not afford for yourself, nor to want what is beyond your reach, is the secret of true happiness in social life. It is the endeavor of the poor to ape the ways of the rich, or to outshine their neighbors, that has brought many an industrious mechanic and honest tradesman to bankruptcy and ruin. True enjoyment does not depend so much upon what one has as it does upon what he can do without.

HARMONY.

Harmony is the key note to success in business. Among partners in trade, or in work of any kind, there must not only be harmony but perfect confidence in each other. Where these elements are wanting rankling discord is sure soon to enter in ending in disruption of bonds, and often in the scattering to the winds of great estates. Persons sensitive to psychic conditions are much more susceptible to inharmonies than others. They can feel the conditions upon entering a room where discord exists among the inmates, and it is often a source of pain to them. The musician whose instrument is out of tune disturbs the harmony of the entire band; so one inharmonious person in the family, or in the business copartnership, will disturb the serenity of all his associates.

———————‡o‡———————

The fatalist may say that man is just what he is made to be, and cannot be otherwise—that whatever he does is the precise thing he is obliged to do, and he cannot help himself. We do not believe it. If true, why seek to improve his condition? Or why should he ever seek to overcome his evil impulses and bring himself into harmony with the higher law of his being? The fact that he *can* improve—that of his own will and volition he *can* mount to a higher stage of being, is a fact that links him to the highest, or All Good, in the Universe. We pity the man who imagines himself as possessing no accountability superior to that of the weather-vane that idly turns to tell which way the wind blows. He might as well have been born a senseless clod.

**
* **

"Let the good angels come in,"—let them come into your hearts, and let them take up their abode in your homes. You have no idea how they will lighten your cares, and roll the stone away from the sepulchre of your hopes and joys. They will bring health and peace, and thrill all your being with the divine harmony of their own heavenly spheres.

THERE COMES A TIME.

There comes a time in the life of every person when he must realize that his brief day of existence is drawing to a close —when the eye loses its lustre, the step its elasticity, and he must feel that he is nearing the inevitable change that comes to all. Have you reached that time, dear reader? If so, you must know that there is not much more of this earth life for you. You must know that the shadows you see in the distance are the mists that hang over the river, beyond which stretch away into infinity the "land of the leal"—the home of the immortal soul. Isn't it about time,—if you have not done so already,—that you began to put yourself in readiness for the long journey? You will need some things to take with you. What have you among your assets that you will want, or that will be of any use to you "over there?" Surely nothing of a temporal character. That you must dispose of, or make proper use of, before you go, or it will weigh you down. Then what have you left that will be of real worth to you when you shall cross over and awaken to the new life on the other shore? Is not the subject worthy of your thought? And would it not be well for us all, occasionally, to close the doors of our souls to the world for a little while, take an account of stock, and see just where we stand?

If every man could only realize how strong is the tie of sympathy between his own spirit and the spirits of those who are near and dear to him in the other life, and how pained they are at his misdeeds, how careful he would be not to wound them by any sinful act. The thought that angel ministrants are ever near to sympathize with us in our sorrows, and rejoice with us in our rational joys and successes, should be a strong safeguard against an evil life, and it no doubt is. Let us welcome all good influences, and ever seek for the "communion of saints."

Who would strike his colors at the demand of the enemy, without a vigorous effort for their defense is no true soldier. The Spiritualist who should become disheartened because he has discovered a fraud in his cabinet, or because his religious and skeptical neighbor "makes faces" at him over the back fence, and calls him ugly names, needs a rap across his spiritual knuckles to brace him up to his duty. With the light and glory of the new gospel shining down upon us, why should any one falter. What is there in the possession of a positive knowledge of what the religious world believes and hopes to be true, to cause one to hide his head in shame, and "deny his Savior?"

POTENCY OF THOUGHT.

How little we do know of the nature or potency of thought. We seem to live and move in an element of thought, that involves and surrounds us as does the air we breathe. In proportion as we are receptive to this thought element, are we able to take in and give expression to thought—not only the thoughts that one's own spirit may shape and give forth, but also the thoughts of other spirits higher in the intellectual scale than our own. All advanced writers and thinkers will admit that their own minds are the keys of the instrument through which the spirit produces its grand melodies, and that if they would give forth the sweetest harmonies they must live in closest sympathy with the divinity within their own souls. True inspiration comes of aspiration and passivity.

Life is a hard journey to those, mainly, who make it so, or whose ancestors have unwittingly made it so for them. The troubles that come to one in this life—the sickness and sorrow, the privations and mishaps—are mostly the natural fruits of one's own ignorance, or the result of one's folly—which are often one and the same.

BEAUTY IN VARIETY.

It is well for the world that all men do not devote their lives to the pursuits of trade. For the truest good of all there must be dreamers. There must be poets, inventors, artists. There must be thinkers and teachers in all the ways and abstractions of life. There must be many men and women who have but little time to plan and think for themselves; their thought is for the welfare of humanity—for the millions who do not think either for themselves or for others. What would wealth be without its adorments of art? What would the world be without its noble army of philosophers, and dreamers, too, if you please; for is not all speculative thought an impulse from the soul realm—the land of dreams? It takes all kinds of thinkers and workers to make a world worth living in. Therefore should all recognize the fact, that each honest toiler, as well as he of great intellectual and executive powers, is essential to the symmetry of the social structure of which all are a part. The more numerous and better enlightened the workers, the more enduring the structure.

If you are miserable, the way to cure yourself of your misery is to minister to the need of some one more miserable than yourself. By arousing in your own spirit an ardent sympathy for others' woes, you will find, ere you are aware of it, your own troubles all forgotten. There is no greater panacea for the ills of life than a lively interest in the welfare of your more unfortunate fellow-beings.

*
* *

A home where love abounds is a place where angels, seen and unseen, delight to dwell. Who would lower the standard of purity of domestic life, or in any manner tarnish the bright escutcheon of home, does a deed that sends a pang of sorrow to the remotest heavens. One of the highest aims of Spiritualism should be to ennoble and beautify the homes of the people.

CONSOLATION IN AFFLICTION.

When trouble and misfortune come—when the realization of great losses sweep over the soul—when the infirmities of age settle down upon the worn-out form—what is there so comforting as the fact of that spiritual knowledge that gives one the conscious assurance that his loved ones on the other side of life are tenderly near to sympathize with him in his troubles. How it bouys up the spirit, and gives to the stricken soul strength to bear the burden of life's ills to the end.   He who has come to the knowledge of spirit communion, and learned to shape his life in harmony therewith, has truly found the " pearl of great price."   For him there is no cloud so dense that he cannot see its silver lining—no grief so profound that he cannot catch a glimpse of the joy and happiness beyond. Duty, however irksome or unpleasant, henceforth becomes to him a pathway strewn with flowers.   He feels that there is a useful lesson in his sorrows, and that they are only for a little while at most.   Where others would yield to despair, he would rise in the strength and panoply of a power that the world knows not of.   He would rejoice and be glad in his afflictions, and, taking up his scrip and staff, would journey on with a light heart to the river's brink.

The spirit world has its own ways for the spread of its golden truths among men.   It bends near to earth, with its mighty hosts of angels, to lift the pall of gloom from the grave —something that the religious teachings of the centuries have not only been unable to accomplish, but which have actually added to the soul's burden the dismal darkness of a false and unnatural theology.   The mighty ones who are moving upon this planet will brook no denial.   The puny opposition of man is to them as nought.   The light of truth is breaking in upon hosts of the children of earth, and will continue to increase, until the world is flooded with its divine rays.

NIGHT OF HORRORS.

From what a night of horrors is not the world awakening— —
has not already awakened—as the result of the development of
the art of printing ! Thought has burst the restraints of a tyran-
nous theology, that so long held it captive and now radiates
the lightning flashes of ideas, from the brightest spirits to the
darkest, even unto the ends of the earth. The past is useful
to us no more, only as a lesson of humiliation to curb our
pride and circumscribe our vanity. The Great Captain of our
Salvation, Universal, Mental and Spiritual Liberty, alligns
humanity with face to the front, and then with the command,
" Forward," takes up the march of human progress down the
ages. It is well for him who knows how to keep step to the
rhythm of humanity.

DIVINE SYMPHONIES.

If we would enter upon the higher spiritual delights of
the other life, when the toils and troubles of this life are ended,
we should bring our spirits into harmony with the divine symphonies of existence here. There is no break in Nature's
plans. There is a perfect uniformity in her conditions for
the happiness of the human spirit, in this world and the next,
and in all the worlds. We cannot live angular, inharmonious
and unhappy lives here, and expect to enter at once upon a condition of exalted happiness " over there." We are spirits now
as much as we ever shall be—not as radiant and grand as we
may reasonably hope to become, but in expression and quality
just the same, differing only in degree. Our true work here is
to sweeten this life by the practice of an everyday kind of
goodness. This it is to draw near unto God.

" Physician, heal thyself." Vice may abound in the land,
bad laws may be enacted for the benefit of the few, legalized
temptations to drunkenness and ruin may exist, in brief, society

may be generally "out of joint," but do not think, O com-
plainer, that you alone can bring harmony out of chaos. The
job is too great. The first and main thing for you to look
after is yourself. Are you living up to your highest conception
of truth—to your best ideal of manhood? If not, your first
work and duty is in your own spirit,—to bring yourself into harmony with the divine in your own nature. Then will you be
prepared to work for the world in a way that will accomplish
the greatest amount of good.

* *

The more one chafes or rebels against his environment—
as the wild bird beats its wings against the bars of its cage—
the greater the pain and unhappiness he brings upon himself.
To wisely plan to improve one's condition, or seek to overcome
unfavorable or inhospitable barriers to one's happiness, is quite
another thing. "What can't be cured must be endured," is
an old and homely adage. But before one consents to "endure" he should first be certain that a "cure" is impossible,
and when found that it is, then endurance, with the best possible grace, becomes simply a virtue.

* *

If the average, self-assumed custodian of other people's
morals or manners, would find a wretch that needs scourging
—one that should be "lashed naked through the world" for
all manner of faults—let him look within. He who would
keep all the weeds and briars out of his own garden has precious little time to bother with those that encumber his neighbor's grounds. Besides, there is nothing in all the range of
reformatory methods quite so potent as a good example.

* *

Let no one center his hopes of happiness wholly in the
future. Heaven is more of a condition than a place. The
soul that is unhappy here need not expect at once to find happiness "over there." It should carry to the other life enough

of heaven to forecast its future. Why should we hide ourselves amid the shadows in a world where there is so much sunshine as there is here.

A NECESSARY EVIL.

Selfishness of a certain kind, under the existing order of things, is a necessity of individual and public life. It is only in a condition of society where all are unselfish that the individual can afford to be like his neighbors. Should he allow himself to be singular in this respect, seeking his neighbors' welfare wholly at the expense of his own, he would soon have but little, except his character, that he could call his own. So it is with nations. To maintain themselves against the rapacity and greed of the invader, they are compelled to appeal to that first law of nature, self-preservation— to hedge themselves within barriers of selfishness. But there is an ideal condition of society where no precaution of this kind would be necessary— where every individual could wisely devote his life to the welfare of his neighbor, and in so doing would secure the largest measure of happiness to himself. That is "the good time coming."

ACTIVE USE.

The faculties of the soul—benevolence, kindness, charity, —which are not kept in active use, will gradually lose their powers of expression; while on the other hand those faculties or qualities which are kept most constantly employed, will become brighter and keener thereby. Men do not become entirely good, or thoroughly bad, in a day. If we live on a low plane, and allow ourselves to think unworthy thoughts, or indulge our bodies in degrading appetites and passions, our natures will expand in that direction, and that, too, at the expense of our higher selves. We can grow in the direction of the true and good, or we can grovel in the gutters and sewers of our natures, as we will. Why will man feed his spirit on husks, and clothe himself in moral rags and tatters, when he might live like a prince?

---‡o‡-----

THE MAN WHO KNOWS.

The man who knows is certainly a far more reliable person to obtain information from than the one who doesn't know, and doesn't care to know. Science represents the latter person in its relation to modern Spiritualism. It considers it beneath its dignity to investigate anything which it cannot weigh in its scales, or reduce in its crucibles; hence, it prefers to denounce the honest claims of modern Spiritualism as the tricks of jugglery, or the creations of a diseased imagination. It was thus in Columbus', Galileo's and Fulton's times; the mossback conservatism of those days was intensely disgusted to imagine that there could be grand facts of nature whereof they were as ignorant as babes. In fact, there are babes whose manifestations of psychic power could scatter their theories and skepticism to the winds.

-----‡o‡-----

POWER OF THE SPIRIT.

What do we know about the potency of the human spirit—its power over disease, its inherent divinity? If the Hindu adept may, by an effort of the will, compel matter to move through space—may even overcome the law of gravitation, by the exercise of a higher law, and hold himself suspended above the earth—what, if any, may be the limit of the spirit's powers? The world has had its stone age, its ages of bronze and of iron, its age of steel, steam and electricity, why may the next step in its onward progress not be the age of spirit? And such, it seems to us, is the age upon which we are now entering. Strange things are happening everywhere, things that teach us that matter may be scattered as with a breath, and instantly reunited—that solids may seemingly be passed through solids

—that even the human form may be made to appear and disappear under the magic power of spirit. Is not the prophecy near fulfillment that mortal and spirit will walk the earth side by side, the latter tangible to physical sight and sense?

CLINGING TO THE PAST.

It is amazing with what tenacity some, indeed most, of our religious sects cling to the past. They shut their eyes to the facts of science and the modern development of spiritual truth, and grope along in the mist and shadows of a superstitious and barbarous past, thus hugging foolish and hurtful delusions to their souls in preference to the beautiful truth. They will accept as truth the assertion of some ancient semi-barbarism, and reject the evidence of their own senses! They will believe the most amazing conceptions of superstition concerning the Creator and his plans, that had their birth in the childhood of the race, in preference to the plain, comprehensive facts of nature, which appeal convincingly to all enlightened minds. Truly, the sinuosities of the mortal mind are a great mystery and past finding out.

OUR STEWARDS.

It is an old saw—"It takes all kinds of people to make a world." For the best interests of the world—or rather for the highest unfoldment of humanity—teachers are needed, who, to attain the highest proficiency in their calling, have no time to enter the lists in the competitive struggle of life for the acquisition of wealth. They must give their lives to their work, and pursue the one high object to the end. The wealth-winners of the world must recognize this fact. They also must recognize the further fact, that is, the Spiritualist portion thereof; (and here is the application of the lesson of this fragment), that but few of them could, and probably none of them would, ever undertake to edit and publish a journal in the interest of the cause they profess to love. Hence, to them, as the custodians of the earth's treasures, may we not rightfully and confidently look for the means for carrying forward this grand work?

CASTING SEED UPON BARREN GROUND.

There is but little use in trying to impress spiritual truths upon minds not ready to receive them. It is simply casting seed upon barren ground. Some skeptical persons seem to think that it is the imperative duty of Spiritualists to convince them of spiritual facts—to overcome them, as it were, with argument—and over-ride their objections. Not so. Let them wait until their hearts become tender with some great sorrow—until some bright light goes out of their lives, leaving their spirits palled in the gloom of the skeptic's grave. Then will they be ready to listen to the Voice that is ever ready to speak comfort and hope to the saddened heart, and open the way to a beautiful communion with their loved ones on the other shore·

The man who readily yields to a hot temper, and thus by his foolishness causes another pain, is sowing a crop of nettles in his spirit that will cause him a world of anguish sometime. They must all be weeded out before the rich harvest of a truly chastened nature can be gathered in. Not to be able to govern one's temper is such a sign of weakness in one as should make him blush for his manhood.

**

"The greatest of these"—of the three Christian graces— "is charity." "Faith may be lost in sight"—so reads a certain ritual,—"hope ends in fruition, but charity extends beyond the grave throughout the boundless realm of eternity." How grandly beautiful is the spirit star-gemmed with this divine light! How its heavenly rays permeate human life! How they enrich and ripen the spirit and draw it close within the great loving arms of Infinite Love.

TENDENCY OF SOCIETY.

It is thought by many social scientists that the tendency of society in America, is toward anarchy. This inference is drawn from the rapid aggregation of wealth and power in the hands of the few, at the expense of the many. The remedy for this condition of things is thought to be found in National- ism. Great trusts can be safely vested only in the hands of the Government, and never in those of individuals, whose aim and ambition is self-aggrandizement. Thus it seems that Bellamy's dream, "Looking Backward," is something more than a dream. The Government owns the public lands; it owns the vast postal system; it owns the canals (now coming into disuse), and the great highways of nature,—why should it not own the telegraph and railroad systems? Why not control, for the best good of its citizens, the manufacture of cloth, lumber, iron and leather? Why should it not own the coal mines, and the oil deposits, and supply their products to the people at a minimum of cost? Corners in these great staples, for the benefit of individuals, would then be at an end; and it really seems to be the only remedy for these evils. Prices of any given staple, under our present system, are not regulated by the supply, but by the ability of a few men to control the supply, and make the prices to suit themselves. This is a crying evil, and one that cannot be safely trusted to competition for its correction. Its only cure is in placing said staples beyond the reach of corporate trusts. Why not?

————‡o‡————

"A wonderful memory," is what the secular papers call it, when a blind colored baby, three years of age, in Chicago, gives the exact population of various cities at various times, and answers readily puzzling geographical questions, and per- forms other astonishing mental feats. There is no more mem- ory about that than there is in young Hoffman's piano playing, or in the writing in various languages by persons who have

knowledge only of one language, such as we have often witnessed. These flashes of inspiration are something more than
memory.

Nature demands implicit obedience of all her children.
She will have no "talking back," no questioning of her ways or
purposes, save but to bring the questioner into truer harmony
with law. The sooner man learns this lesson and adopts it as
the rule of his life, the better it will be for his happiness. The
avalanche that sweeps down the mountain side is utterly mer-
ciless, but no more so than the inexorable laws that govern
human life. Poison kills just as certainly when administered
by mistake as when taken with suicidal intent. Just in proportion as man is ignorant and disobedient will he be unhappy.

What will it matter to the corpse whether it be embalmed and
given a resting place in some costly mausoleum, or whether it
occupies some obscure six-feet of earth—whether it goes back
into the elements to which it belongs in five years or five
thousand. The mummies of Egypt's kings make no better
paper than those of her plebeian water carriers, nor are they
any more respected. The only monument that will survive the
ravages of time, is the one we build in the hearts and memories
of our fellow-beings.

The real things of the spirit cannot be measured or cognized
by the mortal senses. Herein is found the stumbling block of
the materialistic investigator of psychic phenomena. Who
would "discern" the spirit in its true sense, must first exalt his
own spiritual nature, and bring himself *en rapport* with the
world of spirit forces and causes.

What a barren waste is that human life that blossoms with
no generous deeds,—where the rippling laughter of childhood is

never heard, and the sweet voice of love makes no melody in the soul. Better to bear the burdens of poverty for aye, better sickness and sorrow and even death itself, if but the beautiful hope of life beyond and the tender sympathy of one true heart be left.

"AUNTY T ———."

One of the sweetest and grandest souls we ever knew is a sunny-faced, matronly woman, going down into the sunset of mortal life, with a heart bubbling over with goodness. She belongs to no church,—in fact she is a true Spiritualist,—and the only religion she knows anything of, or believes in, is the religion of kind thoughts and good deeds. There was never a sick man, woman or child in the neighborhood where she resided, that doesn't have occasion to bless "Aunty T———," as the young people of her acquaintance all call her ; never a sad, sin-sick soul turned away from her gentle and loving presence uncomforted. How she manages to do so much for others, and at the same time take care of her own home, which is always kept sweet and tidy, is more than we can understand. But, early and late, she is at her task of blessing somebody. If she belonged to a dozen churches, and sub-scribed to all the articles of faith in Christendom, does any one imagine she could be any better woman than she is? And is there a believer in that cold, Calvinistic faith that would con-sign unbelieving souls in the abstract to eternal torment for the glory of God, who could really, away down in his own soul, have the slightest respect, to say nothing of veneration, for a Supreme Being who could make such a woman as this a sub-ject of his infinite wrath? We think better of human nature than to believe it.

All manifestations of nature must be the expression of Thought, the thought of an Infinite Mind, just as invention, art, poetry, etc., are the expressions of human or mortal mind. There is no method in chance, no harmony in chaos, and yet we recognize both method and harmony in the manifestations of nature. The crystal, with its delicate groupings of atoms, the flower with its beautiful arrangement of stamens and petals, the construction of the planets, of systems of suns and constellations, all express method, harmony and thought. Whence comes these expressions of thought? Let him answer, who denies the existence of a Supreme Being.

A PATERNAL GOVERNMENT.

We believe in a paternal and maternal government—a government that cares for and protects the weaklings of the great family. The parent shields the child from danger, and guards and protects its interests. What is man but a child "a little older grown?" Thousands of our people are no more fitted to care for themselves than are children. They become the prey of the greedy and dishonest in many ways. They yield to temptations of vice and intemperance, and become burdens upon the thrifty and virtuous. Why should they not be protected, just as the wise father would protect his child, for their own good, and the good of the rest of the family. We make laws to restrain man in certain matters, thereby recognizing the inability of some to respect the rights of others. Why should any be left to go to destruction? What sort of a government is it that tempts any of its citizens to destruction, as our weak ones are tempted by the thousands of liquor saloons that defile all of our great cities? When man becomes wise enough to be safely allowed to be a law unto himself, then he will need no other protection than that of his own unfolded soul. But the average man is yet far from that millennial condition.

Who lives for earthly pleasure and gratification alone, with appetites and passions unbridled, cannot surely realize that he is dragging down into the mire of his own lower nature, the royal standard of true manhood. Life is too short to live unworthily or unwisely. No one can afford to be profligate of time. And yet how many there are who become bankrupt in health and in character, before they have reached the meridian of their years. A few years hence, and how vain will seem all things that beguile the spirit into ignoble ways.

"FOR SWEET CHARITY'S SAKE."

There are many needy ones in the world—men and women sick and friendless, and helpless orphans—who find it a hard struggle to live. A little judicious help, kindly bestowed, will aid the giver as well as the receiver. It will bring comfort to the one, and an enlarged spiritual nature to the other. God pity the man or woman who never gives "for sweet charity's sake." It indicates that his nature is hard and selfish—that he has no sympathy for his suffering fellow-mortals. Who would like to carry such a spirit into the other life, where, we doubt not, he will find the greatest need of sympathy for himself? Give, though your means may be limited and the amount small. It is not the gift so much as the spirit of it that benefits the giver. If you have nothing of this world's worth to give, then give a kind word of sympathy. There is nothing like it to draw the spirit nearer to the great loving Soul of the Universe.

We can learn to say "No" with a gentle grace that will even inspire a feeling of gratitude in the heart of the one denied. But the negations of many people are generally accepted, if not always so intended, as an offence. How much the thoughtful amenities of life smooth down the rough places, and lighten the burdens which most of us are required to bear. If you cannot grant your neighbor's request, do not refuse him with a stab.

PHYSICAL COURAGE.

Physical courage, when exercised in a worthy cause, is something to be commended—to be desired. But, when it is backed up by no moral courage, there is no more merit in it than there is in the courage of the bull-dog or hyena. The physical bravery of the man that whips his wife, or that assaults old age, or that attacks an inferior in physical strength, is not true courage, but cowardice. Neither is it a commendable courage that prompts one to be tyrannical or overbearing, or quick to resent an insult with a blow, or ever ready to submit moral questions to the arbitrament of physical strength or skill. If the true test of merit in man or woman is found in the bull-dog side of his or her nature, then Sullivan is a better man than Daniel Webster, and Big Bertha a better woman than Sarah Cooper. These are the standards of barbarism— of a false chivalry—that makes heroes of bullies and black-guards. The courage to dare and do in a good cause has nothing in common with that courage that has no sound backing in moral principle.

CHRISTMAS TIME.

The glad Christmas time ! the time for generous deeds—for the exercise of the better humanities ! How the iron nature glows and bends in the white heat of the divine thought of a living Christ. Strip the idea of all supernaturalism ; make him simply and naturally the son of Joseph and Mary ; call the story, if you will, a romance, a myth of the past, and yet the Christ idea remains, and ever will remain, to call forth the best, and the sweetest in human nature. It is then we recognize to a degree, the brotherhood of man — that we are all children of a common Father, who never wearies in his love for us, or in the bestowing of his bounties. The beautiful Angel of Charity, all mantled with the smile of God, walks forth in these glad Christmas days, into the byways of life, carrying

Joy and comfort to the hearts and homes of the poor. Even the poor unfortunate within prison bars opens the wicket of his cell to bid the Divine Guest to enter in. We glory in the spirit of "peace on earth, good will to man," which the celebration of the birth of the Christ-child ever brings to the race.

WHAT CARE WE?

What care we now for the pains we have suffered or the sorrows we have endured in the past. Is nature unkind or God cruel because sickness, pain and death is the common lot of humanity? Is the calamity of the cyclone, or the scourge that lays waste the habitations of men, an evidence of a malign influence at the helm of the Universe? Not at all. Should we not regard all such seeming evils as the efforts of Old Nature to evolve a perfect man? A hundred years from now, what will it matter to us what thorny paths we are now treading with bleeding feet? Shall we not then be able to see, in the clearer light of eternity, what now is hidden from our sight, and know of a verity that all is for the best? The child can not understand the wisdom of parental restraint; but there comes a time when it is made clear to him, and he recognizes it as a blessing in disguise.

THE RIGHT WAY.

"As ye sow so also shall ye reap." There was never a truer maxim. Whether it be of good thoughts and kind acts, or their opposites. If ye sow idleness and dissipation ye reap poverty, disease and early death. If ye sow dishonor, ye reap its sure harvest of shame. This is the law, founded in the constitution of man. It is the code of the moral universe, whose penalties none can escape. The right way is marked by finger posts at every point of deviation; there are guide boards at every pitfall. Therefore, why should any err? Yet notwithstanding all precautions and warnings, many there be whose footsteps are sure to wander from the straight and beaten path. Hence the wrecks of humanity that strew the shores of time—the "frightful examples" to warn others of the dangers of wrong-doing—a mighty multitude moving down to the gates of death. O, it is pitiable !

———————————

There is no life so complete that the eye of Perfection may not see in it many defects. It is this imperfection that makes us kin with all humanity. We cannot separate ourselves from our kind. We are a part of all, and all are a part of us.—each dependent upon every other—each a help or hindrance to his fellows. And this unity of being does not end with this life ; it embraces all conscious intelligence in the universe, from an infant angel to an infinite God, with whom we are all ONE.

*
**

The Spiritualism that has no element of spirituality in it —the Spiritualism of phenomenalism and sensuous excitement solely—is of no more benefit to an individual than the fetichism of the barbarian. It must touch the soul and quicken the finer qualities of the man into activity—it must make him grander, more gentle and charitable, more loving and kind— it must ennoble him in every department of his physical and spiritual nature, to be of any real benefit to him. This is the kind of Spiritualism that comes of the higher teachings from the spirit world.

*
* *

How very, very brief, at its longest, is mortal life ! We scarcely reach years of accountability before we begin to note traces of decay and death. The locks are threaded with silver, the eye loses its luster, and ere long the step becomes feeble with the palsy of approaching dissolution. Look back, ye who have reached life's limit of years ! How like a swiftly fleeting dream does it not all seem ! And what a hollow mockery of happiness is all that ministers to the vanity and selfishness of earth! The bright, shining gold of character is all that is of value to the spirit now that it is about to lay all things else aside, and step out naked into the new life. Is it not so, O Sire?

A WORD IN YOUR EAR.

Young man, a word in your ear. We know you—we have "trod the wine press" of your temptations—have reveled in your hopes and aspirations. If you were driving a pair of high metaled thoroughbreds, how taut you would hold the reins ; how carefully you would watch every motion. No wayside object which might cause them fright would escape your notice. You would hold them steadily to their work to your journey's end. Your passions and appetites are those high-strung chargers, and *you*, your better self, your spiritual nature, are the driver. The drinking saloon, the haunts of so-called pleasure, the temptations to a life of idleness, these are the wayside objects you must guard against, and which will require your constant vigilance. Take care there! Hold a steady rein! The vortex of a wrecked life is at the right, and danger and death at the left and just before you! Angels are watching you. Loved ones on the mortal plane, with eager eyes, are hoping, praying, that you may reach your journey's end in safety. Oh, disappoint them not!

All Nature is throbbing with life divine—the earth, the air, the sea. God is indeed everywhere. Upborne on the crest of the wave of the infinite sea of life is man, the highest and most perfect expression of God in matter. On and on through the ages, from infinity to infinity, the work of man's spiritual unfoldment is ever progressing, nearing but never reaching absolute perfection. How vast the thought! The question with every unfolded soul is not, "What is man that Thou art mindful of him?" but, "What is God that He should be mindful of man?"

UNUSED WEALTH.

It is impossible for one to hold great wealth in possession long unused, without closing the avenues of the spirit to those ennobling graces, those beautiful unfoldments, that distinguish right royal manhood from an intelligent animal. " Ye cannot serve God and Mammon." He serves Mammon in selfishly getting, with no thought of generous giving. It is glorious to be able to give, when such ability finds a generous response in the soul. In the journey and struggle of life there are so many who are unable to bear their burdens alone—and then it so enlarges one's own soul to lend a helping hand to the weak—that it is truly grand to be strong, where strength is thus used for the good of others. But to be strong, to be rich, for one's self alone—ah, that is what shrinks the spirit.

Some people are always looking backward ; they seem to be anchored to the past. Pride of ancestry, tradition of opinion, what has been, is vastly more to them than what is, or what may be. Lucky for the world—for the cause of human progress—that some there are who have but little respect for tradition, or authority of opinion. They prefer to do their own thinking, although they may not always think wisely. They regard it as far more creditable to believe an error, or come to a wrong conclusion, after a careful examination of any given subject, than to accept the truth blindly, without investigation. Of such is ever the grand army of reformers in the world's ways and works.

*
* *

Why plow with a forked stick, or carry your grist to the mill with your corn in one end of the sack and a stone in the other? That is just what all are doing who pin their faith upon the sleeve of tradition. The evolution of humanity from some lower form of life, and that from some still lower form, reaching back through aeons, to the first quivering protoplasm or jellyfish throbbing with divine impulse on the magin of some paleozoic sea, is a fact as well demon. — — — strated as the rotundity of the earth. Hence, the religious thought adapted to the infancy of the race is but mother's milk to the full grown man. And hence, again, the religion that does not keep step to the march of human progress, must needs stand aside and give place to something better.

BELIEF.

'There is no virtue—there can be none—in mere *belief*. It is not what a man believes but what he *is* and *does* that makes the man. If one *believes* all the dogmas of Christianity, and *practices* iniquity, no evangelical Christian will concede to him the possibility of salvation. On the other hand, if one practices every Christian virtue, but reject the dogmas of the churches, they regard him as alike lost to all eternity. Now here is a strange inconsistency. If it is really the *practice* of the virtues that saves the believer, why should not the practice of said virtues save the non-believer? Honest belief is a matter of evidence and conviction. If one has ever been convinced of the truth of a religious dogma, and has no conviction there-of, how is it possible for him to believe? And if he cannot believe why should he be condemned for what he cannot help? If eternal justice is an attribute of Deity, what must the answer to these questions necessarily be?

Trouble, sickness, and sorrow are only for the moment. We never seriously regret these ills when they have passed by. In fact, we very often recognize in these afflictions much needed and helpful lessons of life and duty. The lash of physical pain is often necessary to keep us mindful of the duty we owe to our bodies. When we shall reach the sunlit shores of the Hereafter, and can look back over the varied experiences of our mortal lives, we doubt if we would be willing to part with a single pang, physical or spiritual, we ever endured. They will all be seen to have had their divine uses in shaping our characters for good, and fitting us for the truer enjoyment of life in spirit realms.

————‡o‡————

IN A MANGER.

Christ came to Joseph and Mary, two poor young people of Nazareth, ignoring the ostentation and pomp in which the Jews looked for him to come ; hence, they rejected him. The wonderful manifestations of Modern Spiritualism, bearing to the world the positive proofs of a continued existence beyond the grave, came first to three young people in humble life residing in Western New York. It is nearly always thus, that through the weak and lowly of this world—"from the mouths of babes and sucklings"—come the great truths that confound the wise, and the wise reject them. Truly, "God moves in a mysterious way His wonders to perform." It is not for us to question His methods, but to accept with grateful hearts whatever of good He chooses to bestow upon us.

————————

"Try the spirits," is an injunction quite as necessary and important in these days as in those of St. Paul. It is an injunction, also, whereof Spiritualists should take heed quite as much as skeptics or unbelievers. Above all things should we never surrender our reason or common sense. If some misguided or undeveloped spirit, representing himself as some master-soul of by-gone ages, comes to us with folly in his message, we should exercise our sovereign right of judgment to cast him aside with a word of friendly advice to mend his ways. Plato and Socrates were not imbeciles in their mortal existence and certainly they are not so now.

⁎

What a blessed thing is death, when it comes in the fullness of time to relieve the spirit of its worn-out body. With the old house falling into decay with age, the roof leaky, and the walls mouldy and cheerless, how gladly the tenant—if he has lived wisely and well—goes forth to occupy his beautiful mansion builded for him in the Summer Land. There should be no sorrow in old age, for it is then "we are almost there," and the glad thought should fill the soul with delight. The haven lies just beyond that bank of clouds we call death. See ye not the harbor lights, O Sire, and thrills not your spirit with joys of the home gathering so near at hand?

————‡o‡————

SUNSHINE.

Our lives should be full of sunshine, no matter how hard or humble the lot we are called upon to fill; for in the sunlight of the soul we can all the better bear the ills that may befall us. It is the cheerful spirit that suffers the least in sickness. The shadows of physical pain will often flee away if we confront them in a spirit of gladness, determined to accept whatever comes to us as for our good. Why should we mope and mourn over earthly losses, when such losses may prove riches to us in the Beyond? Surely our houses and lands, and our treasures of gold and silver, will be nothing to us "over there," and unless we use them wisely here, they will doubtless be worse than useless—a millstone to prevent the spirit from rising above the earth.

PREJUDICE.

Prejudice is a terrible bar to spiritual growth. We know a good mediumistic lady, who would, in the privacy of her own home, dearly delight to permit her loved ones on the spirit shore to come near to her, but is positively forbidden by her husband to enjoy communion therewith. This same husband, when their little five-year old daughter was languishing on a bed of mortal sickness, declared that he would prefer that she never recover, than to be cured by Spiritual Science. And now in his childless home, he still nurses his bitter enmity toward those gentle and benign influences, those loving ones, who, in sorrow, are made to turn away from his heart and home. Ah, what tears he may yet shed in this life, what agony of spirit he may endure in the next, for this stubborness of unreasoning purpose, only the pitying angels may know. Old Theology, thou distorter of the truth, thou murderer of helpless babes, what crimes hast thou not to answer for !

BLESSINGS IN DISGUISE.

The storm and the tempest, the lightning's vivid flash, the fierce commotion of the elements, all have their uses in the natural world, to purify the air and clear the sky of clouds. We breathe more freely when the storm is past. The earth seems cleaner, the birds sing with a sweeter melody, the air is fragrant with the new, fresh breath of flowers. So is it with the storms that at times sweep over the human spirit. If we but bow to the blast, we shall rise again in greater strength, and life will have a clearer and brighter outlook than ever before. If that which seems to be an affliction is accepted in the right spirit, it then becomes as a refining fire, burning away the dross and impurities of our natures, and leaving in the crucible of life the pure gold of the spirit. Poverty, sickness and misfortune—all are blessings in disguise, if we but learn to accept them as such.

RIGHTEOUS JUDGMENT.

How apt we are to judge matters outside of ourselves by our own moods of mind ! Thus, when we stand above the clouds, upon the mountain top, all things around us are bathed in the beautiful sunlight ; but when immersed in the shadows of the valley, we see only gloom in our surroundings. This is a dreary, dark, and dreadful world, says the misanthrope. How bright and beautiful is nature, responds the soul aglow with happiness. A few weeks ago, deeply pained at the frauds and impostures practiced in the name of our religion, we wrote, "Truly the evil days have come to our beautiful Spiritualism." Now, in the clearer light of the hilltop, we rejoice that the clouds have rolled away. We wonder if the prospect of a better and brighter home for the GOLDEN GATE has any bearing upon our changing moods of mind !

DON'T CROWD.

Don't crowd ! The world is big enough for all. Keep to the right and don't joggle your neighbor. Thus will you make the journey easier for yourself as well as for your fellow travelers to the grave. The grave ! Did it never occur to you, dear reader, that that is the one place in all creation where everybody minds his own business. There is no crowding there, nor taking an unfair advantage of a fellow tenant in common. The highwayman can lie alongside the honest Granger who has just sold his wheat, without the slightest desire to pick his pockets. The one "ewe lamb" of the widow's heart and home can trust herself there with the cruel spoiler. There is no envy, or suspicion, or hatred in the grave. Parents, what though your children who have passed out of your sight, return not home to you at night, our word for it, they are up to no mischief now. Look for them beyond the shining portals, where death has lost its sting, and the grave is swallowed up in victory.

If the man who poisons his exhalations with tobacco could only realize what a walking stench he makes of himself to all clean persons, he would surely abandon the nasty habit. But he doesn't. He imagines his breath to be as sweet as the " balm of a thousand flowers," when in fact the mal-odor of a tan yard is attar of roses in comparison. Many a sensitive and finely organized wife has no doubt yielded up the ghost on the altar of a tobacco-smirched husband—gone up higher where the air is purer.

"LIFE UNTO LIFE."

The gift of mediumship ennobles or degrades its possessor just in proportion as the latter exercises it for the good of humanity, or for his own selfish advantage. In the latter case he unwillingly yokes himself with all the selfishness of the universe, and undeveloped and mischievous spirits are not slow to avail themselves of the opportunity to practice their mischief through him. But if his beautiful gift is ennobled with a sincere desire for the good of others, and a subordination of self to the higher aspirations of the spirit, it then becomes "a savor of life unto life" to the world. Spiritualism needs more of this kind of mediumship. It is the kind that links the mortal to the angel, and calls forth the purest and holiest joys and emotions of the soul.

GROPING IN DARKNESS.

There are times in the life of every sensitive soul, we care not how highly unfolded, when it seems as though all hope and joy had fled forever—when one can but grope in darkness, and the heavens seem shrouded in impenetrable gloom. It is then one needs some strong arm on which to lean—some true heart to which one can turn for sympathy and comfort, until the clouds have passed away. Happy the mortal who possesses such a friend! These Gethsemanes of sorrow are doubtless a part of the education the spirit needs to fit it for the higher life. It is then the Great Assayer of character stamps upon the burnished ingot of the soul its mint value. Then, let us welcome the cloud and the storm—yea, even the fierce gleam of the lightning's wrath—as the furnace fires of God's loving purpose in moulding us into his image.

Give, if you would be happy—give of kind thoughts and gentle words always; they are often more precious than silver or gold— give of your bounty of earthly treasure; give of the weetness of your own soul; give freely and ungrudgingly, to all whom it is in your power to bless. We are told that "God loves a cheerful giver." We are quite sure that angels do, for do they not always tell us so?

A GRAVE MISTAKE.

It is generally understood among investigators of psychic phenomena that the qualities essential for physical mediumship are quite as independent of conscience or morality as is the gift of poetry or painting. There is a disposition with many Spiritualists to tolerate dishonesty in mediums for the sake of their mediumship. This a grave mistake, and leads to disaster to the cause. And here we should learn to discriminate between the work of tricky or undeveloped spirits, who sometimes use mediums to their disadvantage, and the practice of deliberate fraud, such as the employment of confederates, the use of prepared paraphernalia, etc. In the former case we should be lenient and charitable; in the latter, it is wrong to both spirits and mortals to seek to condone or palliate. Such mediums should be "driven from the synagogue," and made to do penance until they can reform their ways. The medium who cheats in one phase should not be credited or tolerated in any other.

What an unnatural idea of the All-Good has orthodoxy given to the world! Take Calvanism, with its cruel doctrine of election to eternal misery; take that "mathematical contradiction," as Ingersoll styles it, known as the Trinity, which nobody can explain or understand; take the atonement—the shifting of the sins of the world upon the shoulders of a pure and innocent person, and then killing him to satisfy Eternal Justice;—in short, take the infantile stories of the Creator, running through both Testaments, and how puerile they all seem to the enlightened reason. Such, surely, is not the God that all Nature worships.

A person visiting foreign lands finds it necessary for his convenience to change his money into the current coin of the realm whither he goes. Here is a hint to those about to visit the realm of the "Beyond." But how, do you ask, can the traveler, in this case, change his wealth into currency that will be of any use to him "over there?" We answer, he must spiritualize it, that is, convert it into noble deeds for the up-lifting of humanity. He who gives wisely receives. As his deposits diminish here they increase there. Every rich man has it in his power to enter spirit life a prince; or he may go, as goes the galley slave, "scourged to his dungeon" by the lash of his own selfishness.

**

God does not expect us to be eternally praising Him. He has no vanity requiring any such adulation from the children of His creation. Neither does He expect us to go through life mourning continually for our sins. But He does by His Spirit appeal to us to be manly, to be upright, to be charitable and kind, to be true and steadfast to the monitor within, to be wise rulers of the temple we live in, and so live that when the last summons comes, each and every one may leave the world better than he found it.

**

There is no joy like love, no pain like hate. In one blossom all the delights of life—health, companionship, spiritual growth, and at last, and including all, heaven itself. In the other we behold all hideous shapes, phantoms of fear, grim horrors of despair, the fungus growth of disease and death. The man or woman who passes through life unloving and unloved, misses "by an infinite waste of barren years" the road to true happiness.

**

The Spiritualist whose faith is shaken in our grand truths, and who is disposed to reject the whole, because forsooth he may have been deceived by some confederate playing spirit at a materializing seance, would throw all his gold into the sea because he found a spurious coin in his pocket.

A WIDE GULF.

There is a wide gulf betwen the teachings of Jesus and the ironclad creeds of the churches. True, it is claimed that the latter are the natural deductions of the former; but are they? How do we know really what Jesus taught. There were no short hand reporters in his day. It is claimed by wise scholars that no record of the sayings or teachings of Christ was made until some three hundred years after his death. That he taught the principles of love, charity and good will to man, and that he practiced the wonderful gift of healing, we can well believe; but that he ever taught the dogmas of ecclesiasticism we may well question. Christianity, pure and simple, is goodness, all else is the mere speculation of a priesthood seeking for ecclesiastical power. Love is superior to law or belief. Whose heart is full of love for his fellow beings never has time or place to bother with the dogmatic teachings of ecclesiasticism.

SURE INDICATIONS.

The state of one's own spiritual unfoldment is invariably determined by one's expressed thoughts of others. If one thinks kindly and speaks kindly of others, no matter how great or many their failings may be, it is a sure indication of a beautiful spirit. Such an one sees only the good there is in their neighbors — for there is good in all. The worst person living has some good traits — some vritues, that commend themselves to the good, and which such souls invariably recognize, and are ever ready to encourage and uphold. On the other hand, there are those who seemingly take delight in the shortcomings and weaknesses of their fellow beings—to whom an unsavory scandal is a "sweet morsel under the tongue," which they will repeat with an unction that is truly painful to the highly unfolded spirit. Blessed and beautiful is the man or woman who thinks no ill.

ADJUSTMENT OF SELF TO ENVIRONMENT.

It is evidently the privilege as it is the duty of every individual to get out of life all the happiness possible. This can be accomplished only through the possession of a healthy physical body, and a proper adjustment of one's self to one's environment As moral beings we cannot be happy at the expense or unhappiness of another. We can not trench upon another's rights in this respect. Herein is where man differs from the brute. The latter recognizes only the law of might, and its happiness consists only of physical enjoyment. The big dog has no pricking of conscience for robbing the smaller one of its bone. Some men are made so nearly in that way that they can enjoy ill-gotten gains. Whoever can should know thereby that there is something wrong with them, and that they will have a long way to climb before they can reach a perfect manhood.

Spiritualists, of all other people, need to "hold themselves level"—for the reason that they are brought face to face, often, with facts and phenomena of a most startling character. They should weigh well and carefully consider the startling manifestations they are permitted to witness; and especially should they not attempt to force their conclusions, in any dogmatic way, upon the minds and consciences of their neighbors. Everybody needs, and must have, the positive proof in his own experience. He will take no one's word, in spiritual matters, implicitly. The advocate of the phenomenal facts of Spiritualism, whereof he has had convincing proof, should remember this.

FORTUNE'S LADDER.

Some good souls wonder why it is that, with their charitable natures, good intentions, and industrious and temperate habits, they should always be at the bottom of fortune's ladder, while other people, wanting in all these virtues, revel in abundance. They seem to think that in some way Providence is not dealing fairly with them. Now, if the "abundance" their hearts long for were the highest end of being, and there were no hereafter in which to adjust the losses and apparent mistakes of time, they might reasonably conclude that there was some injustice in the divine order of things. But Nature has all space and all eternity in which to strike her balances. In her own way and in her own good time, we doubt not, it will be found that she has dealt fairly by all, and each one will see and realize that whatever his lot in life may have been, that however great the seeming disparity between his own condition and that of others, it was the very best condition for him—best suited to the higher needs of his spirit. In this faith we should live, and therein we could get out of life its highest measure of happiness for ourselves.

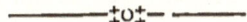

The man who is eternally muck-raking for the evil in his neighbors, sometimes finds his own gutters and back yards exposed and overhauled in a way he little dreamed of. It is not Christ-like to strike back, but there are cases where nature puts in a plea of justifiable homicide, and the world, which is far from just, looks on and commends.

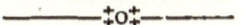

How can we get the best out of life? This is a question of the utmost importance to every human soul. Here are a few simple negations that may help to answer the question satisfactorily. 1st, Not by indulgence in liquor, tobacco, or late hours; or by any abuse of the temple of the soul. 2nd, Not by harboring unworthy thoughts, or thinking unkindly of any human being. 3rd, Not by selfishly shutting ourselves out from the great world of humanity and its pressing needs ; and 4th, Not by barring the windows of our souls to the light and love of the spirit world.

COMPLAINING.

Some one has wisely said, "There are two things man "should never trouble himself about—the unpleasant things he "can help and correct, and the things he cannot." Of course, the evils he *can* alleviate he should set himself at the task of correcting, and those that are beyond his reach it will do him not the slightest good to fret about. Some people waste their lives in complaining, and thereby they invite all manner of causes for complaint. We have known families whose homes were but little less than apothecary shops, so vast was the array of all manner of medicine bottles in sight. The result was that there was some one in said homes always ailing. Whereas, if they would take Shakespeare's advice, "Throw physic to the dogs," welcome the air and sunlight to their bed rooms, and, above all, quit thinking themselves sick ; or, if they are a little out of harmony, forget themselves in the alleviation of the miseries of others, they might soon laugh at their follies and infirmities. The trouble with most people is they think too much about themselves—their aches and pains, their poverty or their riches, their likes and dislikes, when their true way to happiness would be to turn their thoughts away to the great world of wrong and misery around them, and by every effort in their power work to lift the burdens of others.

Sensible minds do not judge Christianity by the horrors of the Inquisition, nor by the cruel wars that for ages followed in its trail, nor by its persecution for opinion's sake, nor by its occasional delinquents from grace; but by the good it has done, for the sad hearts it has made glad, and for the heavy burdens of woe it has lifted from the shoulders of the race. Why should not Spiritualism be judged by the same charitable and righteous judgment? Because bad people sometimes use it for a cloak for unrighteous deeds, therefore should it be condemned? Shall its blessings to the world be rejected, because mediums are not all honest, nor Spiritualists all good and pure?

ACTING ONE'S BEST.

What a world this would be if all would live and act their best—that is, as they could live, if they would, notwithstanding all their imperfections, all their ignorance, and all their tendency to evil. The toper would cease his tippling, and save his earnings to carry joy to his family ; the wrong doer of every description would turn from his evil practices and live in the better side of his nature. Fault-finding, cross-grained husbands and wives would become lovers again, and their children would rejoice and grow up in the sunshine of happy homes. We should then only hear good of everybody. The seller would consult the interests of the buyer, and the buyer of the seller. We should all take a friendly interest in each other's welfare, and together jog along happily side by side to the better country. Is it not glorious to think such things possible?

PITIABLE.

"Charity suffereth long and is kind." One of the most pitiable things in the universe is a man without charity in his soul. He is usually one so puffed up in his own conceit that he becomes indifferent to the ills or trials of another. The prayer of every true soul should be : "Help us, thou pure and shining ones, to bear each other's burdens, and to sympathize with the weak and unfortunate in their troubles and afflictions." Did it never occur to you, dear reader, that you might have been a thief or a drunkard? Is it any virtue of yours that you are not? It is much more to the credit of some men that they are only moderately bad, than it is to others that they are really good. To the latter it may be quite impossible to be otherwise; while it may cost the former a hard struggle not to be worse.

————§o§————

IMMENSITY OF THE UNIVERSE.

Did you ever try to realize the immensity of the universe, of which our little world is the smallest of tens of thousands?— stars so remote that a ray of light traveling at the rate of nearly 200,000 miles a second, would require centuries to reach the earth? The mind is utterly powerless to grasp such distances. Man, of his own powers, is only cognizant of a few things, and those of a certain dimension. Reaching upward with the telescope, and downward with the microscope, he is able to unveil new worlds and countless forms of life that were entirely beyond his grasp before. Think you, with these helps to his eyesight, he has reached the limits of life or space? Far from it. There is still infinitude beyond. The measureless expanse of ether is doubtless filled with life, tangible and real to a finer than mortal sense. And so the Psalmist might well exclaim, "What is man that Thou art mindful of him?" A mere speck on the object glass of God's great microscope.

————§o§————

PURPOSES OF CREATION.

Who that has stood by the bedside of a dying child, and watched its fluttering pulse and labored breathing, but has felt, somehow, that the purposes of creation in that life had been thwarted—that the earth experience which is believed to be necessary for the spirit's highest unfoldment, having been denied in this case, a great wrong had been done to the child— that Nature had not been just or fair in the distribution of her favors. Herein, we think, may be found one of the strongest reasons favoring re-embodiment. Not that it is a reason at all; but it looks somewhat that way to the "mortal mind."

The spirit that seeks earth expression and fails, ought, surely, to have a chance to try again—that is, if the spirit is permitted — — any voice in the matter.

————§o§————

CONTENTMENT.

It is not what one has that brings one happiness, but what one is contented with. There is many a sad heart, worried mind, and sickly body, linked to a large bank account. An elegant home is but a poor comfort to one with a skeleton in the closet. Infinitely better a life of daily toil and a humble cot with health and contentment. A man with a cancer in his throat may be Emperor of Germany, or President of the United States, and where is the peasant, or day laborer, that would exchange places and conditions with him. Give us to know the truth, in health and peace, with a heart in sympathy with humanity, and we care not who rides in his carriage, or revels in his riches.

————§o§————

" With charity for all and malice toward none,"—this was the actuating motive of that grand soul, Abraham Lincoln, in his dealings, as the President of the United States, with those misguided sons of the South who were seeking the overthrow of the Republic. What nobler or better rule of action could one adopt in his intercourse with the world, and especially in his dealings with those he believes to be in error. Suppose you try it, dear reader, for a single day.

* *

An intelligent friend of the writer, working long hours on a small salary—one much given to speculating on the philosophy and wherefore of human existence, — remarked to us, recently, that he had come to the conclusion, that a future life was not desirable. We replied that whether desirable or not, did not change the fact—he would surely continue to live after the change we call death; that the true business of this life is to bring ourselves into harmony with nature, make the best of our opportunities, and do all the good we can, thereby the better preparing the spirit for the activities and enjoyments of the life to come. Looked at in a true light, hard work and even poverty, may become blessings.

PERVERSION OF CHRISTIANITY.

It is not Christianity, but the perversion thereof, that the skeptical world can justly condemn. Christianity, as embodied in the simple teachings of Jesus, is one thing, and as diverted and perverted through the channels of human selfishness, pride, ambition and the lusts of the mortal mind, is quite another. The philosophy and higher teachings of Spiritualism simply divest Christianity of its crudities and imperfections, and restore it to the world in all its original purity and beanty. What is there in the practice and the teachings of the "Man of Sorrows," who "went about doing good," and who "had not where to lay his head," that is in anywise in common with the aristocratic religion of a modern fashionable Christian Church? They are as far apart as the East is from the West. Jesus came to his disciples, in bodily form, after his transition to spirit life. Does he ever come to the haughty purse-proud believers in him now-a-days? In mortal life he healed the sick by the laying on of hands, and plainly taught that "greater things than these," should be done by those who followed him in the spirit. If he told the truth then who are his true disciples now?

In tens of thousands of homes to-day, through one or more members of the household, comes the beautiful inspiration of the angel world. Wives, mothers, and daughters, and oftentimes husbands and sons, in vast numbers, are developing spiritual powers, often where they little dreamed such powers possible. In all such cases, where the aspirations and desires for the good and pure prevail, there is a quiet work of spiritual enlightment and unfoldment steadily progressing, revolutionizing, harmonizing and sweetening family life as none but those thus blessed can understand.

OLD AGE.

"O, the horrors of old age!" exclaimed, a bright lady friend of the writer recently: "To feel that one's youthful "charms are fading away, and the once fair features becoming "wrinkled with age—is it not terrible?" Not at all, we replied, if one's spirit has profited as it ought by its earth experiences. There is no beauty like that of a beautiful spirit. The woman who, at fifty, has not come to realize this fact has lived to a poor purpose, and now learns too late that she has "built her house upon the sand." No one, with the brains of a chickadee, can look into the face of a truly spiritual woman— one who has grown with her years into the higher graces and glories of true womanhood—and ever detect a wrinkle there. But it is a sad thing when wrinkles come upon the spirit.

"SHALL I GIVE UP MY RELIGION?"

"Shall I give up my religion—the religion of my ances- "try—the religion of the Bible—for a belief in Spiritualism?" Inquires some anxious soul first brought face to face with some unanswerable fact of our spiritual philosophy. By no means, we answer. You need give up nothing in your religion that is of the slightest value to you—not a principle of the Golden Rule, nor of Christ's Sermon on the Mount. The *fables* of your faith—such as a belief in a lost world, a vicarious atonement, a literal resurrection of the body, eternal punishment, a personal devil, etc.,—these you will naturally outgrow, because they are all inconsistent with the constitution of the Universe, and man's higher spiritual unfoldment. "But the Bible teaches

these things," do you say? Well, the Bible is the work of
man, in its makeup, at least, else no "revision" would be
necessary. There is surely much of it that could not possibly
be the "word of God," or of that divine inspiration which is
the same in kind through all ages and forever.

*
* *

The higher spiritual development—that is, development
of the greatest use and benefit to the mediums and their immediate surroundings—can come to those only who take the
least thought of themselves, or of the pecuniary advantages
that may accrue to them from the exercise of their gifts. Not that
a good medium, who gives his entire time to others, is not entitled to reasonable compensation for his services, especially if
it is his only means of livelihood; but unless the money consideration is a secondary matter wholly, and the good that he
can do of the first importance, his own spiritual nature derives
no benefit from his gifts.

*
* *

Who values life for its sensuous enjoyment and pleasures
only, will wake up some day to a terrible realization of the fact
that his ships, that sailed away in early life with such bright
hopes, have all been lost at sea—gone down with their rich
cargoes of golden promises and possibilities—to return to him
no more forever. The young woman who lives to be admired
for her physical charms, at the expense of the more enduring
graces of the spirit—who delights in the adulation and flattery
of brainless dudes—feeds her soul upon husks. Spiritual star-
vation with her is only a question of time.

*
* *

What must be the rich man's feelings when he first wakes
up in the world " beyond the sunrise," to find that his pockets
have been picked by the burglar Death, of the keys to his safe
—when he realizes that, forevermore, he can have no more
handling of his gold? How it must sicken his soul to see

his accumulations scattered by profligate heirs, or wasted in unprofitable litigation. Better oblivion than such a fate. How many such we could all name, whose souls are thus chained to "night's Plutonian shore."

———‡o‡———

SOMETHING BETTER.

To denounce one's errors of belief, is not the way to correct one of those errors. You must show him something better in your own belief, something that will appeal to his higher spiritual nature. In the bitter denunciation of the churches, as practiced by some Spiritualists, they are but putting far away the conversion of church members and religionists to the grand truths of Spiritualism. You cannot hurt a fellow man in the most vital part of his nature—his religious opinions—and expect him to love you. You cannot lift a man up by knocking him down. You can win him, if at all, only by showing him the better way, and by walking therein yourself. Don't extol your own religious opinions over those of your neigbor, except by showing and comparing the fruits thereof. This standard of excellence would naturally make us humble. What have we done? What are we doing?

———§o§———

The mighty influx of spirit power now inundating the planet, will, in the fullness of time, bring all humanity under its divine influence. It is the "beginning of the end," foretold by ancient seers—the end of the old in religious thought, the end of oppression and wrong, the end of the retarding influences that have so long bound the souls of men in bonds of error and superstition. The glory of the "new heavens and the new earth," spoken of by John in the Apocalypse, is about to be revealed to the sons of men —is even now breaking upon the wondering vision of thousands of earth's children. "Hosannah to the Lord in the highest—peace on earth—good will to men."

A CONSTANT STRUGGLE.

Life, with many, is a constant struggle; and yet is not that very struggle just the kind of experience needed to bring forth the richest fruits of the spirit?　As bodily exercise makes the muscles strong, so does the push and effort necessary to overcome obstacles in material things give to the spirit the vigor and strength it needs.　Some people think because they have not prospered in worldly ways—have not accumulated wealth, or may even have failed in business—that they are necessarily failures as men and women; when the fact may be that they have won grand victories over themselves—that they have come off conquerors over many things, and have made for themselves a karma that shall be white and lustrous with the glow of divine love and light in the "world beyond the river."　Human judgment is fallible—our plans, in worldly mattters, may fail, and our ships return to us empty laden; but what of that?　Are we to be blamed because the harvest we hoped to reap was blighted, or the worthy venture upon which we risked our all proved a failure?　There is a fruition richer by far than argosies of treasure, and that is the harvest of soul.

"POOR FELLOW."

We heartily concur with the dramatist who said, "Fools are they who seek for happiness and pass by love in the pursuit."　The unmarried man is more or less selfish, especially if he is able to maintain a home, and capable of making some good woman happy.　He spends his days in the keen pursuit of trade, and his nights in a more or less destructive form of dissipation at his club, and, ere long, his kidneys go back on him, and "the wheel at the fountain is still."　No loving wife bends over him with a farewell kiss; no children join the regulation procession that follows his remains to the grave.　"Poor fellow! we shall miss him at the club," spoken between drinks, by some fellow bachelor, is the nearest approach to a sigh of

regret at his departure. The Club is a monstrous carbuncle on the neck of society. In fact, any form of social life whence woman is excluded, is unnatural and wicked. The man who goes through life unmarried, unloving and unloved, misses, by an infinite waste of barren years, the road to true happiness.

DISTRUST.

The very worst condition of mind that one can bring himself into is that of general distrust—that is, to doubt the honor and honesty of every one with whom he is brought into business or social relations. Of course it is well to be cautious against indiscriminate confidence in people one doesn't know, but we hold that if one will endeavor to cultivate his intuitive faculties—his sixth sense—he will not be apt to be deceived. Besides, it is better to be deceived occasionally than to lose faith in our fellow-beings. We should look on the bright side of life, and recognize the good there is in all. Only thus can we best aid the erring up the steeps of life, and at the same time bring our own spirits into the best condition for healthy growth and unfoldment.

CENTRAL POINT OF TWO ETERNITIES.

Which is the most to man's credit—to come down from an angel by some moral cataclysm, like that mentioned in the Mosaic fable of creation; or come up from some type of anthropoidal ape, in accordance with Darwin's theory of development? The latter process is the only one consistent with the idea of Immutable Law, or of that Infinite Energy that is ever pushing upward through matter towards perfection. It is alike creditable to man and his Creator that he should ascend the scale of being—alike discreditable to both that he should make a pitiable failure of himself, after once having been sent forth perfect from the hand of Infinite Perfection. As compared with his barbaric ancestors man has everything to en-

courage him ; but as compared with the Mosaic fable of creation, the outlook for him is far from hopeful. We prefer the
more rational theory, and hold that man is the central point
of two eternities—of the past, up which he has climbed from
an impulse of Divinity ; and of the future, toward which he is
steadily moving forward in the highway of eternal progression.

ADJUSTMENT TO NATURE.

Throughout the universe harmony is the rule, inharmony
the exception. The cyclone that sweeps the earth, leaving
death and desolation in its path; the earthquake that rocks
the foundations of the mountains, burying cities in its awful
throes; the "pestilence that walketh by noonday;" war, famine,
and even death itself, are all efforts of the intelligent forces of
the universe to bring about that harmony which Nature will
have at any cost. Man, in discord with the higher purposes
of his being—out of tune with the divine life,—is a moral
cyclone, a devastating pestilence. He is war and famine—
the Satan of the Old Testament. But once adjusted to the
grand diapason of Nature, he gives forth melody divine in
every thought and action.

How often do we find those living in the slums seeking to
drag their fellows down to their level. Such people are in
much greater need of pity than those whom they would tra-
duce. Whoever lives a clean and correct life need have no
fear of false tongues. He is clad in the armor of truth, against
which the shafts of malice and ignorance fall in vain.

* *

The invisible ether around about us is threaded with spiritual
currents, connecting our own spirits with the outlying world of
spirit forces in the universe—with all that is good, if we will,
or all that is ill—currents that bring us into harmony with the
life of all divinity, or into fierce discord with the shapes and
shadows of moral death. If we would be well in body and

mind, if we would dwell in harmony with our own souls, we must find these higher and purer currents and float upon their crystal surface into the beautiful harbor of rest to which they lead.

————§o§————

THE CHURCH OF ROME.

The only Church now in existence that clings blindly to the past, with no attempt or intention to allow its communicants to think independently upon religious things, is the Roman Catholic, and the creed of that Church is simply crystallized igrorance enthroned in the Pope. If you are a good Catholic you must accept the interpretations of the Church in all religious matters from alpha to omega ; no matter how inconsistent with facts or abhorrent to enlightened reason, you are not allowed to entertain a questioning opinion. It is only by this *ex cathedra* enforcement of its dogmas that the Church of Rome is able to subject to its domination the ignorant masses with which its membership is mainly composed. Such domination is no doubt better for many persons than no sense of moral or religious accountability at all. In fact, it would hardly be wise, in any enlightened community, for the priest to release the strong grip he holds upon the consciences of a multitude of men and women. Hence, as much as we disclaim all censorship or domination of religious opinion in ourselves, we are entirely willing to see such domination forced upon others—upon all who need such restraints and checks upon their undeveloped spiritual natures. Until one can walk alone without trenching upon the rights of others, he must be held by the restraints of the law, or the shackles of the Church. Therefore, before we would pull down the Church, we should build up the man.

————‡o‡————

In the higher life of the soul there are delights that are never dreamed of by the mortal mind—a realm where the inflowing tide of inspiration lifts one above the plane of sensuous

things, and the spirit bathes in the scintillant glory of the
Divine Life.   Would you live in this realm, enjoy these super-
nal joys, live your best in thought and action, and it will surely
come to you.

*
* *

Let no one imagine that all believers in psychic phenomena can be trained to think alike in aught except the bare fact
of spirit existence and return.   The mind is naturally prolific
in theories and speculations, and will indulge therein say what
we may.   The trouble with many Spiritualists is that they are
so wrapped up in their own vagaries that they have no tolera-
tion for the vagaries of others.

*
* *

To accomplish the best work in any line of art or genius
—in painting, sculpture, invention, poetry or music—the gifted
one must lift his soul far above the jingle of gold, and hold
himself close to the heart of his divine inspiration.   The
remuneration will surely come with his success—as a natural
sequence thereof, but not as the inspiring cause.   Would that
we could impress this thought upon the minds of all gifted
instruments for the manifestation of spirit power.

*
* *

We can live like unhatched chickens, in the shell, as
many do, or we can come forth into that larger life of the
spirit which is our birthright.   The former condition is the
childhood of the spirit, the realm of small thoughts and small
things.   Ought we not to rise out of this realm, and learn to
think grandly, and to live grandly—not in a material sense,
but in the grandeur of a noble life and high aspirations?
There be many kings and priests of the Most High who never
lived in earthly palaces.

*
* *

There is no buying nor selling in the land "beyond the
river."   The mind schooled in the ways and tricks of trade
and but little else, in this life, will there have to begin with

the spiritual alphabet, and take its place in the infant class. What advantage can it be to the spirit to be skilled in the — — things of earth for which it will have no use in spirit life? It will have use for all its love, all its generosity, all its purity, all its nobility of character, all its unselfishness—but all that is of the earth earthy it will leave behind.

————‡o‡————

BEFORE THEIR TIME.

How many people die before their time—that is, at or before middle age—passing on to the other life without the full measure of earth experience necessary for their work and development on the spiritual plane of life. Most men live too fast—business men especially. Excitement, worry, late hours, sleepless nights, alcoholic stimulation, etc., all more or less incident to that greed for gain which seems to be a part of our competitive system, soon consume the taper of life, and they pass on to the other stage of existence before they have lived out one-half their years. And what do they gain? What does any one gain who devotes every energy of his life to the acquisition of that which, when attained, he is obliged to leave to others, perhaps to gratify the follies and vanities of thankless heirs?

————‡o‡————

WEALTHY BACHELORS.

Oh, the abominable selfishness of a wealthy bachelor's life! The man who could, if he would, make some good woman happy and establish a beautiful home, with children to gladden their lives. But this would cost money—money to be expended upon some one else than himself; and so he drifts about like the butterfly, from flower to flower, enjoying the pleasant and refining society of good women often, without any expense to himself for their board and clothing! Such men stand wofully in their own light. They are building their house upon the sand, with no foundation of love to support it when the storms of sickness and adversity come. The years glide away all too soon for their earthly pride; old age creeps upon them, and ere long the shadow and gloom of the grave fall across their paths. Death at last claims them for his own, and they glide out upon the silent river from the care of some hired nurse who wonders where he shall find another job. How different the departure of one from some happy home from the fond arms of a gentle wife to close his eyelids in death with her soft, caressing hands.

————‡o‡————

MAN'S REAL WORTH.

Some one has said that a man's real worth in the world is simply that of the business he follows. Gauged by this standard, which we are inclined to think is a just one, what is the rum-seller worth, or the gambler, or the stockbroker, or the usurer, or the professional base-ball player? What is the worth of the fashionable woman, who spends her time and substance in fashion's follies, and in a selfish gratification of her love for finery and display? What is the young man worth who is squandering the fortune left him by an indulgent father in idleness and dissipation? These are the questions which Conscience, the great Judge, will ask of every soul, as it knocks for admittance at the gate of the City Celestial: What use did you make of yourself on earth? How have you profited by your opportunities? It might be well, dear reader, for you to ask these questions of yourself now, and if you cannot answer them satisfactorily, perhaps you may be able to further on.

————‡o‡————

These temples of the spirit, through which the soul finds expression, how important it is that they be wisely cared for. To abuse the body with strong drink, or tobacco, or the gratification of any base appetite, or by riotous living, all tends to deprive the instrument of its fineness of tone, and obscure the light of the soul shining through it. To abuse the body is to trample upon the soul, and hasten the time of its release, all unprepared. Good hours, cleanliness, careful diet, temperance in all things—these are all essential to a well-ordered life, and the highest possible degree of spiritual unfoldment.

THIS OLD EARTH OF OURS.

A kind mother, a lavish and bounteous friend, is this old, old earth of ours. She spreads out her banquet of rare viands and luscious fruits, she unlocks her treasures of gold and silver, and precious stones, and invites man to draw near and help himself. She wafts his ships across mighty wastes of sea, with the magic of her breath, pointing the way they should go with a spirit wand; she lends him the couriers of the skies for his messengers; she gives him, in brief, unstintedly of herself—of the melody of her birds and brooks, of the beauty and fragrance of her flowers, of the grandeur of her starry nights, —and when at last, like a child wearied with its play, he would seek for rest, she takes him in her loving arms and coddles him to sleep upon her bosom.

HOME WHERE LOVE IS NOT.

A home where love is not—where in the wide world can one find a more dreary place? Hearts that ache for sympathy and find it not—that ask for bread and receive a stone,—God pity them! Better that they go their separate ways, and never more rest under the same roof. And yet, in married life, how many unloved wives, and indifferent and unfaithful husbands, may be found; and children grow up in the atmosphere of such homes, all unbalanced and out of harmony with their own higher natures, to add to the world's woe! It is indeed pitiful. But what can be expected when marriage is made a thing of passional impulse, as it too often is, and not of those higher spiritual and intellectual attractions, which alone are lasting and permanent. Love, founded in the higher nature, and on mutual attraction of spirit, will survive the disintegrating processes of time, and grow brighter and sweeter with the years. Only those between whom such love exists has God truly joined together

———§o§———

Can you realize, dear reader, how swift is the flight of time—we mean you who have crossed the meridian line, and have seen what the world is disposed to call your " best days ?" Your best days should be your last days—your days of fruition —your days of ripe experience, of treasured memories. The earth is fading away. You are nearing the silent river, beyond which bloom the evergreen shores of immortal life. You must soon bid good-bye to earth—soon must part with all earthly possessions. Are you ready for the summons?

* *

The seance for spiritual communion should be sacred to the purest thoughts and the highest aspirations of the soul. Every member of the circle should draw near as to an altar dedicated to the living God. Not that one should enter into this holy of holies with a long visage, or a heart draped in black ; but one should draw near in the sweet passivity of a cheerful spirit, bright with the sunshine of hope and joy. It is thus that the good angels can draw nearest to our hearts, and both mortal and spirit receive a baptism of the divine life.

* *

It is never a disgrace, however humiliating it may be, to be deceived. The more honest one is himself, the more honesty he is apt to see in his fellows. Hence, those good, honest Spiritualists who have witnessed the cruel deceptions practiced in public materializing circles, mixed up, it may be, with here and there a few grains of truth, are not to be blamed. They can hardly be made to realize that men and women, whom they have long known and esteemed, could so dishonor them selves as to trifle with such sacred things. The psychic form is all the more beautiful when produced in the atmosphere and — — harmony of the home circle. There let it remain for the present.

SELF RESPECT.

It is a rule that he who would be respected must first re-spect himself. The same is true in a larger or community sense. There are thousands of excellent people in the world, in and out of the churches, who believe in the fundamental truths of Spiritualism. They are mediums for the spirits themselves, or have mediumship in their families. They know that their loved ones who have passed on are not dead, but that they live and love them still, and that they can and do come to them when conditions are favorable. But they would not for the world be regarded as Spiritualists, nor have it known that they are subject to spirit influences. We can not blame them, when we consider how very little many Spiritualists respect their own cause. With the solution of the grandest problem of the universe in their hands—a truth that eclipses conception with its mighty results—they stand around and do little or nothing to command the respect of the world. Shall we blame the world when it reviles?

Who would not rather pass on to the other life in a flush of glory, by making his last act some crowning impulse of grandeur and divine self-abnegation, than die with coffers dis-tended with unused wealth, to corrupt ungrateful heirs, and fill the heart of the owner with sadness in the Infinite Beyond.

What spirit, manifesting through mortal mediumship, ever taught other doctrine than that embodied in the Golden Rule? There are those, it is true, who sometimes come to us, bringing back a bad earthly condition—spirits who have not yet learned the better way—but by kindness and good advice they are generally found to be yielding and submissive to the divine law of unfoldment, and are soon made to recognize their relationship to the Infinite Spirit.   All spirits who are allowed to come to us as teachers, invaribly hold up to us the highest standards of morality.   They teach purity of life and conduct, and endeavor in all possible ways to lead us upward into the light of all goodness and truth.

WHAT CHANGES HAVE COME.

What a change has come over the world since, for the amusement of his debased subjects, Nero fed his hungry lions on the humble followers of Jesus.   The taste that could find satisfaction in such a cruel spectacle was akin to that of the ravenous beasts that fought and struggled in the awful carnage. The world, to-day, possesses no type of humanity so low as to tolerate such cruelties, which clearly shows the upward trend of the human race.   It is only by contrasting great lapses of time that this fact is made prominent.   Thus are we made to recognize the great truth of man's development from lower types of human life, and by which we may logically infer his ascent from the primordial cell, through vast gradations of animal life to his present high estate.   In all this chain of unfoldment we can discover no " missing link "—no break in God's eternal purpose in human progress.   Surely, but slowly, the world is growing better.

One can not judge of the tree by the fungus growth upon its bark, nor of the sea by the debris cast upon the shore; neither can one judge of Spiritualism by the excrescences that sometimes appear upon its surface.   There are depths on depths of grandeur, purity, and beauty in Spiritualism that the world knows not of, and which can never be inferred from the lives and conduct of some who claim to be its champions.   It is a plant that thrives best in the soil of a harmonious home. There to many lives it is a most precious thing, full of all beauty and freshness, and ever exhaling sweetest fragrance.

FAITH AND KNOWLEDGE.

In the Church we are asked and required to believe by faith, and without proof, in what Spiritualists claim they are able to prove, viz., the continued existence, upon another plane of life, of the spirit of man as an individualized, conscious entity. Now faith and knowledge are naturally antagonistic to each other. In fact, they can not long run in parallel lines without converging towards a point of common unity. Faith is a phantom of ignorance that disappears in knowledge. No one will be contented with a belief in a future life by faith, when he once learns that a positive knowledge of the fact is within his reach. And so a multitude of good, religious people in the churches are coming to a knowledge of the truth, through the unfoldments and manifestations of the spirit in their own homes and lives, as well as through the "gifts of the spirit" in other ways.

The man who sees only the good there is in his fellow beings, making no note of their weaknesses or failings, may be deceived and wronged many times and in many ways—he may die in poverty, unhonored and unknown,—yet we would like to be in his place when he wakes in the morning of his ressurection to life eternal it the spirit world.

*
Be of good cheer, fellow traveler on life's journey ! Know ye not that it is only when your own spirit is full of sunshine that your angel friends can draw nearest to aid you and lead you out of trouble? It not only does no good to worry and fret over disappointments and troubles that one can not avoid, but it does positive harm, in that it shuts one out from the

possibility of that help that might come to one through the spirit.   It may require much discipline of the mind to overcome the tendency to worry over what goes wrong.   But how to obtain that discipline and mastery over one's self generally, should be the study of every soul.

*\
* *

The French language has no word that corresponds with the dear old Saxon word, home; and France is a country where home, in its sweet American significance, is unknown. He misses one of the dearest charms of life, who lives, though it be never so grandly, without a home.   How pure the joys and rare the delights, that cluster around the home.   It is not *home* where one sleeps, or eats his meals, unless one's heart is in the place; and what heart ever went into a restaurant or lodging house !   The virtuous home is the foundation of the Republic, the bulwark of orderly society, the stepping stone to heaven.

*\
* *

All who believe in the Bible, believe that Moses and Elias materialized on the Mount of Transfiguration; they believe also ,that on many occasions spirits appeared to mortals, and that even Christ himself came to his disciples and was recognized by them.   Now, if communion with spirits is wrong, why did not Jesus warn his disciples against it?   And why did he do that which, if wrong, he would have condemned in others? Will not some of our Christian ministers answer this question?

*\
* *

The plowshare that remains inactive in the soil becomes corroded with rust.   So it is with the spirit that rests inactive in the soil of the world's needs.   We can grow and keep the spirit bright only by constant use of our faculties.   It is not well to become corroded in our sympathies or charities, for thus we die before our time.   There are too many dead people in the world—dead in all save the mere breath of life—waiting to be buried.

THE SWEET BY AND BY.

" The sweet By and by !"   How many a time and oft have the words, "There's a land that is fairer than day," been sung to the air of "Sweet By-and-by," by those who would draw near the invisible world, while their loved ones on the other side moved aside the vail to greet their idols still on the shores of mortal life. There is a world of comfort in that familiar song, when sung by the true Spiritualist. He knows something of that land so fair, knows that it is a reflex of the beautiful places of earth. He knows if he makes the best use of himself here, that when the trials and struggles of this life are over, he will pass on to his "dwelling place there," a home amid beautiful surroundings, and a landscape as real and tangible to the spirit senses as this earth is to these tenements of clay. Hence, the Spiritualist can sing that song as no one else can, for the words mean something to him. Herein he finds a comfort and a strength that the world knows not of.

Listen, ye heavy hearted and sorrowing, ye weary and o'erburdened souls! Know ye not there is a needed discipline in your trials ; and the time will come when you would not for worlds part with a single pang your hearts have ever known, or a tear your eyes have shed. It is only through fierce heat that the dross is burnt away, and the pure gold left in the crucible. You are the gold in God's crucible. Let him temper you as He will.

*
* *

You cannot detract from the value of gold by discovering and disclosing the spurious coin. The gold remains unchangeable forever. It survives the furnace heat, and retains the quality of its undimmed lustre through all mutations of the chemist's art. It is only the false that fails and disappears in the crucible. The truth lives forever, and grows brighter with the ages.

The frailties of poor human nature ought not to be paraded before the world, to poison the moral atmosphere, and deaden the sensibilities of the good and pure. If one finds a dead dog upon his premises, were it not better and wiser to bury it than to drag it through the streets? Spiritualists expose their sores; other religionists cover theirs from public gaze. In that we think that they are wiser than we.

THE VOICE OF NATURE.

The voice of many-tongued Nature, ever pleading with man, is an invitation to "come up higher." She presents him everywhere in the material world, lessons of infinite beauty, harmony and perfection. She gives to him a wonderfully delicate and intricate machine, through which he may express himself on this external plane of being, and she warns him by terrible penalties not to misuse it. She paints the lily for him as a symbol of purity for him to imitate in the whiteness of his own life. She unfolds to him the wonder and glory of the universe to lead his thoughts upward and outward from the littleness of himself to the greatness and majesty of that infinite power and unity that we call God. She would ever lead him by the hand, as a parent would lead a loved child, into the ways of wisdom, goodness, and truth. Who would go through life heedless of her higher teachings, "builds his house upon the sand."

Storms, in the physical world, clear and purify the atmosphere. What though the fierce lightnings lash the heavens at times, and the mad cyclone toys with the habitations of men. There is, no doubt, a purpose in it all; although not always apparent to the finite understanding. So it is doubtless with spiritual things. Great excitements and commotions are necessary to obliterate evil and fit the spirit for clearer perceptions of truth. The soul that lies at anchor within the land-locked harbor of truth, fears not the storm without.

POWER OF WEALTH.

The power of wealth is most strikingly illustrated in the case of that New York lady, who is said to be the "richest woman in America," of whom the papers make occasional mention. With thirty millions of dollars worth of securities in her possession, the accumulations of which are constantly and rapidly increasing, she nevertheless lives so meanly as to almost deny herself the common necessities of life. She has no thought of the great world around her, except that of how it may be utilized to increase her stores. She never performs a generous act—never gives heed to the plaint of suffering humanity. With a mighty power in her hands for good, she is going down to the grave, and her spirit out into the other life, with the good she could do all undone. Could there be a beggar in the world poorer than this poor woman? What reader of the GOLDEN GATE would exchange his condition for her wealth and her spirit?

———‡o‡———

There is no monoply, or close corporation, of spiritual gifts. There is scarcely a man, woman, or child, to whom some phase of spiritual manifestation is not possible. In fact, the very best mediums are often found in private life, who would no more think of making a commerce of their gifts than they would of selling the sunshine of an encouraging word to a sorrowing soul. And yet we know that whoever must live by his gifts must be paid therefor. We would not oppose paid mediumship, but we would most earnestly encourage the development of mediumship in the home circle.

* *

"Destroy my belief in the possibility of the psychic form," says one, "and I have no further use for Spiritualism." How barren and empty of spirituality the nature must be that finds nothing in the intellectual evidences of another life to console him—nothing in the other and varied sensuous manifestations of psychic power given in the light, and under conditions impossible of deception. But he need not surrender his belief in materialization, for it is a stupendous fact, all the same. And the way is preparing for its manifestation, to those who are prepared to accept it, under conditions far removed from every doubt. Let no Spiritualist become discouraged. None will who *knows* the truth.

*
* *

Spiritualism has suffered more from the public materialization seance—from the antagonism and suspicion of deception it has aroused—than from all other causes combined. The manifestation of the psychic form, as at present produced, is not for the skeptic; and until such time as the element of darkness can be eliminated from the materializing seance, and it can be held under conditions that can challenge skepticism, it should be confined to the laboratory of the spiritual scientist, for private investigation and experiment. There are many places where this phenomenon can be developed and studied to advantage; but it is not in the promiscuous public seance. Spiritualists should refuse to patronize such seances.

*
* *

Man should never lose faith in himself, or his fellow man, nor in the principle of eternal Love and Justice that dominates the universe. No matter what calamities may befall him, or what wrongs may prevail around him, he must still hold fast to the unchanging fact, that the trend of humanity is ever upward, and that right is the outcome of all the moral forces working through the human race. Error is but the friction of the machinery, not yet wisely adapted part to part. But this will disappear as man evolves a higher spirituality, and learns the lessons written in his own soul, by the hand of Infinite Truth.

*
* *

What matters it whether man is the result of one embodiment or one hundred ? If we ever return to this planet for further experiences in the mortal, it will no doubt be for our good. However, but one embodiment at a time is all that should concern us, and how to find the highest and best expression therein.

AMENDING THEIR CREEDS.

Would you pull down the churches? Not at all. We would amend their creeds, and make them vastly more potent for good than now. The fatal mistake of ecclesiasticism is its Procrustean bedstead of creed, established in the comparative infancy of the race, and which is made irrevocable. This creed makes no provision for intellectual growth, none for the revelations of science and none for the more rational demands of man's spiritual nature. The human race can not be bound to the past forever. It has long since begun to exploiter new fields of thought. It has made discoveries that cannot be adjusted to the religious teachings of the church. It demands a new statement of facts and principles. And this the church will be compelled to make, or its Doctors of Divinity will, ere long, find themselves preaching to empty pews. Truth will not suffer by stripping it of its husks, neither will true religion suffer by divesting it of its crudities and adapting it to man's advancing spiritual nature.

LIFT UP YOUR HEADS.

Lift up your heads and rejoice, O ye struggling and sorrowing ones of earth! Though the night has been long and dark, see ye not the roseate tints of the coming day—the day that shall dispel all shadows and shapes of woe, and usher you into a condition of life where honest merit shall have its fair share of all things necessary for the soul's happiness? What if misfortune and poverty have been your lot, remember they are only for a brief season ; and especially should you encourage the thought that in no sense is your true self made richer or poorer by your earthly conditions, and that the only wealth that will last is the sterling wealth of character, which the poor may have as well as the rich, and frequently in greater abundance. Then let the world wag on; do your best; an archangel could do no more.

INGERSOLL.

The spiritual life of the world is in no danger from infidelity or atheism. There would be just as much Christ in the world—that is, the Christ spirit—if there were a hundred Ingersolls where there is now but one. In fact, there is no broader humanity taught, no better lessons of brotherly love and duty than those taught by Ingersoll himself. *Belief* is in no sense essential to goodness. Indeed, the history of the Church abundantly shows that belief has been the basis of wrongs and wickedness untold. There is no goodness that is not of God, and goodness is the common property of mankind. There are but few hearts in which the Christ spirit reigns more supremely than in the heart of Robert G. Ingersoll. The church will yet come to accept the grand truth that he is the truest disciple of Christ who best loves his fellow men.

A GOOD WIFE.

A good wife! What a wealth of joy is embodied in the thought. To feel that though friends forsake, and all the world turn against you, she will stand by you to the end, ever ready to shield and comfort you with a love that is stronger than the love of life—a faith that will outlive death! What rapture of infinite love—what pleasure of all the delights of heaven, can excel this! We know such an one (there are no doubt many such), whose bright intellect, highly unfolded spirit and wealth of all that good men most prize in woman, all combine to make a queen among her sex; and yet so free from assumption of especial merit is she,—from all ostentatious display of her royal gifts and graces —that the lowliest of God's children can ever find in her a wise counsellor and a gentle friend. Her intuition, in the work in which she and her companion are mutually engaged is always unerring, and ever she is patiently and trustingly leading the way to higher and better views of life and duty. We say, we know such an one,—and she is not far away !

SIGNS AND WONDERS.

When the Master was on earth He said that certain "signs and wonders" should follow those that believe, and that greater things than He did should they do. He evidently meant what He said. But what are the "signs and wonders" that attend those who pretend to "believe," in these later ages of Christianity? Do they heal the sick by the laying on of hands? Are they superior to the deadly effects of poison? Not at all. Then how can they be His disciples? The marvelous phenomena attending the manifestation of the spirit, under the name of modern Spiritualism, seem to be a literal fulfillment of the great Teacher's predictions, in many things. Out of the mouths of babes many truths are spoken, and they are made to speak and write in languages whereof they have no knowledge. The sick are healed by spirit power, and many strange signs are given to teach man the true way of life. But only the wise are receptive to the truth.

There is an assurance, an abiding comfort and confidence in a knowledge of spirit existence and communion as enjoyed by all true Spiritualists, that no faith in things unseen and unknown can possibly give. To the true Spiritualist the dark problem of the grave has been solved. For him the future has no terror, and he is reconciled to bear the burdens of life patiently, knowing that thereby he is the better preparing himself for his home in spirit life, and for the companionship of loved ones gone before.

THE HIGHEST GOOD.

The problem of life—how best to attain the highest good —is one that concerns us all. The young man or woman just coming on the stage of action, with bright hopes and high aspirations, is brought face to face with strange and abnormal conditions of life and labor; with systems of religious thought, founded on ancient superstitions, that are at utter variance with all the known principles and laws that dominate the universe; with inconsistencies in law and human government; with error and ignorance of every form. Is it any wonder that he falters and stumbles? He needs a new creed, founded on common sense, and consistent with his own constitution. He needs to feel that he is One with the All Good, and that his first and highest duty is to adjust himself to the universe of which he is a part, and in harmony with which only can he find happiness. Thus adjusted and harmonized, he becomes a mighty power for the correction of the errors and evils which confront him on every hand.

A SETTLED FACT.

One clearly established fact of the manifestation of an independent spirit intelligence, settles the question, with any honest mind, of continued existence of the spirit of man beyond the change called death. Every careful investigator of our phenomena has had proof upon proof of spirit existence, and that such existences are the spirits of human beings who once lived upon the earth. To millions of intelligent people, including many of the brightest minds the world has yet produced—scientists, scholars, statesmen—men in all walks of life—the central truths of spirit existence, and the power of the same persons we have known on earth to return, under proper conditions, and communicate with mortals, is quite as much of a settled fact as is that of their own existence. And what do these returning spirits all teach us? That life is progressive forever ; that man must answer for his own sins ; that there is no endless hell and no vicarious atonement for sin ;——— that each one must work out his own salvation, either in this life or in the next ; that there is time enough and room enough for all ; that there is no greater Devil than ignorance, and no greater hell than man's undeveloped conscience ; that goodness brings its natural reward of happiness, and wickedness its natural penalty of suffering ; and that the whole plan of salvation lies in the simple act of ceasing to do evil and learning to do well.

PROPER EDUCATION.

Children need to be educated in spiritual knowledge and to grow into an understanding of our phenomenal facts. To such children the manifestations of spirit intelligence or power have no terror ; but they learn to enjoy them, and take delight in communing with their spirit friends. A little four-year-old mediumistic boy on being put to bed in a room by himself was told by his new nurse to have no fear as she would leave the door open. " I don't want the door left open," he said. But she left it open all the same. He then called to his mother, who knew the boy better, complaining, " Lizzie has left my door open and spoiled my dark circle." He had his little drum and other playthings upon his bed, and it was his custom after retiring, to have a romp with his little spirit playmates.

" The days that are no more ! " Days worse than wasted in the worls's unholy strifes, days of spiritual darkness and decay, days of sadness and despair ! Happy the spirit that has buried their memory forevermore and come forth into the light and life of the new day. For then it is that man begins to find his own soul. He begins to learn that all earthly experience that does not add to his stature as a spiritual being is more or less hurtful, for the reason that it will, in the beyond, chain him to earth conditions when he should be mounting upward into the higher realms of being. How empty and profit-less will seem many things that engrossed our thoughts here, when we come to caste aside this house of clay.

**

Scatter the seeds of truth wherever the fallow ground of the spirit is ready to receive them, but nowhere else. There is no sort of use in thrusting our facts or philosophy upon people who will meet you with ignorant ridicule and abuse. They are "wedded to their idols." Time and circumstance are necessary to prepare their hearts for the good news, for the glorious gospel of intercommunion of the two worlds, and the beautiful lessons of love and duty that come to us from the higher planes of spirit life. Be patient, it will all come around right in due time.

**

The "Robert Elsmeres," who, breaking away from the faith and teachings of their church, and yet failing to come under the bright light and beautiful philosophy of Spiritualism, are to be pitied. They are deserving of the tender sympathy of men and angels. It is as one who leaves the beaten way for the wilderness, and never quite passes out from its maze and shadows, into the "land flowing with milk and honey" beyond. There is no faith like knowledge, no trust like absolute posses-sion. Herein only is "rest for the weary."

**

Any system of labor reform that does not strike at the liquor traffic, can not be otherwise than a beating of the empty air ; and yet the laboring classes themselves, who are the prin-cipal supporters of the saloons, are the last to join in a crusade against theirs and the world's common foe.

**

Who lives for others lives in the truest sense for himself. Upon the crest of the wave of generous deeds man is borne heavenward. Who exalteth himself shall be humbled ; who exalteth his brother himself shall be exalted.

ON TRIAL.

Orthodoxy in all its essential claims, is on trial before the world. For centuries there were none to dispute; and even down to the last half century there were but few minds strong enough or brave enough to question its demands. The doctrine of the Fall of Man, the infallibility of the Bible, the atonement, an eternity of happiness for those who believe, and endless punishment for those that do not, — these are now the central points of attack from the world's enlightened batteries of thought. The outcome no enlightened mind can doubt — rationalism will triumph and ecclesiasticism be compelled to surrender its untenable dogmas. And what is there that good men should fear in the substitution in the universe of a God of Love for one of implacable hate ? Is it not better for man to be taught that he cannot shirk the consequences of his acts, that he must pay the last farthing of his debt, than to believe that " Jesus paid it all?" And after all, is not goodness, nobility of soul, and uprightness of character the things to be sought for? What has *belief* in the creeds of the churches to do with these qualities in man?

————‡o‡————

We are all building for the future. Every generous act of our lives is a stone in the foundation of that edifice which shall constitute our abiding place in the beyond—not eternally, of course, but for how long we may not know. The character and durability of the edifice will depend upon the kind of material we put into it. If we live narrow, selfish lives, thoughtless of others' welfare, we are building a hut upon the sands, and not a palace of marble walls. Soon it will crumble away and leave the spirit shelterless. The pride and pomp of this life—wealth, station and honor—are nothing but rubbish, all to be rejected by the Divine Builder. In living our best for the future we have but to make the highest use of the present.

CAPITAL PUNISHMENT.

The Bible says: "He who sheddeth man's blood, by man shall his blood be shed." The same book says: "Thou shalt not kill." How can the believers in the infallibility of this book reconcile these two passages? Hanging for murder is a a most brutal business at best. It does not bring back to life the person slain; it does not prevent the recurrence of murder; and then it wastes a human being, which is not good morals, or good economy. To kill to preserve life is more a matter of policy than of morality. It is right, in a certain sense; but it must be done at the moment, under the excitement of fear, or an impulse of justice. The cool, deliberate planning to take life for life, is quite another thing. Isn't it quite enough that the murderer should be deprived of his liberty for life? And then his services might be made available towards undoing, as far as possible, the great wrong committed, and at the same time he might obtain the necessary earth experience to best fit him for the life beyond. One wrong was never yet condoned by the commission of another.

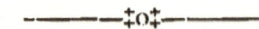

How beautiful is the morning of life, with its bright hopes, its bounding pulses, its glow and sparkle of joy! How grand is middle life with its conscious power, its grandeur of intellect, its mighty play of forces! But more beautiful and grander still is serene old age with its rich argosies of matured thought, its ripe experiences, and its bright anticipation of the life to come. How bright and happy is the home-coming to the wanderer in strange lands. And such is the thought of the home-going to the aged, whose soul ties are anchored on the thither shore.

Until man can so school himself in spiritual knowledge— or attain to that spiritual unfoldment wherein he can think no ill of any mortal, however much he may have wronged him, is he wholly prepared to enter upon the higher life of the soul. Not that we should *love* our enemies, for that were impossible ;— — but we can excuse, and symyathize with, and pity them. We can do them good for ill. We can show them the better way of life in our own life and conduct. We can exalt them by up-lifting ourselves. And this is one of the lessons of our beauti-ful Spiritualism—to bring man into nearness with the divine in his own nature. This is to come under the dominion of Good, which is but another name for God.

IN WISDOM'S WAYS.

We know a bright young girl, tall and straight as an arrow, just entering upon the sober realities of life. Before her is unfolding the marvelous realities of mature womanhood, and the great, restless, uncertain world. Brave and strong of pur-pose, with footsteps firm and eyes peering into the realm of shadows that enshrouds her future, she moves steadily for-ward in the path of duty, guided by the pure light of a white, unsullied soul. What promise of gentle goodness she wears upon her forehead—what prophecy of hallowed womanhood beams in the depths of her lustrous brown eyes! Bend low sweet angels, and take her by the hand. Lead her through green pastures and by still waters. Touch her nature with the divine inspiration of goodness. Fill her soul with kind thoughts, and with gentle promptings to charity, and make her life to blossom with good deeds. What a life of grandeur and usefulness lies before every young woman, if she but wills to walk in wisdom's ways!

The acquisition of wealth may be to one person a means of spiritual growth and unfoldment, while to another it may forge chains of steel that will bind the spirit for ages. It all depends upon the motive for its acquisition, and the uses it is put to when acquired.

REASON.

"Reason," says the matererialist, "is my only guide." And so he sets up reason as his God, and bows down before it, with all the devotion his nature is capable of. Now what is reason? It is the uncertain and oftentimes misleading process whereby the intellect endeavors to arrive at truth. The highly unfolded spirit reaches truth by a shorter route. Let us illustrate : The writer once had some interesting experiments with a Mr. Hutchings, the man kown as the "lightning calculator." We demonstrated beyond question, that he could write down instantly the sum total of long columns of figures, without the reasoning process of adding the figures together. His spirit comprehended the result at once, and it was invariably correct. Man's reason is so warped by diverting influences, he reasons in so many lines and from such a variety of points, that it is but a very poor guide at best. Intuition, when highly unfolded, as it may be, in what is known as the sixth sense, is a far more reliable guide.

Is there anything more beautiful on earth than a happy home, a home pervaded by that delightful harmony, wherein the angels love to meet and dwell? Such a one we dropped into a few evenings ago, together with a score or more of congenial souls, to commemorate the birthday anniversary of the happy head of the household, — the birthday of one who is peacefully gliding down the stream of life, as it widens out towards the great ocean. Earth-life to him has been a success in many ways; certain it is that its evening sky is radiant with the purple and golden prophecy of a glad new day, that shall dawn for him and his dear companion sometime in the sweet by-and-by.

*
* *

True happinesss does not depend so much upon the intellect as upon the affections. In fact, the worse misery one can experience in this world is intellectual misery ; that is, the misery that comes of a keen understanding of those things that conduce to unhappiness. Causes that would prompt some deeply sensitive persons to take their own lives, others, less acute to the agonies of unbridled thought, would treat as trifles. While it is always well to be sympathetic with those in affliction, we should cultivate the faculty of deriving happiness even from our sympathies. In administering to the sorrows and sufferings of others, the spiritual soul can find a sort of melancholy joy.

NEW YEAR.

A new year dawns upon the world. Brings it no lesson to humanity, no suggestion of spiritual help or unfoldment? What argosies of soul-treasure has the year just closed brought to you, dear reader? Have you profited by its lessons, become wiser through its experiences? Has it broadened your nature, made you more liberal and kind, and exalted your views of life? Are you "nearer the Father's house," in its higher spiritual sense, than you "ever were before," or than you were one year ago? If yea, then the new year will open to you radiant with hope and rich with spiritual possibilities. The new year should mean something more to us all than a mere boundary line of time. It should remind us that our days are rapidly gliding away, and that what we do in this earth experience must be done quickly, for "to-morrow we die," or pass on to other scenes and experiences in the great drama of existence.

How many hearts there are in the world aching for a gentle word, and the sympathy of a loving thought—husbands, wives, children, brothers, sisters—living in the chilly atmosphere of indifference to each other's presence, if not of chronic dislike. And thus this world, that should be full of sunshine and joy, is turned into a dismal abode, where all unpleasant and cruel things take root, and grow, and shed their malarious influence to poison the sweet springs of being.

SHORTNESS OF MORTAL SIGHT.

How short is mortal sight! How narrow the range of human judgment! No doubt it will be made apparent to every intelligent being sometime, that the niche he occupies in the universe is just the one for which he is best fitted, and for which he was especially created. This brings us to a recognition of the truth, that in a certain sense, "Whatever is, is right." If it were not so, then wrong is an elemental factor in creation, which cannot wisely be conceded. We come, in the process of intellectual unfoldment, to realize that many things that once seemed wrong to us now appear to be right. It was seemingly a cruel wrong, the betrayal and crucifixion of Jesus, but where would Christianity have been without such betrayal and crucifixion? If there were no sin in the world, what virtue would there be in overcoming evil with good, and where would be the inducement to a noble life?

HALLELUJAH OF GLADNESS.

In the light of the Spiritual Philosophy, life should be made a perpetual hallelujah of gladness. "Sickness and sorrow, pain and death," that are such lugubrious subjects under the teachings of the old philosophies and theologies, are no longer regarded as such by those who have "entered the path," but they become useful spiritual helps and educators—valuable acquistions of experiences to take with us to the other life. We should learn to extract sunbeams from clouds, and joy even from sorrow. We imagine someone will say, "Can one be cheerful with the toothache?" He surely will, if he realizes that a fretful and surly acceptance of the pain really aggravates it as it surely does. We may not all be mental scientists to the extent that a denial of the pain will drive it away, but we can all understand that a cheerful acceptance is certainly a great alleviator of suffering of any kind. It is a sort of flag of truce to meet the enemy half way with a view to compromise.

CHURCH HISTORY.

Through what seas of blood, what Gethsemanes of mortal — — anguish, man has passed in his struggles for spiritual and intellectual freedom. The history of the church for ages, and down almost to the beginning of the present century, is a history of terrible persecutions for opinion's sake. And yet was the church to blame? Was it not rather the undeveloped spiritual and intellectual conditions of the race? The church is an effect and not a cause. It is just what man makes it. In the dark ages it was the expression of his benighted spiritual nature, the same as it is now the expression of a higher spiritual unfoldment. We might as well quarrel with our own childhood, or with the barbaric conditions of our ancestry, as to waste our breath in berating the church for its past cruelties, or its present shortcomings. What we most need, as Spiritualists and Liberalists, is to turn our faces from a dead past to the front of the living present, and, guided by the star of Bethlehem that shines for all, follow it to the eternal Gateway of Light.

The strong owe a duty to the weak—the well to the sick. Our system of competitive industry gives to the strong in acquisitive wisdom the same advantage that the physically strong possess over the weak. We would, in the latter case, deny the right of the strong to trample upon the weak ; but we recognize and encourage the exercise of those powers and faculties that enable one man to dominate the labor and acquisitions of others to his own use. But this should not release the latter from the responsibility and duty he owes to his weaker brother.

*
* *

The seasons come and go—Winter and Spring with their wealth of flowers, and the hills and valleys robed in a mantle of green—Summer and Autumn with their golden harvests

and luscious fruits, to gladden the hearts and homes of men—
but with all her mutations, the old, old earth remains forever
young.   So it is with the immortal soul, attuned to the divine
harmony of existence.   There is no such thing as age to such
a soul.   It is ever unfolding and never losing its immortal
freshness and beauty.   It is the end of life to grow, and not
to languish and die, spiritually.

GET THE BEST.

If you would get the best out of life, spiritually or physically, you must learn to live in harmony with your own soul.
Thereby you come into sympathy, or rather, your nature becomes receptive to the spirit of the All Good.   Once fully
under the dominion of this spirit, the body can know no sickness, the spirit no real anguish.   Peace, like a tidal wave of
inspiration, will bear you ever on its sun-kissed crest, and all
the heaven there is in God's universe will be yours.   How, do
you ask, can this state be attained?   By kind thoughts and
generous actions ; by noble endeavor to do your best in all
things ; by rendering good for ill—love for hatred ; and by
constant aspiration for the interblending of the divine life with
your own.

HOW TO INVESTIGATE PSYCHIC PHENOMENA.

He who would investigate psychic phenomena to the best
purpose, and the best results, should approach the subject with a
passive and gentle spirit of earnestness and simplicity.   The mind
should be divested of all skepticism founded upon mere assumption of facts, or preconceived opinions of any kind.   He should endeavor to realize that Nature has her own ways and methods
for the accomplishing of her ends, and that in these ways and
methods she never consults mortal man, or stops to consider his
opinions.   In this spirit, and with an earnest desire for truth, he
will find the spirit world alike earnest in its efforts to convince

him of the truth of spirit existence and return. He must remember that he cannot dictate or command the spirits in any way. Also, that they are eager to convince only those who are truly willing and ready to be convinced.

DELUSIONS.

To the man who has no knowledge of astronomy, the idea of the rotundity of the earth is a foolish delusion. Can't he see that, with the exception of the unevenness of the earth's surface, that it is flat? Doesn't he know that if the earth "turned over" it would spill all the water out of the ocean? Should we deride him for his ignorance, or endeavor to enlighten him as to his errors? That is just where the great mass of mankind stand with regard to spiritual truth. The spirit-world is to them an undiscovered country, a great flat, resting, in a figurative sense, upon the backs of four elephants, etc., with the balance of the foundation not clearly defined! That is the condition of most of our clerical defamers.

LIBERALISM.

We have no sympathy with that so-called Liberalism, that does nothing but deride and denounce the things which millions of other people are disposed to regard as sacred—the Liberalism which at the same time, does nothing itself for the uplifting of the race. The mighty charities of the church, misdirected and sometimes hurtful, as they no doubt are, are vastly more beneficial to those that practice them than is the practice of no charity at all. The church teaches its members to *give*, and they do it with a lavish hand, as the many costly church edifices of every large city bear witness; while Liberalism with its multitudes of followers, gives nothing but emptiness to the world; and its champions, save and except an occasional mighty genius like Ingersoll, are often obliged to go to bed hungry.

FOOLISH PRIDE.

. How much misery might be averted in this world, if man were freed from the slavery of the foolish pride that prompts him to excel his neighbor in those things that are in no wise essential to his true happiness. If A can afford to gratify expensive tastes, and B cannot, it is not well for the latter to make himself unhappy deploring his depleted exchequer. Neither is it wise in A to excite envy in the mind of his neighbor by an ostentatious display of his own advantages. We should seek to help each other along in the journey of life, ever remembering that at the station just ahead, where we shall all embark for the country Beyond, no factitious circumstance of wealth or fame will count for aught in securing favorable accommodations. It will no doubt often be found there that "the first shall be last, and the last first."

Who fails to get the best experiences out of this life, misses a golden means of happiness in the next. And there is nothing that helps one to such experiences so much as a kind and thoughtful regard for the welfare of others. Who takes no interest in his fellow men, but shuts himself up in his own shell, bent only on his own happiness, is making for himself a condition—(a Karma, the Theosophist calls it)—that will be likely to cause him no little inconvenience in the life to come. It pays to be generous, to be manly, to be considerate of others, even in this life; but vastly more in that land where character is the only passport to companionship with angels.

If the infinite Creator made a mistake in the creation of man, as he must have done if the doctrine of the "fall of man" be true, then what becomes of the infallibility of the Creator? Is it not more creditable to both man and his Maker to believe that the former, through an infinite process of evolution, has come up from some lower but analogous type

of animal life to his present high condition, than that he was
created "a little lower than the angels," but by disobedience
fell from his high estate? There is some virtue in rising but
surely none in falling.

EVIL THOUGHTS.

Evil thoughts sting and hurt the spirit whence they eman-
ate, even more than they do the object towards which they are
directed. We cannot think ill of anyone without connecting
ourselves, in a certain sense, with all the ill in the universe.
We thereby place ourselves in the current, as it were, of unfriendly elements. We become receptive to evil influences,
and to all that retards the growth and advancement of the
spirit. The result is an inharmonious condition, often result-
ing in sickness and premature death. We all ought to live to
ripe old age, in the full possession of health to the last. That
many do not, is no doubt mainly due to their ignorance of the
laws of life and health. They drift unconsciously into these
inhospitable currents, and suffer the ills thereof, without realizing that they have the remedy in their own hands.

GRAND MARCH.

Fall in for the grand march of ideas! Humanity is coming forth from the old, and emerging into the new. For centuries, man has been taught to think according to rule—to
take his religion from labelled bottles, put up and sealed in
the misty past by pious but unschooled religious apothecaries.
Just as though he was not a progressive being, and that what
was good for him in his infancy would be sufficient for him for
all time. He has now reached a period of unfoldment wherein
he must have a reason in and for his theology, and wherein he
is no longer content with the childish fables and fairy stories,
in the name of religion, that filled the needs of his infancy.
Fall in, then, for the grand march of truth!

ONE WORLD AT A TIME.

"One world at a time," says the Materialist. "Live while ye may, for to-morrow ye die." And by death they mean a dreamless sleep — an unconscious cessation of being. If we live the true life — live for the attainment of the highest end of being — it doubtless matters little whether we believe in a future life or not. But the trouble is, it were almost if not quite impossible to live our best with no broader outlook than that which bounds the limit of our mortal years. What to us are the woes of the world—what the plaints of the overbur-dened, "the slings and arrows of outrageous fortune" to the struggling ones — if our own paths are made smooth down to the vortex whence we must needs plunge into oblivion! It is the something beyond "must give us pause." Hence, we would amend the Materialist's refrain by substituting, "Both worlds for all time and eternity.

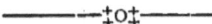

What would not the mother, bending over her dying babe, and prayerfully watching the fluttering away of its little life, give to *know*, in very truth, that there were fond arms ready and waiting to enfold it to a loving heart, just over the line that separates the visible from the invisible—and that nightly, perhaps, when separated from its earthly body, it will be brought to her own seemingly empty arms, for the strength and nourishment necessary for its spiritual growth? What a comfort is this thought to all mothers who have found the truth.

The mole burrows in the dark earth; the owl and the bat come forth with the shades of night to seek their prey;— so the mind, beclouded in ignorance, and on evil bent, gropes in darkness, hiding from the light of the spirit that shines for all. Come forth, O brother man, into the light, and live to honor thy being — worthy of thy immortal destiny.

GLORY OF FORGETFULNESS.

It is glorious to forget, when forgetfulness means the obliteration of unprofitable recollections. And such are the recollections of all things that destroy happiness, or retard the growth of the spirit. Has the world gone wrong with you? Forget it, and look to the future for better things to come. Has your friend betrayed you, or your enemy sought to injure you? Seek to so live that in time to come the regret will be theirs and not yours. Has death robbed you of your idols, and deep sorrow mantled your life? Remember that in some of God's "many mansions" you will find them all again, where the pain of parting will be known and felt no more. Remember that there is abundant recompense for all life's woes— sometime—and somewhere.

The true life—the life of the soul—the only life that is eternal—is within the reach of all. All that pertains to this animal existence—the appetites and passions—the greed for gain—the earthly ambitions—must all die out and disappear sometime. They are all "of the earth earthy." Only the "things of the spirit"—the virtues, loves, humanities, the higher aspirations, the outreachings for truth, and for the spiritual unfoldment that shall bring one into unison with the angelic hosts and the heart of the Infinite—these only will live forever.

How empty and profitless must seem all things of earth— all unused wealth, all pride of name or station, all "pomp and circumstance" of life—to the man whose feet are cold with the creeping chill of death, and who realizes that with a few more faint pulsations his heart will be silent forevermore. That time will come to all, and, in the course of nature, to many of us soon. And yet how prone we are to live as though the day were far hence, and all our needs centered here. The harvest is ripe, gather ye in the sheaves; "for the night cometh when no man can work."

MORAL DISEASE.

The tendency to commit criminal acts is a moral disease, and those afflicted therewith should be treated as humanely as we would treat those who are afflicted with mental or physical maladies. Not that we would go to the extreme of absolving the criminal from all accountability for his acts; for that accountability, however slight it may be, is the leverage whereby we would work his cure. At the same time we would throw around him those benign and humane influences best calculated to stimulate his moral nature. It is much easier to arouse the better nature of undeveloped man by kind treatment, than to suppress the evil side by harsh means. Our prisons should be made schools of reform, and the prisoner should be restored to liberty only when such reform is effected; and once cured of his malady, no more odium should attach to him than to a discharged hospital patient cured of small-pox.

To one who has sought the spiritual unfoldment of his own nature, and come closely in rapport with the spirit world —who can hold daily communion with his own loved ones in spirit,—he finds therein, and in the sweet assurance of a happy time to come when he shall join them in the Beyond, a joy and satisfaction that he would not exchange for aught that earth can give.

**

" There is only a thin veil between us," so thin that many with clear spiritual vision can see the forms upon the other side ; and often the veil is swept entirely away, and we are permitted to greet them face to face. A grander truth the world has never known, Our facts and philosophy demonstrate beyond reasonable question that "if a man die he shall live again." How puerile, then, the efforts of the ignorant and prejudiced to ignore this truth, and cast reproach upon its believers. The narrow bigots of the pulpit, who believe in continued existence without proof, and revile Spiritualists 'for demonstrating the fact of spirit existence, ought to hide their heads for shame.

————‡o‡————

A MOTHER'S LOVE.

Who can measure the depths of a mother's love. There is no grief so terrible, no pain so keen, as that which comes to the mother's heart as she anxiously watches the fading away of the life of the darling babe she pillows upon her bosom. "Oh pitying God," she cries, in the agony of her bursting heart, "is there *no* help?" But no answer comes to her from the depths profound. The fluttering pulse grows fainter with each gasping breath, and then all is still, save the wild wail of her own dispair. She sees not the loving mother angel bending down by her side to gather the little cherub in her arms. She hears not the sweet notes of loving welcome that hail the newly-born spirit, as it opens its pretty eyes upon the delights of its beautiful spirit home. All is dark, dark. In this hour of her woe, "not all the preaching since Adam," can give to her such comfort as the positive knowledge that Spiritualism brings, that her babe still lives, and will soon come to nestle again in her own loving arms.

————‡o‡————

What is there more beautiful in all of God's universe than a beautiful soul? An unselfish soul—a gentle, loving, sympathetic soul—a soul that is ever seeking the good of others—these are all beautiful souls,—souls that the shining ones delight to draw near to—souls that have become one with the divine soul. We all know such souls, and we ever find special delight in being known by them.

THE INEVITABLE.

It is very hard for man to reconcile himself to the inevitable. He cannot understand why he should be compelled to occupy a weak, sickly body, while his neighbor is strong and robust;—why his child should be taken from him, and his neighbor's left;—why he should struggle on in poverty, toiling early and late for the bare necessities of life, while his neighbor revels in affluence. If he could only realize how little difference, really, there is between the condition of his neighbor and that of himself, with the advantage often in his own favor, he would cease repining. Wealth has cares and anxieties that poverty little knows. Health of body and mind; capacity to enjoy the beauty and grandeur of nature; love, with all its sacred ties and promptings; aspiration, hope, the pleasure of knowledge, the true gladness of existence,—which are about all there is of this life,—are quite as much, if not really more, the property of the poor man as of the rich. Lift up your head, O my struggling brother, and be glad.

The very best indication that Spiritualism is making rapid inroads upon the conservative thought of the age, and sapping the foundations of error, is the bitter and ignorant hostility it has aroused among the crystallized fossils of old theology. It is a glorious fact that all preachers of the Christian gospel are not of this class. Some of them have the good sense to see that Spiritualism embraces all that is good in Christianity, in addition to which it furnishes the skeptical world with the positive proof of spirit existence, that survives the destruction of the earthly body.

The rich man who possesses the good sense to become the executor of his own estate, and wisely disposes of the same, will not have occasion to worry himself, "over there," about what he might have done. With his earth work all accomplished, he will go on at once to higher enjoyments and richer experiences.

A WIDE DIFFERENCE.

It is one thing to believe in spirit communion, quite another to be a truly spiritual man or woman. Hence, among Spiritualists, or those claiming to be such, we find nearly all grades of meanness and unworthiness. This is not the fault of Spiritualism, but of poor, undeveloped human nature. A fault which all true Spiritualists should seek to overcome, first in their own natures, and next in the natures and lives of their neighbors. We make no pretension to goodness. It would be egotism and selfishness in us combined to think that we possessed any virtues superior to those of our neighbors. And yet, we humbly believe, that before we would seek to rise by pulling some one else down, or injure another in his good name or in his business, we would, to borrow one of Sam Jones' forcible figures of speech, "trade ourselves off for a yaller dog, and then hire a Chinaman to kill the dog."

The lesson which the Teacher seemed to regard as one of the utmost importance, and one which he enforced upon his hearers and followers upon all occasions, was that of charity. He regarded one who had no charity in his heart for the weaknesses and shortcomings of his fellow beings as one who came far short of the kingdom — that is, of that state or condition of spirit conducive to the truest happiness in this life and the next. Of the three graces, Faith, Hope and Charity, a certain ritual declares—"The greatest of these is Charity; "for faith may be lost in sight, Hope ends in fruition, but Char- "ity extends beyond the grave throughout the countless ages "of eternity."

The facts and philosophy of Spiritualism are inseparably united. They must necessarily go through the world hand in hand. The philosophy without the phenomena would tax the credulity of men as never did the myths and fables of superstition. It would be the old impossibility of intelligent belief by faith. We must substitute knowledge for speculation, and knowledge of spirit existence and its power to return can only come with the positive manifestations, as given through our mediums. Hence, there should not be the slightest occasion for inharmony among Spiritualists on this point. Each phase of Spiritualism is a " part of one stupendous whole."

*
* *

There is a satisfaction that comes to the soul with the knowledge that life is continuous beyond the grave, and that there are none lost in an orthodox sense of everlasting punishment—a satisfaction far beyond aught that words can express. It takes out of the heart the rankling feeling that the plan of the universe is a stupendous wrong, and fills it to the brim with reverence for the Creator. It reconciles one to life and duty, and strews the most rugged pathway with flowers. Let us be glad and rejoice that there is love enough in the heart of God to save all His children.

*
* *

Spiritualists can never know how much of real joy there is in their beautiful philosophy until their own spirits are brought into harmony with the divine spirit of love and charity for all. The mere acceptance of a belief in the facts of spirit phenomena is of no benefit to any one, without the adaptation of one's life to the teachings that come with such phenomena. But entered into in the right spirit, and with the soul attuned to the harmonies of the higher life, there is in this new gospel such a wealth of joy as no tongue can express.

*
* *

The following idea of God was given through a child-medium of eight years, the daughter of a friend of the writer:

"Tell us what you know of God." "We have never seen God, and do not think any one ever has, or will see Him." "Please give us your idea of God." "Take everything that exists—*everything* —and God is the Life, the Soul and the Spirit of it all." Could a Talmage have given a better answer?

———‡o‡———

GIVING WHAT ONE DOESN'T WANT.

There is but little, if any, virtue in giving what one doesn't want, or what one can give and never miss, or can spare without any inconvenience to himself. That kind of giving, although commendable, is never very highly inspiring to the giver. The giving of the " widow's mite," spoken of in the Christian Scripture, was a far grander act, in a spiritual sense, than the giving of thousands by others who have tens of thousands to give. Neither is there much virtue in post mortem benevolence ; for that is simply giving away the property of others ; it belongs then to one's heirs, if he has any; if not, then it belongs to the State. Ownership of earthly possessions lapses with the last breath. A disposition of property for charitable purposes by will is a good deal like the proposition of Artemas Ward, to sacrifice all his wife's relatives on the altar of his country, before the Union should be dissolved ! The good we would do in this world we should do now.

———§o§———

We are all, more or less, subject to psychic influences both from the seen and unseen world. It should be the study of every life to understand the nature of these influences, and to so school his own spirit as to be positive to influences for evil and negative or receptive to the good. In this happy equipoise of soul man can steadily move onward and upward to better and higher conditions of spiritual unfoldment, even unto companionship with angels.

A NEW MEANING.

Read in the light of the new Gospel, the old Hebrew melodies of David have a new meaning. In fact, the old and revered writings of any people become luminous with spiritual light, when once our spirits become illuminated with the light of truth. They are the poetic inspirations of races of human beings just emerging from the darkness of barbarism, embodying often grand lessons of life that are as good to-day as they were when uttered centuries ago. " A new commandment give I unto you," said Jesus, "that ye love one another." Can any better advice than that be given to the world in these modern times ? Can the attrition of the ages, or the erosion of time ever wear out or deface the " Golden Rule ? " It is thus with all truth that has its origin in the higher spiritual nature of man.

That is a selfish, narrow love that would exact more than it would give. Indeed, it is not the highest love that would demand any return. Such is not the love of a mother for a wayward child; nor of the wife who clings devotedly to a cruel or worthless husband. It is not the love of a soldier who gives up his life on the altar of his country; nor was it the love of Him who died for humanity. If it is glorious to give something for nothing, how much greater the glory for giving good for ill. The spirit that has attained to such divine hights has reached the vestibule of the temple where dwells Infinite Goodness.

Who that has come into the truth—into loving nearness and companionship with the spirit world—and learned the beautiful lessons of life and love that angels teach, would exchange the precious satisfaction it gives to him for all the treasures of earth ! It is something to live by—something to light the way through the dark valley to the sun-kissed hills beyond.

INCENTIVES TO A BETTER LIFE.

While thousands of people flock to hear Moody and Sam Jones, and many others recognize in those men a power for usefulness in the world, yet the number of attendants upon their ministrations who take much stock in their statements of religious creed—that is, in the fall of man, the vicarious atonement, a personal devil, etc.,—is comparatively small. If sinful men can be induced to forsake their evil ways and become better citizens, better husbands and fathers, in no other way than through the preaching of Sam Jones, or any other revivalist,—if a belief in hell fire, literally, is necessary to save a man from drunkenness, or stealing, or wife-beating, we would give him the fire, and make it hot. We have no quarrel with evangelical religion. While we think it is much more creditable for a man to live an upright life from a sense of duty than from any fear of post mortem consequences, we will not quibble about the ethics of the question, if only men are made better.

Nature presents to man many problems, many strange manifestations, which she expects him to investigate, and to deduce therefrom a lesson for his benefit. To stand upon the border line of some phenomenon, afraid to go forward—as do some timid souls with regard to the wonderful facts of Spiritualism—is indicative of moral weakness or cowardice. There is no forbidden fruit in the garden of Nature. All is for man's use, for profit or instruction. He who would find the truth must seek for it with untiring diligence, and never allow any bugbear of superstition to intimidate him from the search.

How rapidly the years glide away—youth, manhood, age —the three milestones in the journey of life, that seem so very far apart in childhood, are but a step from each other as we look backward. First a pulsating germ, then a conscious entity struggling in the coil of destiny, then a helpless clod trundled away to the. ash heap! Oh, marvelous mystery of being! Well may we ask, Whence cometh man, and whither goeth he?

In many ways human life has its counterpart in outward nature. In some lives we see the tempest and the whirlwind; in some the shifting sands of the desert and the restless tumult of the waves; in some the calm and beauty of the summer sunset; in some the grandeur and glory of the mountain peak. In others still we have the melody of birds, the murmur of the rippling brook, the fragrance of the flowers, and the soft airs of spring. But whatever type of life may be thine, dear reader, let it not be wanting in that divine sweetness that makes it one with God.

How much better is wisdom than riches,—not the wisdom that plans only for time, but the true wisdom of the spirit that lays its foundations in truth and builds for eternity. Think ye not, O mortal, ye whose life is wholly wrapped up in the garments of earth, that when you come to lay aside those garments, you will blush at your own nakedness? What is the flitting phantasm of the full span of mortal years, to the countless æons of infinate duration beyond! Shall we feed the spirit on husks to gratify the vanities of earth? Shall we live that we may die, or die that we may live?

" Would you put away the Bible?" inquires a good sister, whose heart had been touched with the new gospel, but who still clings to the religion and teaching of her fathers. Certainly not; we would put nothing away, or out of the life of the world, that is of any use to humanity. There are many golden lessons in both testaments that the world needs to-day as never before. There are some things, in the Old Testament especially, that we would not care to perpetuate;—for instance, the cruelties and debaucheries said to have been perpetrated by the consent and at the instigation of the Lord of Hosts. We do not believe the Lord ever countenanced murder or rapine in the past, any more than he does to-day. God speaks to man by inspiration just the same in one age as in another.

SLAVES TO ENVIRONMENT.

We are all slaves, to a greater or less extent, first, to heredity, second, to early training, and next to environment. While we recognize the mighty power of the spirit to overcome these conditions, in time or eternity, we must ever bear in mind and ever acknowledge their potency in diverting man from the straight and narrow way of rectitude, honor, temperance and spiritual independence, which his better nature and higher impulses tell him is the true way of life. A better knowledge of this fact would teach those who have been blest with better conditions to exercise the broadest charity towards their less fortunate brothers. If you are better than your neighbor, pause and consider whether or not you might not have been worse, had you been in his place. Humility is a virtue that but few of us are overstocked with.

Death comes to the aged as a gentle and loving friend. It touches the tired heart and its pulses are stilled. It kisses the eyelids of care, and they are lulled to sleep. It fans the brow with its cool breath, and it finds repose in the bosom of Mother Earth. A little while, and the morning of a new day will break upon the world.

* *

Titles and wealth count for naught in the country whither thou goest. There will be none to do you honor because of any earthly distinction you may have enjoyed here. The king, the prince, and the beggar are no longer such, but only the man, the brightness of whose aura, or lustre of whose garments will depend wholly upon his purity or nobility of character. There are many people who believe, or think they believe, this truth, but who live as though they expected the hosts of the spirit world to bow down before them when they shall land upon the other shore.

————§o§————

COME UP.

Come up out of the cellar, O brother sojourner in the City of the Mortal! Do heavy cares weigh you down? Are you worrying or borrowing trouble over what you cannot help? It does you no good to mope, or go down into the cellar of your nature, where all is dark, damp and dismal. That is not the way to bear the load. Your angel friends cannot help you there, because they cannot reach you. They would have you come up and out into the sweet sunlight of the spirit, where they can see the trials that beset you, and assist you in removing them. If you do your best, and then fail, you have real cause for rejoicing. You will yet be crowned victor in the home of the immortals, if not in the land of Beulah.

————§o§————

Blessed be the man who finds heaven in this life, for then he has something that can never be taken from him. He need then have no apprehensions concerning the future, for he has brought the future, with all its treasures of delights, into his own soul. Life henceforth becomes to him a living joy. The nearest and most direct road to this condition of happiness is by doing good to others.

* *
*

The believer in our facts whose Spiritualism is all upon the external plane—that is, in the pleasures of sensuous phenomena—with no high aspiration for the uplifting and unfoldment of his own spiritual nature—misses the lesson of the divine purpose in his earthly discipline by an infinite waste of barren years. It is not by beholding the goal from afar, but by manfully running the race, that we may win the prize.

A RELIGIOUS WAR.

"The next war," says an alarmist friend of ours, "will be a religious war." If so it will be a bloodless war, a war of opinions merely. There are but very few persons who have enough of the kind of religion that would prompt them to fight to force it upon the consciences of others, and the number is daily becoming less. Let Rome, for instance, undertake it, and all the world, Protestant and Pagan, would rise up against her. Let any one of the Protestant sects, or all of them combined, attempt the sublime folly, and they would have to encounter all manner of liberalism, with Rome added. Public opinion is stronger than law, hence the folly of attempting to force any law upon the people that is distasteful to them. We say to all souls, overburdened with the idea that the people are to be deprived, by religious intolerance, of any human right, or reasonable liberty, Don't you believe it.

Every rich man, if he is reasonably wise, will be the executor of his own estate. Then he can make just such disposition of it as he would like. His wealth will not be at the mercy of probate courts, nor scheming lawyers, nor unworthy heirs—after he passes out and on. To look down from one's future abode and behold the careful accumulations of one's lifetime of years scattered to the winds by rollicking relatives, who are only too glad to get their fingers on the old man's coin, can not afford the spirit a very great measure of comfort. Why wait until it is everlastingly too late, but do the good now that will give to the disenthralled spirit the blessing of rest a little further on.

*
* *

The spirit world has undertaken a mighty work—that of uplifting and spiritualizing the world of humanity that is excluded from the churches. It ought to have the "God-speed" of the churches in this work, but it has not. They seem to prefer that man shall go to hades unless he chooses to go to heaven by their especial lines. They denounce Spiritualism for the shortcomings of its believers, forgetting that it is working up valuable material that they have had the short-sightedness to overlook and exclude.

ERRONEOUS BELIEF.

There are many good people who really believe that our liberties are in danger from religious intolerance—that the efforts of a few cranks to fasten a law for Sunday observance upon the nation, and to force the Bible into the public schools, will surely succeed if not met with vigorous resistance. They seem to overlook the fact that there is a silent resistant force in modern civilization which renders all such efforts absolutely futile. It is impossible for the race to go back into the swaddling clothes of its infancy. Not but there may be those who would seek even to re-establish the inquisition, or re-enact the blue laws of the early American colonies, but with the aggregate of enlightenment against them, which is steadily broadening and increasing, they might as well undertake to check the onward flow of the gulf stream with a sand-bag, or trip up a cyclone with a feather.

TRUTH.

The truth should be the goal of all philosophy—of all religious thought. No man should be so wrapped up in his own conceit as to imagine he has all the truth. He cannot afford to deceive himself, and certainly, if he is honest, he would not deceive others. It may be humiliating to him to be compelled to cast down his idols, and surrender his cherished opinions; but his readiness to do so, when convinced of the truth, is the true gauge of manly honesty. What matters it if one happens to be wrong, if he is only willing to be set aright. It is dogmatic adherence to the wrong, in the face of reasonable evidence to the contrary, that makes the angels weary of their task in the reformation of humanity.

————§o§————

LIKE ATTRACTS LIKE.

He who lives on a low plane, and indulges in unworthy thoughts, naturally attracts to his atmosphere spirits upon the same level of life, and he therein finds helps to a downward course. Hence, the natural tendency of all who thus live is to gravitate from bad to worse—to sink to still lower levels in the scale of being. On the other hand, he who aspires to the better life—says to his lower nature, "Get thee behind me, Satan,"—will receive help from the spirit to overcome. If he looks upward, with an earnest aspiration to rise, he will ever find a friendly hand reaching downward to help him. And so it is, that there is no standing still in life's journey. We are either ascending the hights, or descending into the dark valleys. In the latter case through what agonies must the spirit pass in its backward turning to the light no one can know.

————‡o‡————

ALL TRAVELERS IN LIFE'S JOURNEY.

Ought we not to school ourselves to look with tender compassion upon the undeveloped spirit that can do another a wrong? Only think of the long journey before such souls— the path beset with thorns, which they must walk with aching hearts and bleeding feet, before they can reach the higher life of the spirit. We are all travelers in life's journey together; the strong should assist the weak—should help them to bear their burdens with patience and humility. Can he ask for help or strength who is unwilling to impart help or strength to those weaker than himself? And what is the one who would do wrong to his fellows but one who is weak, and needs help to overcome the evil in his own nature? Let us ascend the hights of being, not grope in the shadows.

ON TO OTHER CONQUESTS.

There are too many mere believers in spiritual phenom-ena in the world, and too few whose lives have been made sweeter and more beautiful by an acceptance, first, of the facts of Spiritualism, and next, by squaring their lives according to the higher teachings of our beautiful philosophy. It should be the ambition of all believers in the intercommunion of the two worlds to bring themselves into harmony with the higher and finer symphonies of the divine life of the soul. Why should anyone be content to go through life forever "seeking for a sign," especially when he has had a thousand signs, and knows of a certainty that the spirit survives the death of the body? No wise or thoughtful person will content himself with the simple possession of a spiritual fact, however great or important it may be. He will soon begin to correlate it with his own spirit, and then pass on to other conquests.

How often, with the new year, thoughtful men—men encased wholly in the affairs of earth, but who sometimes think beyond the present,—how often do such men, with the opening year, resolve better things. Bad habits are cast off, and many good resolutions recorded on the tablets of their minds, which all too often fail to take root in the spirit. A little while, and they drift back into their old ways, and not even a vestige of their good resolution is left, to indicate that they ever thought of "entering the path" that leads to the higher life.

* *

The man or woman who cannot rise superior to the petty passions of hatred towards an inferior, for any real or imaginary wrong done to them, shows themselves to be no better or nobler than the object of their uncharitable thought. There is much they will find it necessary to overcome in their own natures before they are prepared to "enter the path" of spiritual growth. There is only one way to true happiness, and that is by the exercise of the spirit of forgiveness and gentleness. It may not be really possible to *love* one's enemies, but it *is* possible not to hate or despise them. Until we can render good for evil we are not the children of Light.

WHAT HE MOST NEEDS.

What every Spiritualist most needs is the uplifting of his own spiritual nature. When once he *knows* that the so-called dead live again, and that under certain conditions they can hold communication with mortals, then should he set himself at the task of preparing himself for that higher life, by bringing himself into harmony with the Divine spirit in his own nature. This he can not do by unworthy thoughts and practices. He must get beyond the everlasting seeking-after tests. The test is to arrest the attention of the skeptic, not to transfix it for all time to that one object. And yet, how many Spiritualists there are who seem to stop right there. There are many instances in nature of what might be regarded as arrested development. Such instances ought not to be found among those to whom the new gospel has come.

The life of man is the life of the mere animal, when prompted by no impulse to a noble end. To live and toil, to buy and sell, and struggle for earthly possessions, and all that the physical man may be cared for, and revel in the delights of earth, with no outreaching for the higher life—in unfoldment of the spiritual nature—no aspiration for the divine life, which is the perfection of existence—is to live and die as the brute dies. Such an existence is unworthy an immortal soul.

How swift the gliding years! Increasing, seemingly, with the momentum of time, until the landmarks of life—the birthdays and the holidays, the days of gladness and the days of woe—blend into each other, like the wayside objects to the traveler by the lightning express. And so we are speeding onward from youth to manhood, from manhood to old age, and thence out into the night of death, and the sleep that wakens upon a new day.

ON WHAT HAPPINESS DEPENDS.

If man could only realize how much his happiness here and hereafter depended upon the unfoldment of those faculties for which only will he have use in the life beyond, think you he would be a laggard in well doing? What use in the beyond, for instance, will he have for the exercise of the acquisitive faculties — for the knack of money-getting, to which so many devote their lives, — a very useful faculty, we concede, when' coupled with generosity and benevolence, but when not, a very millstone about the neck. What use will he have for unkind thoughts, for uncharitable behavior, for meanness of any kind? A nature trained to the indulgence of evil thoughts or habits will find itself, sometime and somewhere, compelled to pass through furnace fires of discipline to fit it for the better life.

INHARMONIOUS THOUGHTS.

How very little we know of the subtle and unseen forces, the exquisite life principles, that control these bodies of ours. The nerves are so extremely sensitive that they may be affected even by unkind and inharmonious thoughts, which, reacting upon the body, produce headache, loss of appetite, indigestion, etc., disturbing all the currents of being. Some persons are so sensitive as to be conscious of the cause of the disturbances affecting the physical health; others are affected all the same without realizing the cause of the trouble. Spirits on the other side of life, especially those who are skilled in the art of communicating with mortals, understand these things much better than we do. In entrancing their mediums they often find conditions in the way of perfect control that the mortal would never think of, and they understand dealing with those subtle forces much better than do mortals.

GIVE IT TIME.

If Spiritualists were more deeply schooled and grounded in the philosophy and religion of Spiritualism, they would rank higher among the world's reformers, because they would then carry their faith into their works. The attention of many intelligent people on a low spiritual plane of life—Atheists, materialists, and sometimes people of questionable morality and practices—is arrested by the phenomenal facts of Spiritualism. They are forced to admit the truth of spirit existence and return, and henceforth they are called Spiritualists. But they are so only in name, until their natures become quickened by the Divine Spirit, and they ascend into the higher realm of being. Spiritualism is doing for these people what no other system of philosophy or religion could do. But we must give it time for the leaven to work.

He who would win the race must fix his eyes upon the good, and press forward for the prize. Man is surrounded with so many temptations to a life of indolent ease—so much to encumber his spirit and weigh him down,—and then Necessity steps in with her imperious demands, which can be attained often only by hard contest, in a field of fierce competition, with others struggling for the same end, that it is not surprising that so few are able to climb the upper heights of being in this life. But is it not well to "try again," and with a firmer purpose?

* *

As night shuts out the light of day, and covers earth with a pall of gloom, so unkind thoughts shut out the light and love of the Infinite Spirit, that would otherwise stream into the soul, filling it with a radiance and glory all divine. If we would live in the warmth and glow of spiritual truth, we should seek patiently for the path, and walk steadily and truthfully therein.

————————❖o❖————————

QUESTIONS.

A correspondent writes: "Will you please answer the following questions:—(1) What is Soul—is it material—of what kind of Matter is it? (2) What is the spirit of Man—is it material and of what kind? (3) What is Thought—are thoughts material—how tangible are they?

1st. We understand soul to be the material covering or body of the spirit, just as the physical body is the covering of both soul and spirit. When the spirit, which is the conscious *ego*, leaves the body, it takes its house to live in with it. This is what is termed the spirit body, and it is composed of the finer emanations of the physical body—has weight, substance and tangibility,—that is, to spiritual sense. We must remember that there are many forms of matter of which our physical senses are indifferently cognizant. Why may there not be infinite varieties and gradations of matter entirely beyond the ken of our physical senses, as indeed, we know there is in some directions, as science has demonstrated?

2d. The spirit of man we regard as the divine essence, which, acting upon matter, manifests intelligence. This may be a still finer form of matter, for ought man may know.

3d. Thought is the expression of the spirit through matter, bearing with it something of the substance through which it passes. Thus, thoughts are things, or rather, they become things whenever they seek expression. Their degree of tangibility may be measured by the force and power with which they impinge themselves upon the consciousness of others.

We do not think any of us know much about matter or spirit, or whether they are not all one in essence, but differing in degree. When we know more we shall be glad to say more.

MUSTERED OUT.

Note the gray heads in any of our public audiences—the large number of men and women who are on the down grade, and rapidly nearing the silent river. The fierce combat and struggle for life is nearly or quite over with them, and, with tired hearts and bleeding feet, they are waiting for the ambul_ance to gather them in. And yet we know there are many to whom gray hairs bring no regrets. They have "fought the good fight," and are glad that they are nearing home. Not for worlds would they have it otherwise. Get ready, old soldiers of the grand army of life,—ye are about to be mustered out. Square up your accounts with the commissary department, polish up your uniform for the last grand review, and patiently wait marching orders for home! There are many loved faces at the window watching for your coming.

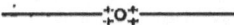

"Excelsior!" shouldbe the motto of every Spiritualist. No one should be content to sit down in quiet satisfaction with sensuous phenomena. All should seek for the mountain height of spiritual unfoldment and delight; they should ascend the ladder reached down to them from the angel world, resolved to become one with the Divine Spirit—fit companions for the highest and best in God's beautiful realm of individualized spirit intelligences.

Love is the panacea for all ills. It will heal all sorrow, cure all strife, bind up all broken hearts, solve all problems of social or civil discord, and lead the race up out of the wilderness of error and inharmony, and out into the promised land flowing with the milk and honey of peace and plenty. To bring the entire race under the dominion of love, it is only necessary for each individual to place himself in harmony with the higher law of his own spirit.

When the clouds and rubbish shall be swept away from our beautiful Spiritualism, the light of its glorious truth will shine forth brighter than ever.   Spiritualists have no one but themselves to blame for the prominence that has been given to the delusions and falsities that have been practiced in the name of Spiritualism by some persons possessing but very little, if any, real mediumship.   No honest mediums, of whom there are many, need fear the most thorough investigation.

**
* *

What is there more beautiful in all God's universe than a beautiful soul—a gentle, loving nature, bubbling over with kind thoughts for all humanity, and ever finding expression in generous deeds.   We have known and still know many such. Some have passed on to realms of light and love, and are now of the shining one ; and some, with their brows encircled with a halo of glory, are waiting trustingly on the shores of time,— golden grain ripe for the reaper's sickle.

* *

Good average sense should teach a man that the condition of mind and quality of action that produce the greatest measure of health and happiness in this life is the right condition and action to cultivate and practice.   There is nothing so promotive of health as temperance in all things, and nothing that affords so much lasting satisfaction as good deeds done to others.

* *

"The truth, the whole truth, and nothing but the truth." How often we hear these words mumbled over in our courts, and in other places where official oaths are administered, making no more impression, often, on the mind of the affiant than if uttered in Choctow.   And yet they contain the pearl of all earthly knowledge—all that is desirable in science or religion —the true end and aim of all research.   This is the priceless gem that all should seek for

www.ingramcontent.com/pod-product-compliance
Lightning Source LLC
Chambersburg PA
CBHW030644030726
47497CB00006B/1950